Greetings

from inside Your Book of Spells

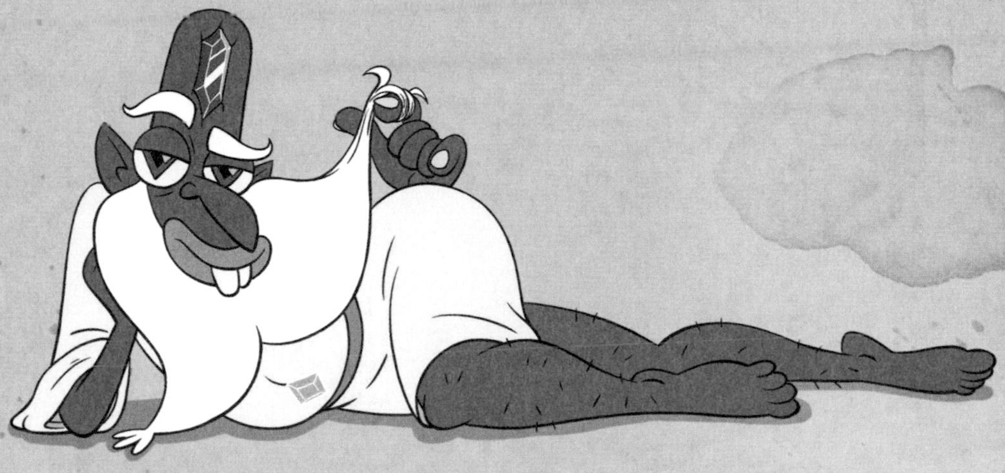

Welcome to your new Magic Book of Spells! I don't know who you are, but you can write your name here, and I'll try to remember you:

Mikayla!

I'm Sir Glossaryck of Terms, at your service, m'lady!

I'm here to help you reach your potential. I live inside your book. This message is just for YOU, and it changes depending on who happens to be the owner of the book. Sometimes I'm REALLY welcoming, and sometimes I really don't have the juice; it's like I can sense when the new princess is kind of a dud, and I sorta glaze over.

If she's a dud, it's just a waiting game, really, until she gives the book to her kid or she gets eaten by a centaur—whichever comes first.

If I'm super welcoming, it usually creeps people out, so either way, it's probably lose-lose for you.

Anyway, let's take a moment to calibrate your book to you personally.

1. Cover your right eye, and with your left eye, focus on this spot:

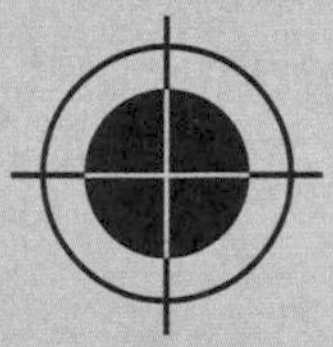

2. Cover your left eye, and with your right eye, focus on this spot:

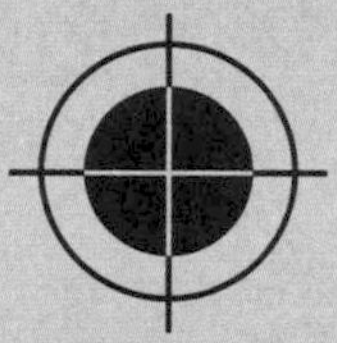

3. Now look at both spots with both eyes at the same time. If you are able to focus on them both, congratulations! You are a goat or a rabbit. This book will work properly for you.

4. If you are not able to focus on both of them at the same time, repeat steps 1–4.

Now that your book is either calibrated or not, we both know you really came here just to learn all about me.

All about Glossaryck

I've existed forever, but I was born quite some time after that, long, long ago. Just like yours, my birth was traumatic and brutish, but unlike you, I remember every detail of it! Imagine if you had to carry that around with you!

But, I digress. . . . So, yes, at some point after I existed and before my birth, I was called into being by one queen or another to assist with Mewmanity's need for understanding the Realm of Magic. I knew from the future that in order for people to be reading, I'd have to create books in the past, so I made this book and helped the first queen learn to read by writing inside. I liked the book so much I took out a mortgage and moved in with the silkworms I used to weave the pages.

They also weave my robes and my undies. And far be it from a little old book man to just dole out all his beauty secrets, but since you're a Butterfly, you're gonna need all the help you can get. The reason this beard is so white is that it's coated in silkworm slime. Works great in ear and pit hair, too, but don't get it in your mouth or you'll turn into a skeleton.

I'm serious. Not one drop.

Anyway, before you know it, I fell in love with myself and the two of us (me and myself) had some kids: Heckapoo, Omnitraxis Prime, Lekmet, Reynaldo the Bald Pate, and Rhombulus.

I put them in charge of managing the contact points between the queen and the Realm of Magic—Heckapoo for interdimensional transit, Omnitraxis for space-time, Lekmet for entropy, Reynaldo the Bald Pate for enforcing orderliness, and Rhombulus for warfare. I made the mistake of giving them free will, and I pay for it every day.

Anyway, at some point, you, me, and the kids are going to be working together as the Magic High Commission, keeping a watchful eye over magic in the multiverse. If you're not a princess or you're some kind of hairy birdling or lizard man, then you probably won't be on the Magic High Commission, but to you I say kudos on stealing this book!

A Note on the Contents of ~~My Stomach~~ This Book

You're going to encounter glyphs and symbols in this book that will befuddle and frighten you.

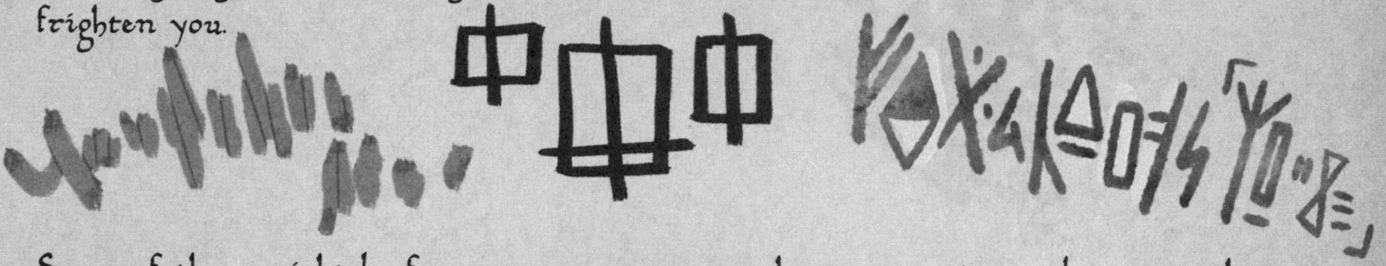

Some of these might be from one queen or another attempting to learn another language, or some might be a bit of food that got squished when I fell asleep on it. You know how it is when you have some food but you're also in bed and you wake up and the food is like glue because you were all warm in bed, and it remelted the cheese on the pizza, which then sticks to the sheets? It's called <u>heat transfer</u>, whereby an object with a different temperature from its surroundings will reach thermal equilibrium.

The formula for it is as follows:

$$\frac{Q}{t} = \frac{kA(T_2 - T_1)}{d}$$

Shout out to MAH BOY Jushtin for this equation!

Pay attention to all the scribbles, and good luck figuring out what any of them mean. I only speak one language, and it's this one. When people come here all speaking a different language, I'm like, "You wanna be in this book, you better learn the language of this book or go back to where you came from!"

It never works; they always stay and fill my pages with their own languages.

So you figure it out.

Or don't? I can't read a lick of it and I get by fine.

Speaking of lick, why don't we flip ahead to Comet's chapter, where you can bake me one of her pies. It's really the best part of the book.

How to Use This Book

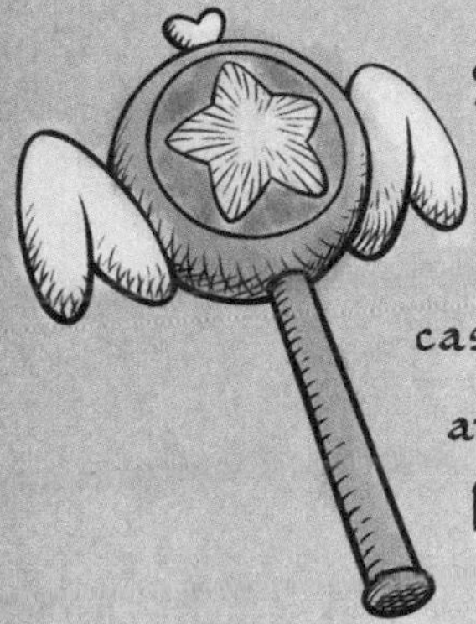

So first you're gonna wanna have a wand.

Your grandmothers have done their best to transcribe spells they cast with their wands. There are some great spells in here, and there are some that aren't even spells. Using the wand as a hammer or gravy ladle isn't magic, although admittedly, gravy IS magic.

Try the spells that are well-documented and start simple. I recommend starting with the often overlooked Levitato in Grandma Crescenta's chapter. But I know you're gonna just go right straight for Skywynne's Warnicorn Stampede.

MOLDING
ACHERS
NURSING HOME

Go ahead. It's gonna be a mess. Be sure you point your wand away from yourself. Also, don't point it at that building over there.

Once you've cleaned up the mess and ~~buried~~ tended the wounded, flip back to this page and continue from here.

Make Your Own Entries

Like any failed relationship, this book is only as bad as what you put into it. So don't be shy! Your chapter awaits you at the end of this book. Make your own comments there, and take advantage of empty pages to enter your own spells. Include as much information as you can, or if you want things to go horribly, make the spells dangerous and/or cryptic.

If all else fails, fall asleep on this pizza.

It's so warm. . . .

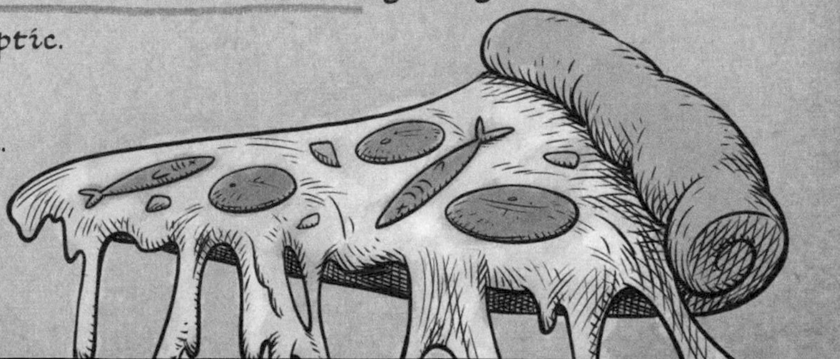

SKYWYNNE
QUEEN OF HOURS

Ticktock, the clock talks,
but secret are its powers.
The only one to break its spell
is Skywynne, Queen of Hours.

The Era of the Hourglass, year 1–

Oh, dear reader, where do we start? Let's start at the beginning. As the children's tale goes, our people came on a boat, found the land of Merwni, made it great (it's not that great), and worshipped the Stump (I mean, not me, I'm a non-believer!). We fought off the wicked monsters (well, we didn't, we are still fighting them every day). They say long, long ago, the very first queen found the sanctuary, and she was so brilliant, beautiful, brave, and strong that the magic came to her. It formed a wand that was every bit as wonderful as she, and it was her destiny to rule the land of Merwni.

Now I, Skywynne Lavender Butterfly, am queen—the 27th queen, to be exact. I am 17 years old, which is young for a queen. You might think my mother is dead, but she is not. She found ruling to be boring. She is now retired, living in our beautiful vacation home inside of a volcano. She says the unrelenting heat does wonders for the skin.

Apart from being young, I have some other disadvantages as a new queen. For one, I am small. I am neither strong nor beautiful, but I hope to be brilliant. I am of the opinion that the queens of the past have not done such a great job ruling over our people. We have faced famine and countless monster raids. Half of our people were pulled down into the Underworld a century ago by the Lucitors, leaving the royalty plagued by scandal, shame, and general incompetence.

Speaking of which, on the night of my Wand Passing ceremony, my mother made it a grand event, hiring jesters, songstrels, and mimes from around the land. She also hired some trained (not-so-trained) dragons. They got loose and burned the stage to ashes. It was utter chaos! As the dragons made their way to the castle, I yelled to my mother, "Please, save the Magic Book of Spells!" I was worried it would burn; it was always my dream to learn magic and add to its (mostly) scholarly pages. My mother, Lyric, hopped on her magic wand, a beautiful thing in the shape of a broomstick, and rode away. But the castle was burning at an alarming speed. Back then, the castle was constructed of flammable wood, some of it made from the body of the First Stump (which I still say was just a stump).

After several agonizing minutes, my mother returned from the fire, slightly charred but smiling. She had retrieved The Great Book . . . . . . of Fashion. Ugg. She thought that more important than the Magic Book of Spells?!

As we started work on the new castle of Mewni, what would eventually be a beautiful onion-style domed structure made of less burnable bricks, I would stay up at night thinking about what we had lost. The Magic Book of Spells! All the history of the queens! And Glossaryck! Oh, poor dear little weirdo that he is. It was somewhere in that dark time that I vowed to be a better queen than my mother. To rebuild, to push the limits of magic, and to make a new Magic Book of Spells! Which is what, dear reader, you are reading now.

My mother is visiting and insists I place this in the new Magic Book of Spells. She thinks that my ambitions to pursue magic are wonderful, but that I cannot ignore the other duties of royalty, like choosing the fashion for my reign. Here is a page from The Great Book of Fashion. It has been used by every queen to decide what her people should wear. I do not care—I closed my eyes and flipped to a random page. What you see above is the result. My mother thinks I should have chosen something more slick, but I believe this is just fine, and who cares anyway?

I remember the day of my Wand Passing ceremony like it was yesterday. I was excited and terrified all at the same time! It was a day I had long waited for, but alas, just before the wand reached my hands, the dragons got loose and burned down the castle. The ceremony was postponed a month and held with just my mother, my father, and myself on top of the smoldering ashes of our once great castle of very flammable wood.

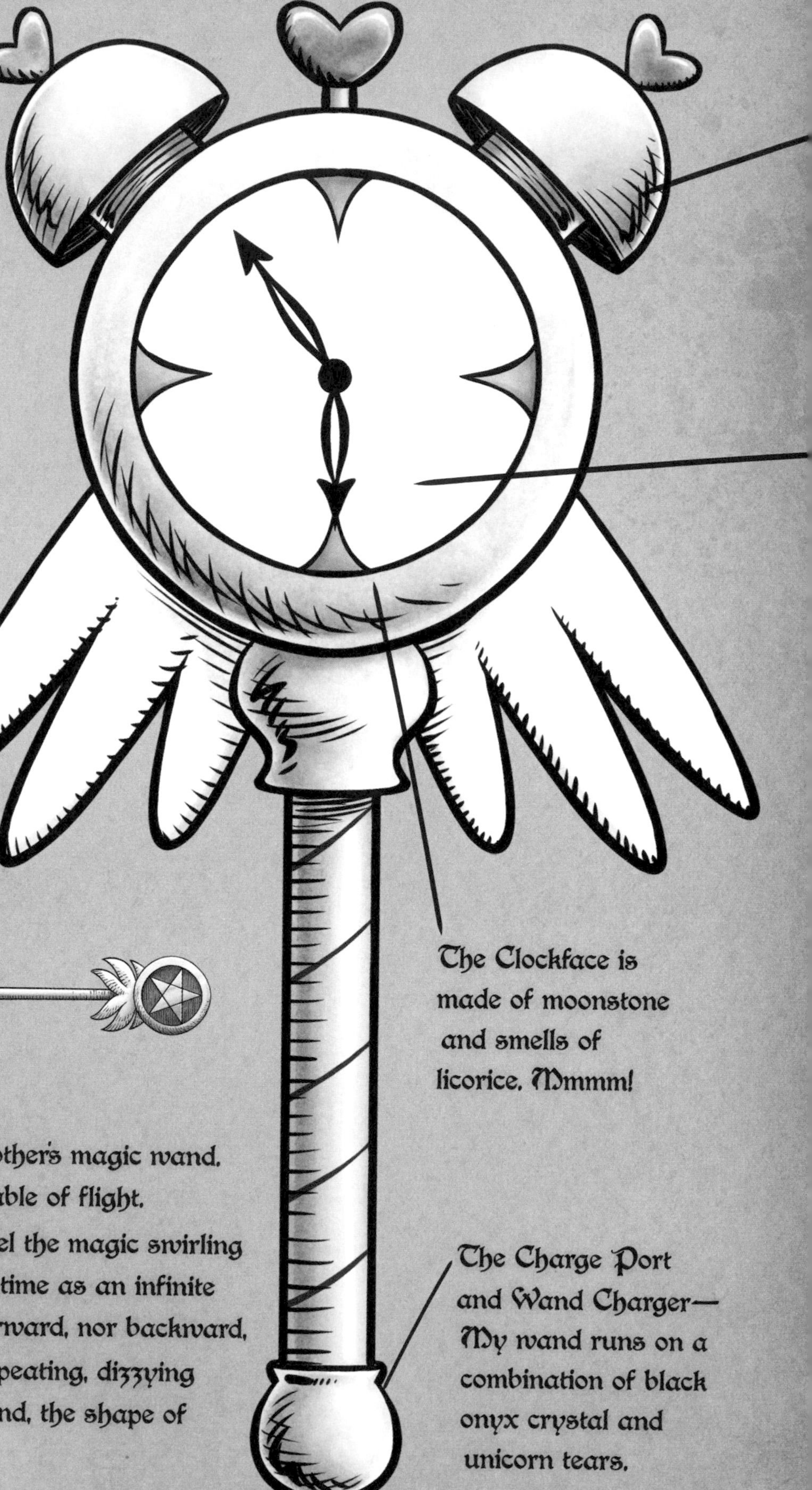
The Clockface is made of moonstone and smells of licorice. Mmmm!
The Charge Port and Wand Charger—My wand runs on a combination of black onyx crystal and unicorn tears.

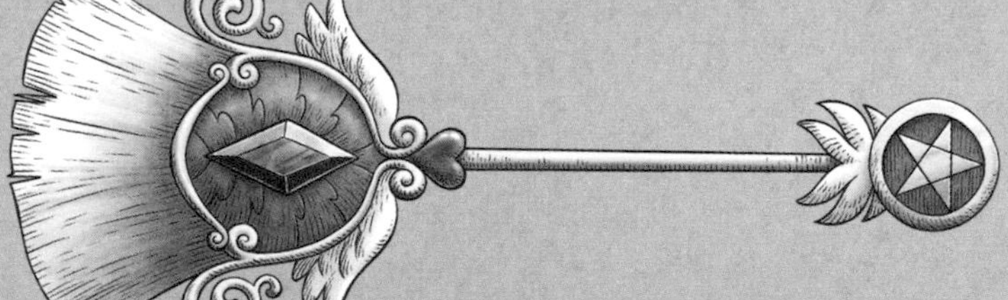

I had always admired my mother's magic wand. Long, slender, clean, and capable of flight. When I grabbed it, I could feel the magic swirling around inside me. I could see time as an infinite paradox, going not eternally forward, nor backward, but around and around in a repeating, dizzying circle. My destiny set! My wand, the shape of a clock!

The Ringing Bells—
My wand has a unique feature: ringing bells on the top. These bells make a sound that can only be heard by dogs, ferrets, and pig-goats.

The Millhorse—
My wand is powered by the same Millhorse who ran my mother's wand, Bartholomew the Brave. He is quite an old horse, but still strong.

The Crystal—
My crystal takes the form of the hands of the clock. It may not look very crystal-like from afar, but if you look closely, the hands are made of black onyx.

Skywynne Queen of Hours

Aureole Sign: Silkworm
Height: 5'

Attributes

Strength: 16	Dexterity: 5
Intelligence: 18	Constitution: 18
Wisdom: 20	Charisma: 7

Skywynne is one of my favorite grandmas! She was rebellious and had some pretty wicked spells—kind of like me!

Skywynne's chapter is also the only chapter Star actually read all the way through.

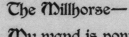

The Era of the Hourglass, year 2–

Hello, dear reader. Much has happened, and you'll be glad to know that time has been on my side! I have been quite busy creating spells, some of them even useful! I'd like to tell you the origin of a particular one, for it is quite an entertaining story.

I had been ruling for two years, mainly overseeing the rebuilding of the new castle, which was going painfully slow. My people were at their wits' end, distrustful of the royalty, sick of living in tents, but far too lazy to put in the real work of castle rebuilding. It was then that my mother, Lyric, came by for a visit. She brought along a prince, one of many, I'm afraid. This prince was named Dip Kelpbottom of the Waterfolk, and he really was a dip. In frustration, I spun around, pushed the two of them out the door with a blast from my wand (while muttering, "Infuriating repeater"), and got back to dealing with the problems of my inherited kingdom.

The next day, my mother returned with Dip Kelpbottom, and again, I kicked them out! The scenario went on like this for weeks, her returning with Dip and me kicking them out. The fact that she never seemed to have any memory of having already done this made me even more frustrated! And to top it off, the kitchen staff had given me the same meal of creamed corn and smoked fish every night! I was about to blast them, too, when suddenly, I realized that time must be repeating itself!

I was a bit frightened, but mostly impressed with my abilities! What use could this spell have? And then it occurred to me: I could trick my people into rebuilding the castle themselves with no memory of it! The very next day, I told my people that if they picked up a brick and trusted me, we could restore Butterfly Castle in just one day! They were suspicious, of course, but decided to give it a try. Little did they know that "day" was actually five years of hard labor! The castle was completed, bigger and more beautiful than ever. All the Mewmans had a new home inside, and most importantly, I won them over. They dubbed me Skywynne, Queen of Hours and paraded me around the grounds.

What to Do if You Want to Repeat Time

To repeat time, grab your wand with your pinky out. Think of something frustrating—like how your mother believes a man is of any importance—and power up your wand as you spin around once clockwise, uttering the phrase, "Infuriating repeater." Then blast! You will find time repeating itself over and over again. When you want it to stop repeating, simply do the spell backward. Blast, spinning once counterclockwise as you utter the phrase, "Gnitairufni retaeper." Power down your wand with your thumb pointed out, and you will find time acting normal again.

Uses for repeating time:

- Studying for an exam.
- Getting the most out of your vacation days.
- Getting to know someone when you are too shy to speak to them like a regular person.
- Tricking your peasants into rebuilding your burnt-down castle.
- When you are not sure of the right thing to say to someone who probably doesn't know you exist and wish to try out a bunch of different things, so you hopefully sound exciting and they will remember you better. ("Hello" doesn't get much response, and "I like your muscles" feels awkward, so you'll eventually settle on, "How's the weather?")

The Era of the Hourglass, year 3—

I have been very busy ruling Mewni and creating spells. It seems I have been a good queen thus far! My people have a place to live, safe from the monsters in the Forest of Certain Death. We are closed off but not hungry, as I have learned how to make food out of pure magic. Every day the people flood the town square, and I create a storm cloud of tasty treats that rain down on my people.

While experimenting with coming up with a new spell, I accidentally deleted gravity! Everyone on Mewni (including myself) began to float up, up, and away! I tried my trick of just doing the spell backward, but in this case, it only made things worse; we all started flying away even faster! But I collected myself and remembered that gravity is a consequence of the curvature of space-time caused by the uneven distribution of mass/energy. My spell had stopped Mewni from rotating, so everyone was floating away! I had to get Mewni spinning again, and then the centrifugal force would pull the inhabitants back to Mewni! Gravity was restored!

What to Do if You Want to Create Food

Hold your wand to your stomach and think of something you want to eat. You may not know what you want, but if you wait long enough, your stomach will tell you. Raise your wand into the air and send a primary blast into the clouds, calling out the food you want. If you want glowberries, call out, "Glowberries!" Then watch as glowberries rain down on the streets. If you don't want to eat the food yourself, this spell will be difficult to perform, and you might make mistakes. Once I tried to make pigeon pie for my people, but I was really craving dragon-berry tarts. What rained down were pigeon-berry tarts, and they were disgusting.

This spell makes something you can put in your mouth, chew up, and swallow, but I wouldn't say it's food. Quick! Skip to Comet's chapter and make me a pie!

What to Do if You Delete Gravity

115

1. Power up your wand to a count of 115 so it is extra charged.
2. When you have enough power, call out, "Rasberry ribbon lasso."
3. Lasso the planet.
4. Pull it in the direction you want it to spin.
5. Watch as gravity comes back and everyone lands safely on the ground. (In all honesty, many will not land safely.)

CAUTION
MUST GROW VINES
FROM SOMETHING
ORGANIC.
DON'T USE PLAS
OR METALS

What to Do if You Want to Move Time Forward

To move time forward, hold tight to your wand and utter the words, "Shooting star, push me far, oh, shooting star." This spell will push you forward in time exactly 10 minutes. This spell is beneficial if your mother decides to throw you a party full of eligible young princes and you do not wish to be there. At said party, I repeated this spell 16 times.

10

What to Do if You Open

PANDORA'S BOX

DO NOT OPEN!

Well, first of all, DON'T OPEN IT. Although if you are reading this, I assume that, like myself, you have opened it and are in big trouble. You will find it sucks objects in through one end of the box (my personal assistant, my pet pig-goat, some of my hair) and starts spitting horrifying evil cockroaches out the other. The only thing to do is think fast, use your dimensional scissors, cut a rift, and throw the wicked thing in! Better hope you picked a dimension free of intellegent life.

I have no idea where the box came from. I found it in the ashes of the castle; it probably belonged to one of my great-great-great-great-great grandmothers. If only I'd had the original book of spells or Glossaryck to warn me, but alas, I had neither. I opened the box.

What to Do if You FREEZE TIME

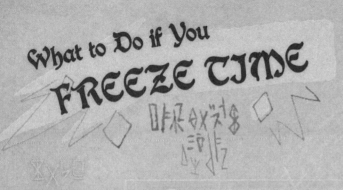

Freezing time is easy, unfreezing time is not. To freeze time, all you need to do is wag your wand around and say, "Easy peasy time freezy!" Then enjoy your freeze day! As you know, being queen is exhausting, having to answer everyone's questions and fix everyone's problems. It is good to have some "me time," you know? With my freeze day, I rearranged all the castle furniture to my liking, read a very long book, and snuck into handsome Sir Gem-robin's house to smell his freshly laundered shirts. A beautiful day! The problem is unfreezing time.

You may think you can wave your wand and simply say, "Easy peasy time un-freezy!" but you cannot. It does nothing. Don't even try. To move time forward, you must physically go to the Plains of Time and push the Wheel of Progress.

1. Take out your dimensional scissors and cut a rift to the Plains of Time.

2. Use your wand to get the Wheel of Progress started again. (This will look like a big hamster wheel.)

3. Avoid touching anything, especially clocks and time spirits.

4. Once the wheel is turning, Father Time will return and keep the wheel running for you.

5. He may give you sad eyes, but running on the wheel is his job. Tell him to quit being a baby about it.

Update by your girl Star! Finding Father Time may not be that easy now because he's off exploring the universe or whatever. At least he's happier now. I fell for the sad eyes.

What to Do When You Raise the Dead

I'm assuming that you have been tempted to raise the dead. I know it was one of my first thoughts when I started experimenting with my magic. I always imagined how fun it would be to see them rising from their tombstones. You may think this has to do with turning back time, but it does not. What this spell does is raise the dead from the Underworld for a little mischief and fun.

RIP
RIP
RIP

To raise the dead, follow these simple steps:

RIP

1. Find a graveyard.
2. Stand on the grave of the deceased you wish to reanimate.
3. Stick the handle of your wand into the ground.
4. Lightly touching the top of your wand, dance around in a circle, muttering this incantation: "Spirits of Mewni's core, from this moment you will sleep no more! Fly out from where your head doth rest, and wake up from your deadly nest. Travel onwards into the night, and give the wanderers a fright. When you have had your fun, return so little harm is done."

Please be aware that there are different kinds of undead. This list will help you identify which kind you are raising.

<u>Ghosts</u>—The classic long-dead, see-through creatures that look like floating white sheets. When you run through them, you will be momentarily chilled to the bone. I recommend raising these on a hot summer's night. Very refreshing.

<u>Zombies</u>—Zombies get a bad reputation as being brain eaters, but I find this not to be the case. They are often grateful for the opportunity to be raised and will gladly help you with any manual labor you need to do, such as building unicorn stables.

<u>Spirits</u>—These are the mischievous ones. They enjoy pranking and humiliating anyone around them. They are mostly harmless, but you'd better keep an eye on them, or you will find yourself elbow-deep in grapes they insist are eyeballs. It's very annoying.

<u>Dead Clowns</u>—These are the worst. Stay away from any and all dead clowns. They are absolutely terrifying, with their painted faces and meat noses. They also <u>will</u> eat brains, so my recommendation is to leave them in the ground.

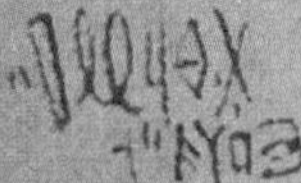

The Era of the Hourglass, year 4—

The neverending duties of being queen are starting to get to me. Every day I make food for the peasants, and do they ever thank me? No! They just want more and more! They are looking round as corn cakes! The daily rain of food has made such a mess of my beautiful castle courtyard. The food has also attracted monster riffraff, and they have been invading the villages and causing nothing but terror in my poor plump people! Plus, worst of all, Sir Gem-robin now has a girlfriend! I suppose I only have myself to blame. I have been trying to speak to him for 4 years and have only had the courage to ask him about the weather!

I was in a bad way. To make myself feel better, I used my dimensional scissors and traveled to Dimension 811. I like this dimension; the only life on 811 is some rock moss and some very stupid fluorescent worms. It's quiet, and a perfect place to push the limits of what one's wand can do. . . .

What to Do When You Explode a Dimension

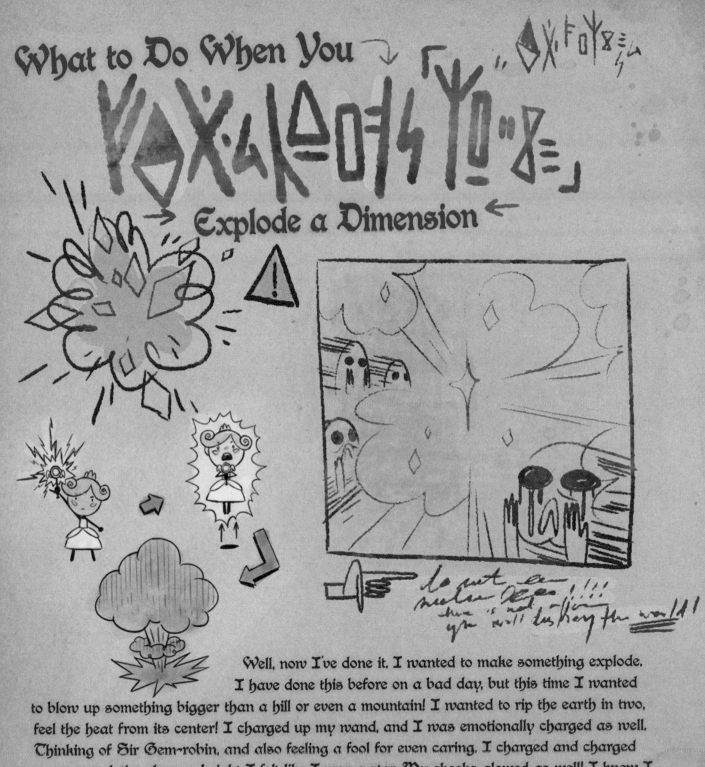

Well, now I've done it. I wanted to make something explode. I have done this before on a bad day, but this time I wanted to blow up something bigger than a hill or even a mountain! I wanted to rip the earth in two, feel the heat from its center! I charged up my wand, and I was emotionally charged as well. Thinking of Sir Gem-robin, and also feeling a fool for even caring, I charged and charged up my wand, the glow so bright I felt like I was a star. My cheeks glowed as well! I knew I must be dipping down for the first time! What a wonderful feeling, a feeling of so much power! I powered up and up, the glow from within me burning brighter and brighter! I was floating high up in the air! When I couldn't hold on to it any longer, I let out a mighty blast . . . and Dimension 811 was no more.

The Era of the Hourglass, year 10—

Well, I know you have not heard from me in many years; indeed, a lot has happened. I was quite devastated by my actions after blowing up Dimension 811. It may have only been a dimension of moss and worms, but I truly miss those moss and worms. Having that much power shook me to my core. I do not think any queen has pushed the limits of magic as much as I, and I hope no other does. The power is too great. I was falling into a pit of despair, only emerging once a day to make food for my people and then retiring to my quarters. One day, my mother came by and told me I was trying too hard, expecting too much. That I shouldn't try to solve all the problems of Mewni—it has far too many—and that I should really brush my hair.

I almost agreed with her, but something inside me shouted, "No! I can't lie idle! I am Skywynne, Queen of Hours! If I have the power to blow up a dimension, I can fix one, too!" Inspired, I ran out of the room. I announced to my people that I was no longer going to make food for them out of magic! At first they were horrified, but then we got to work. I cleared out some of the forests around the castle, scattering the monsters that lived there, making room for my people! We planted crops (mostly corn). It wasn't easy—often they complained—but eventually, they could feed themselves, and they were happier for it. In just five years, our population doubled. The castle grounds became too crowded, so we took over more and more of the monster territory. I taught my people to fight so that they could defend their land. It was a glorious time.

With the burden taken away of having to wait around for food to fall from the sky, my people were free to make art! We sang, we painted, I opened the Skywynne Institute for Unmagical but Somewhat Gifted Children.

It was such a beautiful and marvelous time! I was elated! I also heard a rumor that Sir Gem-robin was newly divorced. I went to his house, the one I knew so well from my former days of freezing time and sniffing his shirts. I knocked on the door, and when he answered, I kissed him! We were married the following year. My mother wanted to throw a grand party, but I said no way. Sir Gem-robin and I eloped in private in a quiet rocky dimension I found, surrounded by fluorescent worms. For you see, dear reader, after exploding Dimension 811, I found some of the worms in my shoe. I planted them in Dimension 812, a dimension previously void of life, and they are doing marvelously.

The Era of the Hourglass, year 13—

The most incredible thing happened today! Glossaryck has returned! I opened the book to write a new entry (That's right, I'm back to my spells again!) and there he was! Eating pudding, of all things, and getting it all over the pages of my beautiful book!

It turns out he had not burnt to ash in the fire! I asked Glossaryck where he'd been, and all he would answer was, "On vacation." Apparently, he hasn't changed at all.

He also told me my new book was lovely and he was going to live in it! He introduced me to some of his pets who would also be living with him, three silkworms named Silky, Stinky, and Sassafras. He told me they would be helpful if the book was ever burned again. He had some other pets, too: Stormy the centipede, Simone the beetle, and Sally the earwig. I welcomed them to the book. Of course, you know of my fondness for bugs.

He then asked me to introduce him to my daughter. Daughter? I told him I didn't have a girl, but a beautiful son named Jushtin (two years old now!). He just scratched his beard and asked if I was sure. I told him I know the difference between boys and girls, thank you very much. Then he went back into the book for a nap.

I may not have a daughter, but my son has great potential for magic! I can see it in his eyes. I sometimes even let him hold the wand, which takes the shape of a cane. I believe one day he will be a mighty magic wielder, like his mom. I feel like I have achieved a lot as queen. I am looking forward to the day when little Jushtin rules Mewni and perhaps I can retire to the royal vacation home inside the volcano.

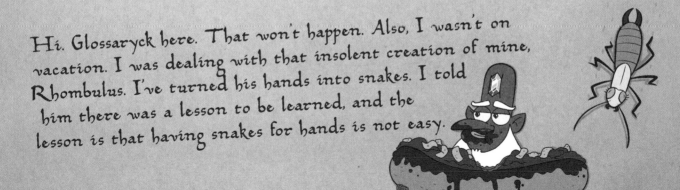

Hi. Glossaryck here. That won't happen. Also, I wasn't on vacation. I was dealing with that insolent creation of mine, Rhombulus. I've turned his hands into snakes. I told him there was a lesson to be learned, and the lesson is that having snakes for hands is not easy.

I have done it! I have created my greatest spell to date, perhaps the greatest one I will ever create. It is called the Warnicorn Stampede. I have taken the classic Warnicorn Transformation Spell and altered it with Stampede, multiplying the original warnicorn into a herd of warnicorns and then giving the herd locomotion. To make a Warnicorn Stampede, you must do a complicated incantation dance. I have drawn it out here.

TIP

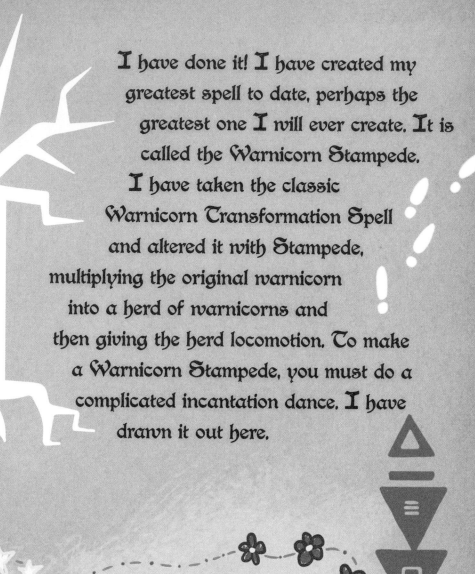

You can't be lazy on the incantation dance. When she says hold your wand "way up," you better hold it way up. I feel like this spell is a little overly complicated, but the end result is cool!

INCANTATION DANCE

1) Grasping your wand, cross your arms.

2) Hold your wand up, way up, and twirl.

3) Charge up your wand and strike a pose.

4) Charge up your wand and strike another pose.

5) Leap into the air.

6) Bow down.

7) Twirl one more time.

8) Strike one final pose with your wand above your head and call out, "Warnicorn Stampede!

Pulled this from a story about me in the Mewni Times!

9) Enjoy watching as your Warnicorn Stampede annihilates your enemies.

JUSHTIN
THE UNCALCULATED

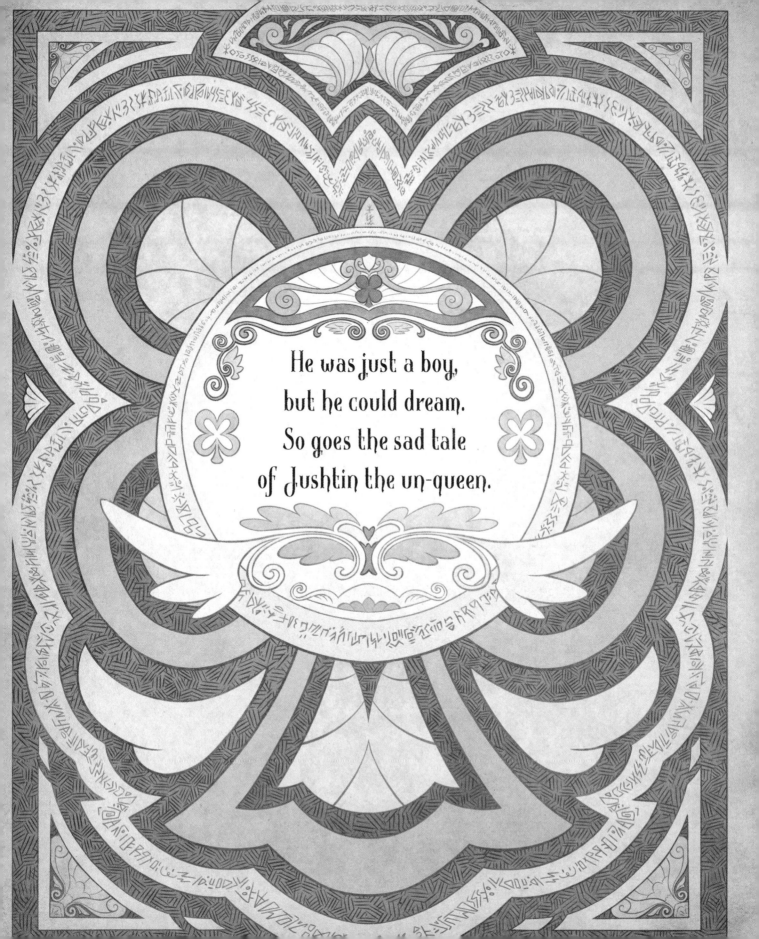

He was just a boy,
but he could dream.
So goes the sad tale
of Jushtin the un-queen.

Jushtin the Uncalculated

Aureole Sign: Bog Slug
Height: 6'

Attributes

Strength: 10	Dexterity: 3
Math: 20+	Constitution: 3
Wisdom: 4	Charisma: 4

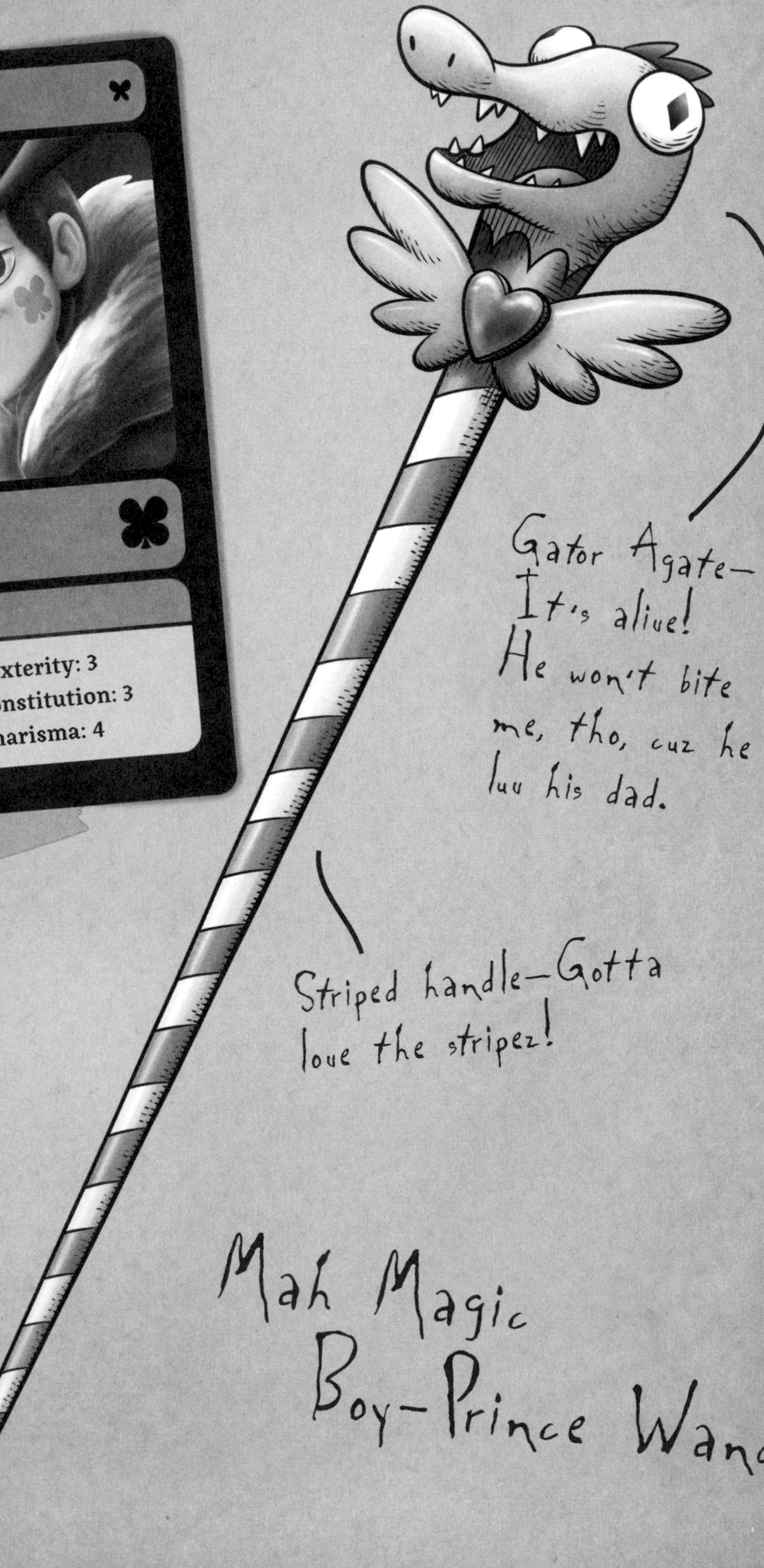

Gator Agate—It's alive! He won't bite me, tho, cuz he luv his dad.
Striped handle—Gotta love the stripez!

Mah Magic Boy-Prince Wand

Favorite BEVERAGE
HELLO
MY NAME IS
Jushtin
Favorite SHADEZ
My favorite music
My BFF, Prince Sazmo
Pea-Pea
Mah Ride (I WISH . . .)
THA CRU
Sazmo
Viscount Tinbenz
Whizzbag
MY MATH TUTOR

Let's reset tha Mewni calendar!!!

DAY ONE, YEAR OF THE JUSHTIN

Yo, 2 day is gonna be historic becuz Prince Jushtin has tha magic book now.

You may have heard about me from my mom's chapter (LUV U, MOM). I'm Mewni's new ruler and I am tired of the image of Mewni not being a destination. Me and mah cru are gonna put Mewni on the map!

It's gonna be so lit the light will be like a star and we'll measure the wavelength changes of the light the party's emitting with ma favorite Doppler equation:

$$\Delta \lambda / \lambda = v/c$$

Mewni is gonna be the new home for hangin' with your cru and useful equations!!!

Shout out to mah cru!!!

We're the Boy-Prince Cru and this how we roll—it's me; Sazmo of the Dock of Unending Torment; Pea-Pea, prince of Musty Mountain Caves; Viscount Tinbenz of the Spider Bites, and old Whizzbag of Garbage Beach!

If you want to put yer cru on the map u r gonna need a ride that says "put this cru on the map." To get a ride like this u will need a chariot.

(It can look dumb like this one. It's okay, we r gonna make some modifications.)

SPELLS

Yer gonna need some horses. Here is a spell for when you are with yer cru in the barn and you are trying to put wings on a horse. (This made Pea-Pea laugh at first but then the horse kicked him and Pea-Pea cried.)

Hold yer wand out and say, "Wings"! And point it at any old horse, okay?

Once you got your winged horses tied up to your chariot, yer ready 2 mod yer chariot. This spell will make a special extra-comfy seat for Whizzbag when he has his "creaky knees," as he calls them. I call this spell Creaky Knees (duh):

Point your Magic Boy-Prince Wand at the seat and say, "Creaky knees"!

Now yer chariot has flying horses and a seat for your elders. Ms. Jannis always sez respect your elders. NE wayz yer chariot is ready 2 fly. Before you take off, be sure to use this equation to calculate for lift, where the coefficient of lift is gonna be the tilt of them wings!

$$L = (1/2)\ d\ v^2\ s\ CL$$

Jushtin,

Stanfred found your Magic Book of Spells at the bottom of the UH-OH bin where we put the horse droppings in the stables. It's your book, and I really shouldn't have to intervene here, but it's impossible for me to imagine a scenario wherein your book would naturally find its way into the UH-OH bin. Needless to say, Glossaryck was utterly traumatized. This book will be a historical record—maybe the most important record of our family's magic, and I implore you to take better care of it. Use your good judgment.

Love,
Mom

Oh that's where i left it so dumb LUV U 2 MOM.

FINAL DAY—YEAR OF THE JUSHTIN

Oh, woeful morn.

Mother has revealed to me that she is with child. Her nursemaid read the moon-pond and believes the child will be a girl, so Mother came into my chamber and woke me from a brilliant slumber full of dreams of GOOD TIMEZ W/ MAH CRU.

"Jushtin, my sweet baby boy prince, it is with great sadness that I must take from you your Magic Book of Spells and your wand, or Magic Boy-Prince Wand as you call it. You see, soon you will have a sister, and she will be the rightful heir to the Mewni throne," she began. She told me of the nursemaid's premonition and then, choking back a single tear, Mother took my book and wand and left my chamber.

Through the crack in the chamber door left ajar, I could see that she was jumping up and down with joy, hugging the book and wand as though they were long-lost children. I can only imagine that this joy was some sort of mask for the pain she was feeling at having to take from me my natural birthright to then give to this unknown child, who is yet but a speck in the ether.

Oh, Mother, take off your mask and weep with me.
My heart is like a black hole.

Let us weep together as we measure this black hole's gravitational radius:

$$R_g = 2GM/c^2$$

SOLARIA
THE MONSTER
CARVER

A castle stormed is a hero born
with might and strong as steel.
Kneel the void before her
and the crushing force she wields.

THE WAND OF AGGRESSION

THIS WAND HAS SEEN ME THROUGH MANY BATTLES. IT IS AS IF IT WERE AN EXTENSION OF MY OWN ARMS.

NOTE I.

ETERNAL FIRE—THE FLAME THAT GIVES BREATH TO THE CAUTERIZING POWER OF MY WAND

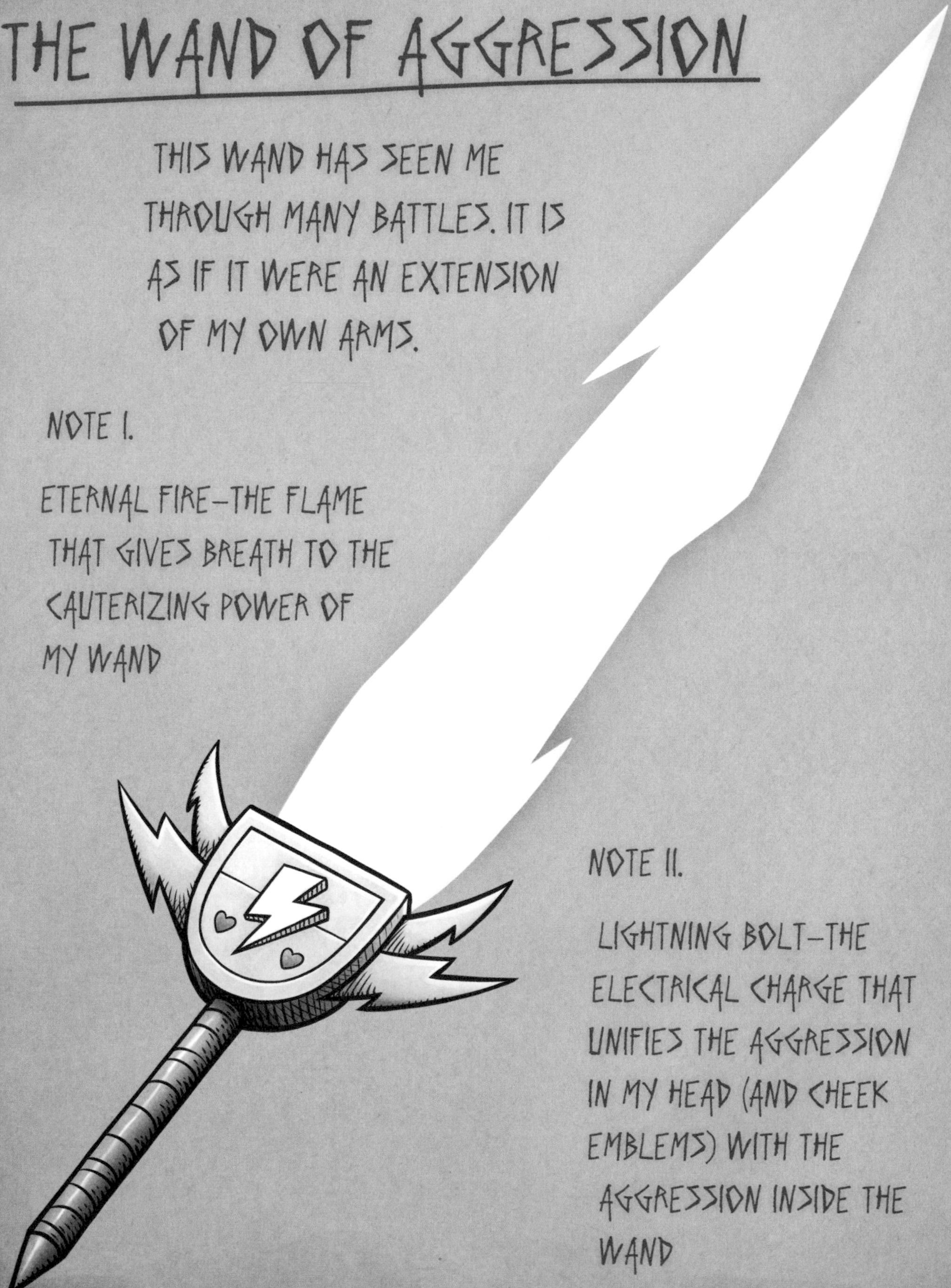

NOTE II.

LIGHTNING BOLT—THE ELECTRICAL CHARGE THAT UNIFIES THE AGGRESSION IN MY HEAD (AND CHEEK EMBLEMS) WITH THE AGGRESSION INSIDE THE WAND

NOTE III.

MILLHORSE—BARTHOLOMEW THE BRAVE—THE FINEST MILLHORSE ANY QUEEN COULD ASK FOR. HE HAS SERVED ME BRAVELY FOR YEARS AND MY LOVE FOR HIM IS UNCONDITIONAL. LOYALTY ABOVE ALL ELSE!

THE GREAT MONSTER WAR

VOLUME 1
THE ASSEMBLING TEMPEST

BOOK 1

FROM MONSTER TO MONSTER
WAR 690 – WAR 705

BOOK 2

THE ATTACK ON CLOUD KINGDOM
WAR 705 – WAR 713

BOOK 3

MEWNI REGAINED

WAR 713 - WAR 719

APPENDIX 1: MISCELLANEOUS

MAPS AND DIAGRAMS

CHAPTER 1

THE FOOLISHNESS OF THE QUEENS

AS THE YEARS PASSED AND THE MEWMANS BECAME A GREAT AND POWERFUL FORCE IN THE LANDS OF MEWNI, THE MONSTERS GREW JEALOUS OF US, BARRING OUR FURTHER SETTLING OF THE COUNTRY. THEY BLOCKED US FROM FOUNDING NEW VILLAGES IN PARTS OF THE LAND WHERE BEFORE ONLY MONSTERS DARED TO TREAD—WHILE, AT THE SAME TIME, DEMANDING THAT WE TREAT THEM WITH MORE RESPECT. A TRUE DICHOTOMY. WHY SHOULD WE RESPECT A CULTURE THAT DOES NOT RESPECT OUR OWN?

IT IS THE RIGHTFUL DUTY OF EACH OF THE QUEENS OF MEWNI TO EXPAND OUR REACH AND GIVE OUR SUBJECTS A BETTER WAY OF LIFE, REGARDLESS OF WHETHER OR NOT THE MONSTERS SEE THIS AS AN INCURSION INTO WHAT IS "RIGHTLY" THEIRS . . . AND IT HAS BEEN—UNTIL MY REIGN—THE QUEENS' FOLLY TO NOT AFFORD THE MONSTER THREAT THE DIRE SERIOUSNESS IT DESERVES. THE QUEENS BEFORE ME HAVE BEEN TOO LAX, HAVE LET THE MONSTERS GET AWAY WITH TOO MUCH.

BUT I, SOLARIA, WILL NOT ALLOW THAT TO BE THE CASE DURING MY REIGN. THE MONSTERS WILL COME UNDER MY THUMB AND LIKE IT—OR THEY WILL BE WIPED FROM THE FACE OF THE LAND.

Solaria the Monster Carver
Aureole Sign: Lion Dragon
Height: 6' 3"
Attributes
Strength: 20
Intelligence: 13
Wisdom: 13
Cold Determination: 18
Constitution: 20
Charisma: 13

I tried giving myself this haircut when I was feeling unqueenly. Solaria got away with it. But I don't think it's really for me.

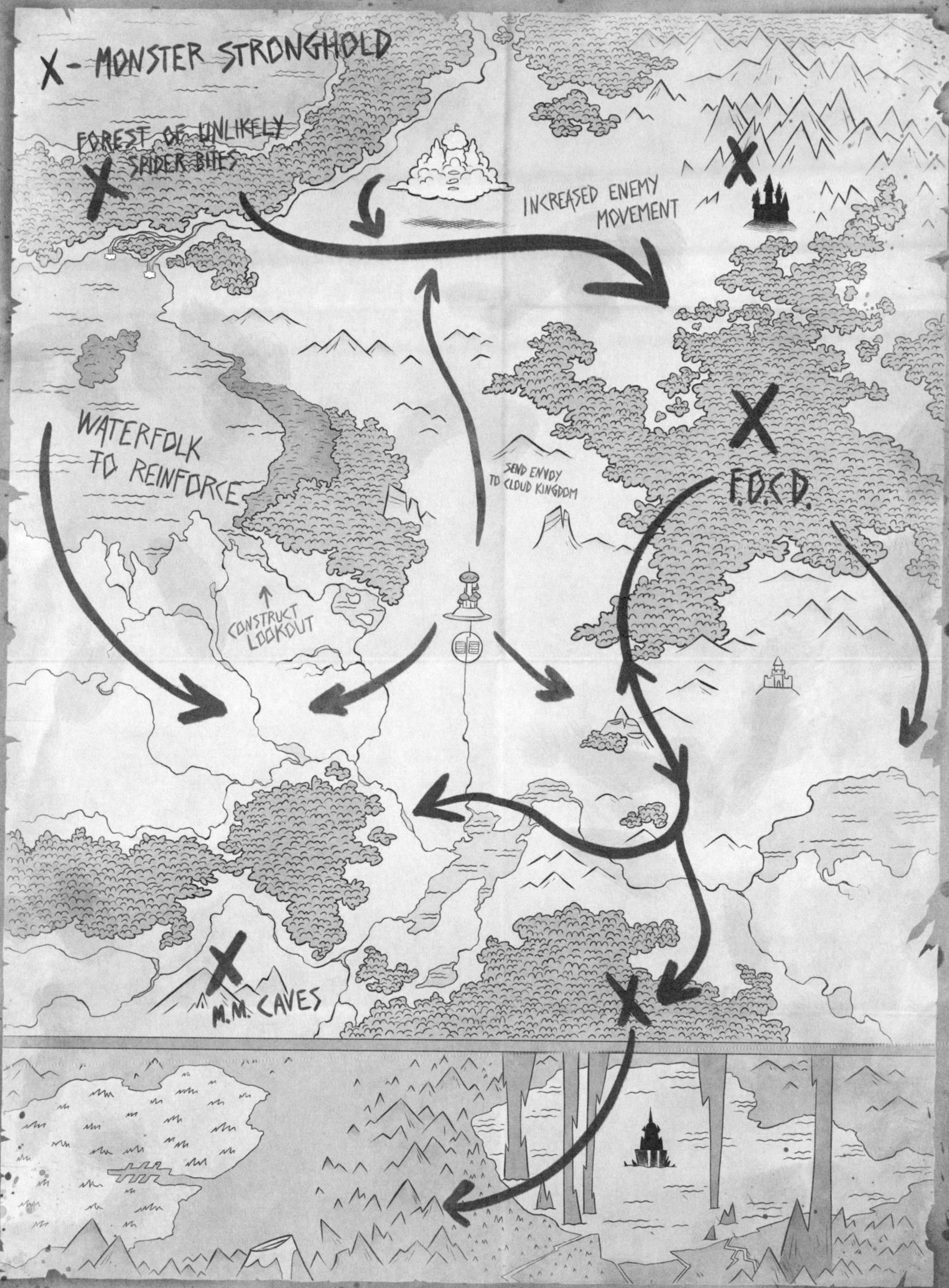
X - MONSTER STRONGHOLD
FOREST OF UNLIKELY SPIDER BITES
INCREASED ENEMY MOVEMENT
WATERFOLK TO REINFORCE
SEND ENVOY TO CLOUD KINGDOM
F.O.C.D.
CONSTRUCT LOOKOUT
M.M. CAVES

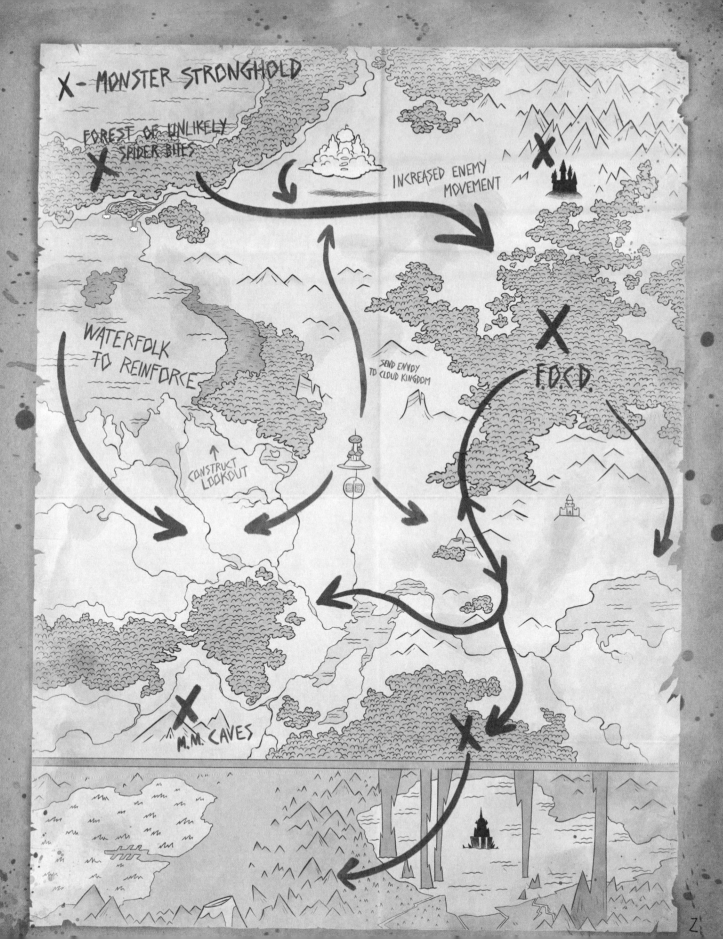

LETTER FROM THE SECRETARY OF THE MONSTER PEACE COUNCIL

Queen Solaria—

All efforts to peaceably parley with the monsters have failed—and now they will no longer allow us safe passage back through the Forest of Certain Death. As of this writing, the monsters were unwilling to meet our demands—and, therefore, we were unable to entertain theirs. It is with a sad—and hardened—heart that I must inform you that war with the monsters looks inevitable. Do with this information what you will, but know that your subjects are loyal men and women such as myself, who are willing to die for their queen. We will try to return to our queen's side, but the journey is long and dangerous since we cannot venture safely back the way we came.

I do fear that this message may never reach your eyes, so I have sent three of my fastest raven scouts (with the same message) in hopes that one of them will find a way to breach the monsters' ranks and reach Butterfly Castle.

In Eternal Orderliness,

Alphonse the Worthy
Secretary of the Monster Peace Council

CHAPTER 11

CREEPING EVIL

I BELIEVE THAT THE MONSTERS ARE JEALOUS OF OUR ACCOMPLISHMENTS AND THAT THEY MUST WANT OUR MAGIC AND POWER FOR THEMSELVES. THEY HAVE RAIDED OUR OUTLYING SETTLEMENTS—THE ONES FARTHEST FROM BUTTERFLY CASTLE—AND MANY MEWMAN LIVES AND HOMES HAVE BEEN LOST. WE CANNOT STAND BY AND ALLOW THIS TO HAPPEN. WE MUST GATHER OUR STRENGTH AND CREATE AN ARMY THAT IS UNPARALLELED IN ALL OF MEWNI'S HISTORY.

I PITY THE MONSTERS. THEY HAVE NO INKLING OF THE SLEEPING DRAGON THEY HAVE JUST AWOKEN. I, AND MY TRUSTED COUNCILLORS, WILL CONVENE THE MONSTER WAR COUNCIL—AN ENTITY THAT HAS NOT BEEN CALLED TO ORDER IN A CENTURY—AND THEN THEY WILL BE VERY SORRY, INDEED.

****

THE MONSTER WAR COUNCIL WAS CALLED INTO SESSION THIS MORNING. TWO OF MY MOST TRUSTED COUNCILLORS, HECKAPOO AND ALPHONSE THE WORTHY, SPOKE FIRST. THEY URGED THE OTHER MEMBERS OF THE COUNCIL TO VOTE FOR WAR WITH THE MONSTERS. ALPHONSE SPOKE ELOQUENTLY, SHARING HIS HORRIFIC EXPERIENCES ON THE PEACE MISSION HE HEADED TO THE FOREST OF CERTAIN DEATH, WHERE ALL TWENTY MEMBERS OF HIS PARTY LOST EITHER THEIR MINDS OR THEIR LIVES.

AFTER HIS HARROWING TALE, A VOTE WAS CALLED AND THE RESPONSE WAS UNANIMOUS:

WE ARE GOING TO WAR WITH THE MONSTERS.

CHAPTER III

A NEW MAGICAL ARMY

WAR IS DARK BUSINESS—DARKER THAN ANY OF US REALIZED. OUR SOLDIERS ARE NOT EQUIPPED TO HANDLE THE ONSLAUGHT FROM SO MANY SIDES. IT SEEMS THAT WHEREVER WE LOOK, THERE IS A NEW EVIL RISING UP TO ATTACK US. WE ARE OUTNUMBERED AND UNDERPOWERED. IF WE DO NOT WANT TO LOSE WHAT WE HAVE, WE MUST FIND A NEW WAY TO FIGHT. WE NEED A NEW KIND OF WARRIOR, ONE WHO CAN MATCH THE MONSTERS IN STRENGTH AND CUNNING.

UNTIL NOW, THE MAGIC HIGH COMMISSION HAS BEEN WORKING ON THIS PROBLEM. BUT RECENTLY I HAVE DISCOVERED THROUGH CAREFUL RESEARCH THAT A COMBINATION OF THREE OLD SPELLS—SPELLS ONCE KNOWN TO THE QUEENS BUT THAT DISAPPEARED WHEN BUTTERFLY CASTLE BURNED DOWN AND THE PREVIOUS BOOK WAS DESTROYED DURING MY MOTHER'S REIGN—MIGHT BE THE KEY. I HAVE PORED THROUGH HUNDREDS OF MAGICAL TOMES AND I BELIEVE I HAVE FOUND MANY PIECES OF THESE SPELLS SCATTERED INSIDE FIRSTHAND ACCOUNTS WRITTEN IN TWELVE OTHER BOOKS. THESE ACCOUNTS ARE TOLD BY MEWMANS WHO SAW THESE SPELLS USED BEFORE BY THE OLD QUEENS.

ONCE THE THREE SPELLS HAVE BEEN FULLY RECONSTITUTED, WE WILL BE ABLE TO CREATE A SUPERPOWERED MAGICAL ARMY. ONE THAT WILL BE THE BASIS FOR OUR NEW FIGHTING FORCE, AND ONE THAT I KNOW WILL BE UNEQUALED IN THE ANNALS OF HISTORY. TO THIS END, I HAVE REMOVED MYSELF FROM THE BATTLEFIELD—WHICH IS MY TRUE PLACE AS LEADER—AND NOW I SPEND HOURS LOCKED AWAY IN A LONELY TOWER AT BUTTERFLY CASTLE, DEVELOPING THESE NEW/OLD SPELLS.

WE WILL START TESTING THE FIRST OF THESE SPELLS—B.E.A.R.—ON OUR WILLING PEASANT VOLUNTEER ARMY BEGINNING TOMORROW MORNING. I HOPE, THROUGH PRACTICE, TO LEARN HOW TO WEAVE ALL THREE SPELLS TOGETHER INTO A TRIPTYCH SPELL, WHICH WILL CREATE OUR SUPERCHARGED ARMY!

I was MIA for all this. I don't dabble in politics.

THE SOLARIAN METAMORPHOSIS
A TRIPTYCH OF THREE SPELLS

B.E.A.R: BRUTE EAGER ATTACK ROAR

FOR BRUTE STRENGTH AND EAGERNESS TO ATTACK
WITHOUT THE BINDINGS OF FEAR

TWO GROWLS
THREE SLASHES OF WAND
ONE SECOND-FINGER PRICK
(ON SHARPENED WAND BLADE)

FOR SPELL PERMANENCE DRINK THREE DROPS OF HONEYSUCKLE NECTAR AFTER COMPLETING SPELL, AND NO LONGER WILL YOU FEEL FEAR IN BATTLE.

B.O.A.R.: BLUNT OFFENSE ARREST RETORT

FOR BLUNTING OF CONSCIENCE IN BATTLE

ONE HOWL
TWO SWIRLS OF WAND
ONE THUMB PRICK
(ON SHARPENED WAND BLADE)

FOR SPELL PERMANENCE DRINK THREE DROPS OF LIZARD BLOOD AFTER COMPLETING SPELL, AND NO LONGER WILL YOU HAVE A CONSCIENCE IN BATTLE.

R.A.P.T.O.R.: RAGE AGGRESSION PANIC TORPOR OLFACTORY RESPONSE

FOR ENHANCEMENT OF ALL SENSES IN BATTLE

TWO HAWK SCREAMS
TWO JABS OF WAND
ONE BIG-TOE PRICK
(ON SHARPENED WAND BLADE)

FOR SPELL PERMANENCE DRINK THREE DROPS OF PIGEON BLOOD AFTER COMPLETING SPELL, AND YOUR SENSES WILL SOAR IN BATTLE.

ONCE A PEASANT VOLUNTEER HAS GONE THROUGH ALL THREE PHASES OF THE SOLARIAN METAMORPHOSIS SPELL, THEY ARE ENDOWED WITH A WEAPON HARNESSING THE ETERNAL FLAME OF MY OWN WAND OF AGGRESSION; THE MARK OF THIS BLADE IS TERMINAL, PARTICULARLY FOR MONSTERS.

MINA LOVEBERRY WAS THE FIRST PEASANT TO VOLUNTEER HER BODY FOR MAGICAL EXPERIMENTATION AND SHE WILL FOREVER AND ALWAYS BE MY MOST TRUSTED SOLARIAN. MAY SHE LIVE AS LONG AS FATE ALLOWS!

CHAPTER IV

THE TAKEOVER OF CLOUD KINGDOM

TODAY WE HAD BOTH GOOD NEWS AND BAD: THE SOLARIAN WARRIOR ARMY HAS TAKEN BACK A WIDE SWATH OF LAND FROM THE MONSTERS, BUT WHILE OUR BACKS WERE TURNED, THE MONSTERS DESCENDED ON OUR ALLIES, THE PONY HEADS. CLOUD KINGDOM HAS BEEN OVERRUN WITH MONSTERS.

****

MY SOLARIAN WARRIORS—STRANGE TO THINK THESE MEN AND WOMEN WERE ONCE COWERING PEASANTS BEFORE MY MAGIC WAS WORKED UPON THEM—ARE BRAVE AND UNSTOPPABLE. LATE LAST NIGHT, I LED THEM INTO COMBAT AGAINST THE DREADED MONSTER HORDE AND, TOGETHER WITH THE PONY HEAD RESISTANCE, WE WAGED A BLOODY BATTLE THAT ENDED WITH THE MONSTERS' RETREAT.

TONIGHT, WE CELEBRATE BY BURNING THE BODIES OF THE MONSTER DEAD ON A GIANT PYRE AND DANCING WITH WILD ABANDON UNTIL THE SUN RISES OVER THE CHARRED EMBERS, EATING AND DRINKING OUR FILL UNTIL WE FALL INTO UNCONSCIOUSNESS.

CHAPTER V

THE ASSAULT ON BUTTERFLY CASTLE

THE MONSTERS WILL NOT BREAK THROUGH OUR DEFENSES. THEY WILL NEVER SET FOOT IN BUTTERFLY CASTLE . . . UNLESS IT IS OVER MY DEAD BODY.

****

A TRAGEDY WAS ONLY BARELY AVERTED TODAY—MY YOUNG DAUGHTER, ECLIPSA, WAS ALMOST KIDNAPPED BY A MONSTER. SHE IS THE LIGHT OF MY LIFE, THE APPLE OF MY EYE . . . AND AS IT IS ONLY THE TWO OF US (I HAVE NEITHER TIME NOR INTEREST IN TAKING A KING)—TO LOSE HER WOULD BE THE END OF ME.

SHE IS AN INTELLIGENT CHILD AND SHE LOVES TO DISAPPEAR INTO THE SECRET RECESSES OF THE CASTLE. WE OFTEN LOSE HER FOR HOURS AT A TIME . . . BUT ALWAYS SHE RETURNS TO HER ROOMS FOR DINNER. THIS DAY, NO ONE—NOT EVEN MYSELF—COULD FIND HER. I FEEL RESPONSIBLE FOR THIS BECAUSE SHE BEGGED TO GO WITH ME THIS MORNING TO PARLEY WITH THE LEADER OF THE MONSTER HORDE—A STRANGE SIZE-SHIFTER WHO CAN BARELY SLOBBER ITS OWN NAME—AND I DID NOT DEEM IT SAFE FOR HER TO ATTEND.

DESPITE MY ORDERS, THIS MERE BABE (MAY I REITERATE AGAIN HOW INTELLIGENT SHE IS?) SNUCK OUT OF THE MAGIC BARRIER IN ORDER TO FIND ME. INSTEAD OF HER MOTHER'S ARMS, MY DAUGHTER FOUND HERSELF IN THE CLUTCHES OF AN EVIL MONSTER HELLBENT ON HER DESTRUCTION. HAD WE NOT ENDED THE PARLEY EARLY (WITHOUT SUCCESS—THE MONSTER HORDE IS IRREDEEMABLE), I WOULD NEVER HAVE COME ACROSS THE KIDNAPPING IN PROGRESS . . . AND I WOULD HAVE LOST MY DARLING FOREVER.

TO MY UTTER SHAME, I WAS TOO OVERWHELMED WITH SHOCK TO END THE HORRID MONSTER'S LIFE AND IT ESCAPED. POOR ECLIPSA WAS BESIDE HERSELF FROM HER NEAR ESCAPE FROM DEATH, AND SPENT ALL THE REST OF THE DAY IN TEARS.

MONSTER ANNIHILATION TECHNIQUES

LIZARD MEN

NOT SURE WHAT TO DO WITH THESE ONES . . . BEST TO JUST EXPLODE THEM AND SPREAD THE PIECES AS FAR APART AS POSSIBLE. THEY ARE HAPPIER THIS WAY.

SLIME MEN

DO NOT TOUCH THESE SLIPPERY BEASTS. A SPELL WORKED FROM FAR AWAY IS ADVISED, POSSIBLY SOMETHING THAT BURNS THEM TO A CRISP OR SENDS THEM TO ANOTHER DIMENSION. THEY ARE SO MUCH HAPPIER THIS WAY.

KAPPA

A COWARDLY, MEAN-SPIRITED SORT. A SIMPLE DISEMBOWELMENT SPELL WILL MAKE THEM RUE THE DAY THEY WERE BROUGHT INTO THIS WORLD. I PROMISE THEY ARE HAPPIER THIS WAY.

FROG MEN

THESE CREATURES DESERVE NO MERCY. TO END THEIR MISERABLE EXISTENCE, YOU MUST MINCE THEM INTO TINY PIECES. BELIEVE ME WHEN I SAY THAT THEY ARE HAPPIER THIS WAY.

CONJOINICANS

THESE CREATURES, TOO, DESERVE NO MERCY. THEY ARE AN ABOMINATION TO THE EVER AFTER. TO END THEIR MISERABLE EXISTENCE, YOU MUST FLAMBÉ THEM WITH YOUR SWORD WAND. THEY ARE MOST DEFINITELY HAPPIER THIS WAY.

CPS: CRYSTAL PULVERIZING SPELL*

THE CRYSTAL PULVERIZING SPELL IS A FAVORITE OF MINE. IT WORKS ON ALL CRYSTALS, ESPECIALLY THE CRYSTALS RHOMBULUS SHOOTS FROM HIS HEAD AND SNAKE HANDS IN ORDER TO TRAP EVILDOERS. THIS SPELL IS VERY HELPFUL WHEN RHOMBULUS ACCIDENTALLY CRYSTALLIZES A MEWMAN IN THE HEAT OF BATTLE.

ONE COCKEREL CROW
ONE SWISH OF WAND
ONE RIGHT EARLOBE PRICK
(ON SHARPENED WAND BLADE)

REPEAT BACKWARD:
ONE LEFT EARLOBE PRICK
(ON SHARPENED WAND BLADE)
ONE WAND SWISH
ONE COCKEREL CROW

*GUARANTEED TO PULVERIZE ANY AND ALL CRYSTALS YOU MAY ENCOUNTER WHILE ON YOUR JOURNEY

CHAPTER VI

THE MAGIC HIGH COMMISSION: THE HECKAPOO ASSIGNMENT

WE ARE STILL UNDER ASSAULT FROM THE MONSTER HORDE. THE DAYS ARE LONG AND EXHAUSTING. THOSE OF US TRAPPED INSIDE THE CASTLE AWAIT THE ARRIVAL OF THE SOLARIAN WARRIOR ARMY, WHICH IS FORTHCOMING. BUT MORE MONSTERS ARRIVE AT THE SIEGE EACH DAY, AND IT HAS BECOME APPARENT THAT WE NEED HELP FROM BOTH THE LUCITORS AND THE PONY HEADS. AN ALLIANCE MUST BE REACHED, OR BUTTERFLY CASTLE MAY FALL.

I HAVE ASKED HECKAPOO TO ASSEMBLE A DIPLOMATIC TEAM TO GO AND ASK FOR THEIR HELP. MY STRANGELY FABULOUS MATH GENIUS OLDER BROTHER, JUSHTIN—WHO RULED (IF ONLY FOR A SHORT TIME) BEFORE ME—HAS VOLUNTEERED TO BE OUR ROYAL ENVOY. HECKPAOO, JUSHTIN, AND ALPHONSE THE WORTHY WILL USE DIMENSIONAL SCISSORS TO SECRETLY LEAVE THE CASTLE. I HAVE ABSOLUTE FAITH IN THEIR ABILITIES.

HECKAPOO'S DIAGRAM OF DIPLOMACY

N
W
E
S
CLOUD KINGDOM
MEWNI
UNDERWORLD

CHAPTER VII

OPERATION WAND LIGHT

After a decade of fierce and bloody battle, the success of Heckapoo's diplomatic mission has brought Butterfly Castle back from the brink. Warriors from the Underworld and the Cloud Kingdom joined with our Solarian Warrior army and sent the monsters into a full-scale retreat—but only to the Forest of Certain Death.

The Magic High Commission has drafted a resolution that calls for a ceasefire with the monsters, but I am against it. Monsters are lesser than Mewmans and should not be afforded the same respect that we accord the Pony Heads and the Lucitors of the Underworld. I believe a ceasefire would only encourage the monsters. . . . To my mind, annihilation is the only true course left to us.

I am crafting a spell that will turn my wand into a weapon of mass destruction, called the Total Annihilation spell.

CHAPTER VIII

THE WAND IS NOT AGLOW

OVER THE LAST FEW YEARS THERE HAS BEEN A SIGNIFICANT DROP IN MONSTER BATTLES TO BE FOUGHT—AND THOUGH I AM STILL THE GENERAL IN CHARGE OF THE SOLARIAN WARRIOR ARMY, MY TALENTS ARE LESS NEEDED. ALSO, I HAVE FAILED AS A MAGIC WIELDER. I HAVE KEPT MY ATTEMPTS AT THE TOTAL ANNIHILATION SPELL A SECRET . . . BECAUSE ALL MY ATTEMPTS HAVE BEEN FAILURES. I DON'T EVEN FEEL COMFORTABLE COMMITTING THE SPELL TO THIS BOOK—PERHAPS I'LL FIND A WAY TO LEAVE IT FOR LITTLE ECLIPSA SO THAT IT'S AWAY FROM GLOSSARYCK'S ALL-SEEING EYES. GLOSSARYCK, IF YOU'RE READING THIS NOW, KNOW THAT I AM MAD AT YOU. GLOSSARYCK WILL NOT HELP ME BECAUSE HE IS APOLITICAL. I TRULY BELIEVE HE IS MAD AT ME FOR SPURNING THE MONSTER CEASEFIRE AND, INSTEAD, KEEPING MY SOLARIANS AT WAR WITH THE MONSTERS. HE DOES NOT UNDERSTAND . . . THE MONSTERS WILL FOREVER COME AFTER US. THEY WILL NEVER STOP UNTIL THEY CONTROL ALL OF OUR LANDS AND HAVE TURNED US INTO THEIR SLAVES.

ONLY I HAVE HAD THE FORESIGHT TO SEE THE FUTURE. ONLY I KNOW THAT BLOODSHED IS THE ANSWER—BUT, SADLY, THIS IS WHERE MY CHAPTER ENDS. MY DEAR ECLIPSA WILL NOW BE THE OWNER OF THE BOOK AND WAND. HERE IS A DRAWING SHE DID AS A CHILD, ONE I KEPT NEAR MY HEART IN BATTLE. IT WAS MY TALISMAN AND IT KEPT ME SAFE THROUGH ALL MY ADVENTURES. . . .

I LOVE YOU
MOM

DRAWING BY ECLIPSA, AGE 7

ECLIPSA
THE QUEEN OF
DARKNESS

Eclipsa, queen of Mewni,
to a Mewman king was wed,
but took a monster for her love
and away from Mewni fled.

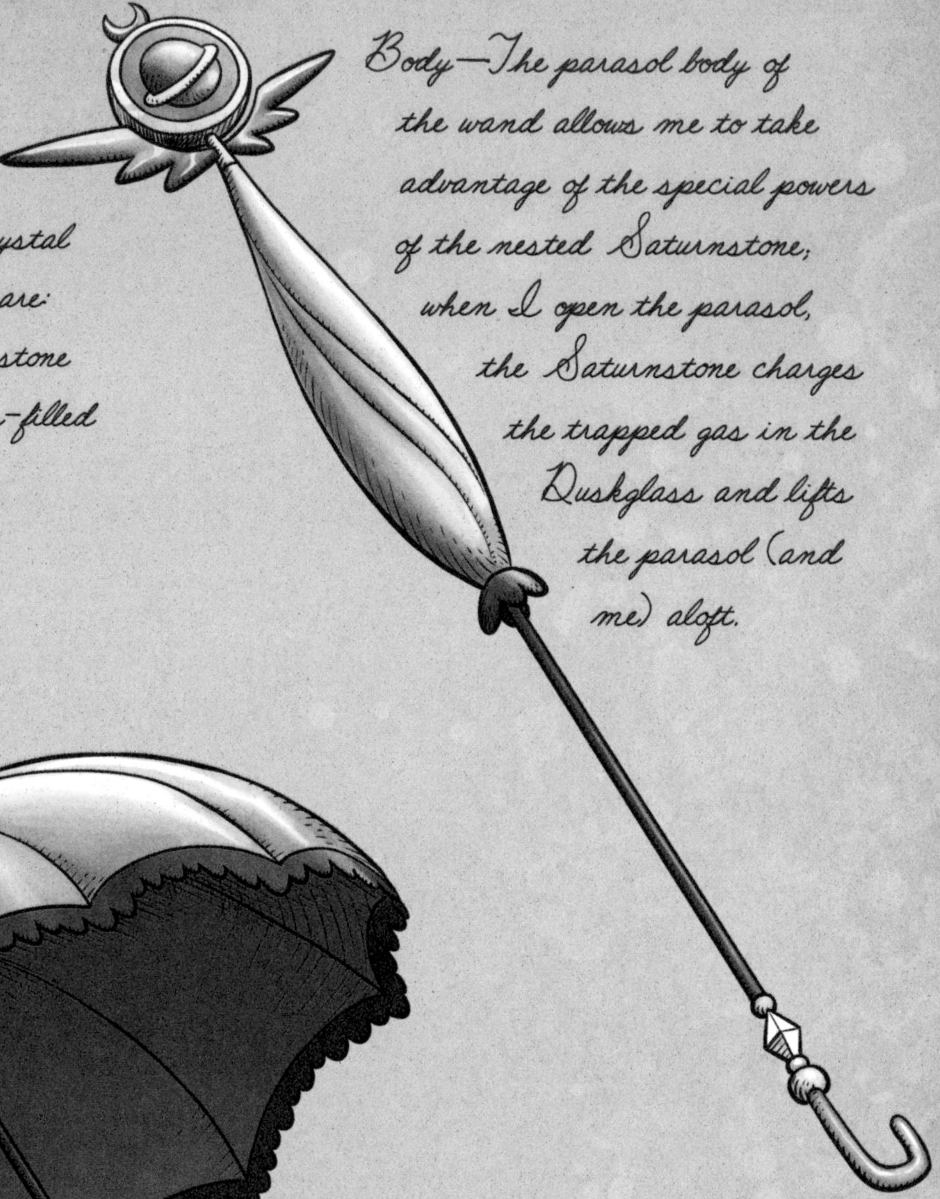

Body—The parasol body of the wand allows me to take advantage of the special powers of the nested Saturnstone; when I open the parasol, the Saturnstone charges the trapped gas in the Duskglass and lifts the parasol (and me) aloft.

Crystal—My crystal is actually quite rare: a nested Saturnstone inside a clear gas-filled Duskglass.

Handle—the gem at the handle of my wand is a Whisperstone, which has the power to "speak" to other stones. In some attacks, I can fire from both the Saturnstone and the Whisperstone, allowing for a forked attack.

Millhorse—Orion the Brindle.

Eclipsa the Queen of Darkness ✗✗✗✗✗

Aureole Sign: Demon
Height: 5' 2"

♠

Attributes

Strength: 14
Intelligence: 18
Wisdom: 16

Dexterity: 15
Constitution: 18
Charisma: 18

I read her spells. . . .
NBD.

I've had my wand and book for several months now, and it's been hard to know what to put in here. My mother says it's a place of truth. She assures me that as long as I have this book, it will be mine and my secrets will be accessible to me only.

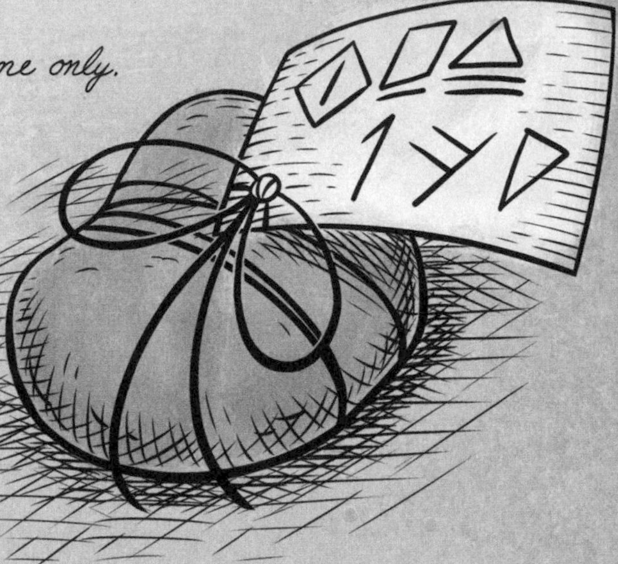

She's encouraged me to treat the book as a trusted friend. It's integral to ensuring that what ends up in here will be of use to the future queens. I, of course, want to fulfill this part of my duty as princess and ultimately queen, but I'd really like to just use this book for myself right now. Mother says that it's a good place to start, so I guess this will be a lot more like a journal than anything.

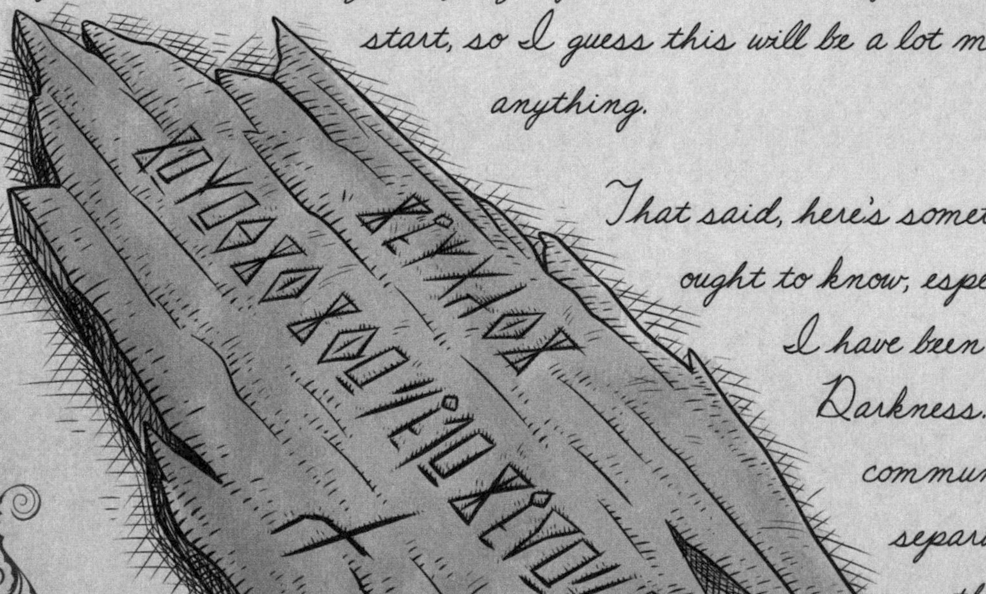

That said, here's something NO ONE ought to know, especially not Mother. I have been seeing the Prince of Darkness. Really, we never stopped communicating since Mother separated us back during the assault on Butterfly Castle. She thought he was attacking me. . . HA!

We have continued to leave secret messages for one another throughout the kingdom during all this war and destruction, and ultimately, when this is over and truth wins out, the chronicle of our enduring love will be a great lesson in resilience to any future princesses.

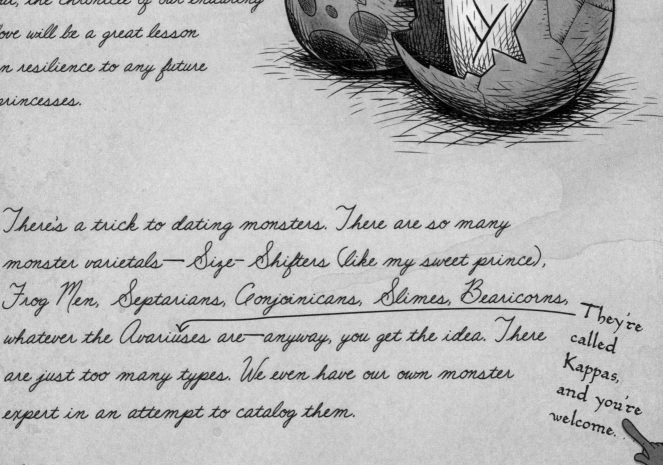

There's a trick to dating monsters. There are so many monster varietals—Size-Shifters (like my sweet prince), Frog Men, Septarians, Conjoinicans, Slimes, Bearicorns, whatever the Avariuses are—anyway, you get the idea. There are just too many types. We even have our own monster expert in an attempt to catalog them.

They're called Kappas, and you're welcome.

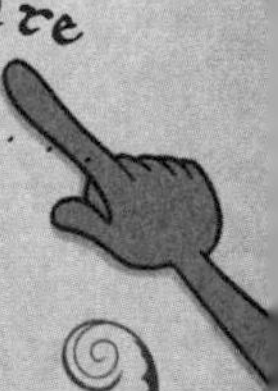

I've dated them all, and if you're an adventurous princess like me, then you're probably eager to see what the monster community has to offer by way of men. Your interest alone won't be enough to prepare you; you need to know your monsters.

Eclipsa's Monster-Dating Guide

Slimes

Dateability score: 5/10

Dating Pros:

* They are very nice.
* They are all called Slime, so you'll never forget their name.
* Their mucus can heal a rash or allergic reaction.

Dating Cons:

* They are very nice (Zzzzz . . .).
* They are all called Slime, so you won't be able to tell them apart, really.
* Their mucus can cause a rash or allergic reaction.

In general, you can have a good time on a date with a Slime, but you can also have a good time at home in your pajamas.

Septarians

Dateability score: 9/10

Dating Pros:

* Looks good in a suit.
* Looks good in a swim suit.
* Attractively aloof.

Dating Cons:

* Not so fond of magical Mewman girls.
* Probably wants to kill your mom.
* Your friends will all have a secret crush on him.

Look, these guys are creeps and you should stay as far away as possible, but if you're like me, you'll ignore this advice—it's worth it.

Whatever these are

Dateability score: 4/10

Kappas! They're called Kappas!

Dating Pros:

- They're pretty unfriendly, so you'll never have to worry about your best friend being a third wheel when you go out.
- They're rich, if you're into that.
- They're sorta vegetarians, except for bugs. Are bugs meat?

Bugs are my only friends.

Dating Cons:

- Too many siblings.
- Needy and narcissistic, great combo (thumbs-down).
- They're braggadocious and have little-man complexes.

This is going to seem like a weird suggestion given the low score here, but you must try dating one of these little guys. It's endlessly entertaining, and by endless, I mean until the end of the single date you will go on with him, after which you'll kindly let him know he shouldn't expect a second date.

Frog Men

Dateability score: 3/10

Dating Pros:

- Hmmmmm . . .
- Having trouble with this one . . .
- They can destroy your adversaries?

Dating Cons:

- Just about everything.

Look, I gave it a try, honestly. I would have given him a zero, but I decided he deserved at least a 3/10 because he said "excuse me" after he coughed up and re-ate a dragonfly.

Size-Shifter

Dateability score: 9/10*

Dating Pros:

- All of the muscles ♡
- Emotionally available
- Size-Shifters tend to be great at tight two-part harmonies

Dating Cons:

- Eats people
- That hair . . . is it long? Is it short? Is that a ponytail or a bun up there?

The Prince of Darkness is a Size-Shifter, so naturally I have a soft spot for them. The people-eating is usually a red flag for most—justifiably so, I recommend trying to get him to go vegetarian. You can reward him with smooches for each consecutive day free of people-eating. The hair? You'll have to let it go.

*Could almost be 10 but I don't want it to go to his head :)

Conjoinicans

Dateability score: Left Side 7/10, Right Side 4/10

Dating Pros:

- When one gets tired, the other one can rub your feet. It's basically like an infinite foot-massage if you rig it right.
- They love their moms.
- If one is boring, you can focus on the other.

Dating Cons:

- Conjoinicans are demons, so you have to deal with the rage and fire. Sometimes it's hot . . . in a bad way.
- They don't always get along, so sometimes the date feels a bit like a therapy session.
- They cry at sad plays and their tears are boiling acid. Something to look out for.

You'll want to decide what kind of gal you are: a left-side or right-side kinda gal. The right side is a bit slower and more needy. The left side is more spontaneous, but you'll never get flowers from him. I'm obviously a left-sider, but I do like the right's cute neediness on occasion.

165 ♠

Despite the war, Mother said it's very important to continue our traditions, so we had the Silver Bell Ball yesternight. Once again, there's an unspoken pressure for me to connect, as Mother says, with the little (though he's quite portly) boy—Prince Shastacan of the Spider Bites.

Uncle Jushtin married Duchess Recluza of the Spider Bites, and we gained nothing from it.

"It's good for our kingdoms to come together; the Spider Bites have resources that could benefit the Butterfly Kingdom," Mother says. What resources? Regular, repeated bites by slightly venomous spiders? No thank you. "Oh, the welts from the spider venom go down eventually . . ." she says.

I understand her position; taking a king is arbitrary. She just went out to sea with Alphonse and nine months later I was born. To her, the king is just throne candy—someone to sit there and look fancy and powdered next to the queen. But even so, consider this:

Lord Styneworthe and Lady Sinew of the Spider Bite Family
request the pleasure of your company in celebration of their son

Little Lad-Prince Shastacan

in his debut into Adult Society.
Please join us on the Seventeenth of Sagnog at six-thirty for food and dancing.
Spider repellent will be provided for the first one hundred guests who RSVP.

Is this someone who is going to make the right impression on the kingdom? I danced with him out of obligation, and he smelled of a musty old coin purse. Not my kink. Plus, he's a bit of an algae-chewer—I understand it's a bad habit and I certainly have my own, but I really find algae teeth to be quite appalling.

I also read his mind while we were dancing. It's a little spell that I created and I refuse to share it, so don't expect to find it in here. Needless to say, there was absolutely <u>nothing</u> going on in there. He wasn't even thinking of how irresistible my rose-oil perfume is. . . .

I'm not sure I'm the key to the Spider Bite/Butterfly Kingdom accord. I just don't share Mother's point of view when it comes to love. I'm not sure she needs to have a real connection with another, but I do.

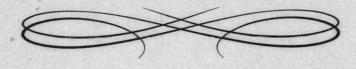

I do magic for myself. I know that goes against the tradition of our society, but it could be argued the queen can't tend to the needs of the kingdom unless she has tended to her own.

These spells are NOT for everyone, but maybe you will find them useful.

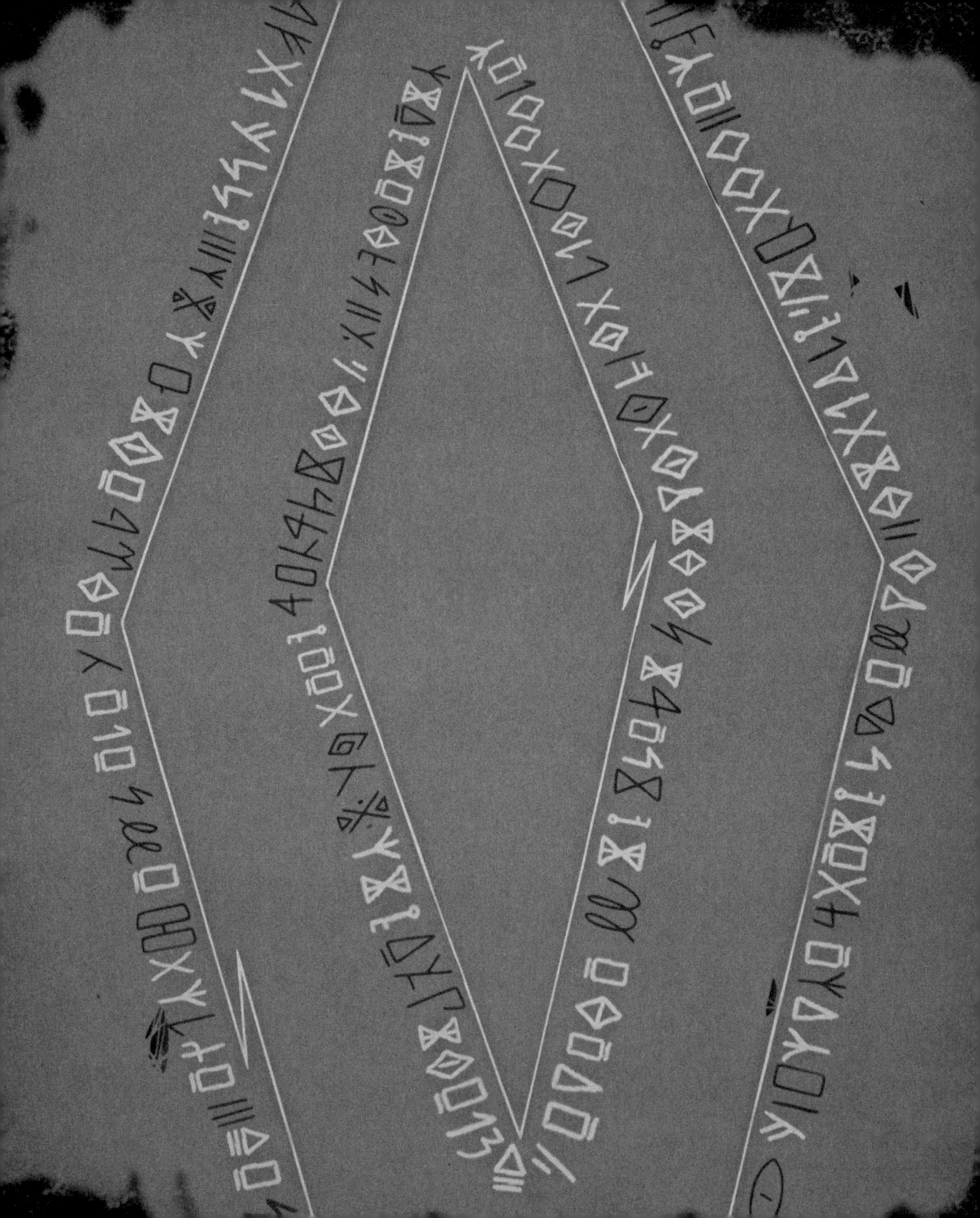

THE ALL SEEING EYE

Midnight Shriek

This spell creates a piercing, soul-freezing sound in the mind of whomever you cast it upon. I've tried this spell on myself and it's a truly horrifying sound, and no one else can hear it but the adversary. It's effective for stopping them in their tracks.

Grip your wand as close to the base (charging port) as possible.

You need the center of gravity of your wand to favor the end pointed at your adversary. Swing your wand back away from your casting arm and call out "Midnight!"

Then swing it in the opposite direction, calling out "Shriek!"

Ouroboros

This spell will make your adversary eat his or her own feet. It's good for if you want them to stop talking or stop walking.

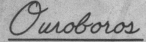

Hold your wand straight up to the sky and allow the upswing to pull you aloft as you say "Ouro—"

And then "boros" as you land, swinging your arm down and pointing the crystal at your target.

Low Self-Esteem Nightmare Dream

Just like it sounds, this spell comes in handy when you need to disarm your adversary by clouding their brain with a sea of unwanted negative self-speak.

Like all good insults, this is an acute attack. Grab your wand with both hands (best to start with a two-handed grasp until you've mastered this one), point it at your opponent, and murmur "Low Self-Esteem Nightmare Dreams." Once you get good at it, you can wiggle your fingers a bit to make yourself seem really witchy!

Hypnoslumber

This spell will make your adversary sleepwalk away from you. Effects can last for eternity or a few minutes, depending on the constitution of your adversary.

Hold your wand out in front of you, with your arm straight. Make swirling motions with your arm from the shoulder.

Say or think the word "Hypnoslumber" repeatedly. You may need to say it aloud at first to master this spell. You'll know it's working if a large spiraling disk starts to form in front of you.

Once the disk is the diameter of your shoulders, it's ready to cast. Point your wand at your adversary and the disk will form a beam. Be careful with this step! I misused it once and sent Uncle Clovis sleepwalking off into the woods.

Body Swap Spell

This is a wordless spell; the point is to do it silently. You don't want your adversary to know you are casting.

Hold your wand aloft and stand on your tiptoes. Tilt your head back and stretch from your toes to the tip of your wand. When you feel you can't stretch any more, have the intention of body-swapping deep in your heart, and exhale.

If you do this correctly you will be lifted off the ground, and you and your target will swap bodies. You won't feel any of their pain, so it's a great opportunity to have them run into the fireplace or a wall of nails.

Things have taken a turn for the worse. Mother is . . . gone. It happened quickly. The monsters ambushed her camp in the night and the entire battalion fell. Both sides lost many in the battle. I haven't even had time to mourn, and already the wheels are in motion; Mother's will has me betrothed to Shastacan, so it's unavoidable. He will become my king and move into the castle in a fortnight.

Thank heavens for the lock on this book. I feel it's the only place I can truly be myself. The Mewni Army along with the Solarians made a profound strike against the monsters last night, and I guess I should have comfort from it, but I don't. The Prince of Darkness wasn't harmed; we met secretly this morning at the old shipping canal beneath the Rose Tower. It's obvious that the recent turn of events is going to strain our relationship, even though the Prince of Darkness had nothing to do with the ambush—he was opposed to it—and he knows I am opposed to the Mewman aggressions toward monsters. He asked if I was going to pursue my mother's agenda with the monsters. It's a fair question, but not one I can even begin to answer now.

For levity, I told him about my first night with Shastacan. I asked Shastacan to remove his boots because I don't like them to be worn indoors, and to my surprise, I found that he doesn't wear socks. He explained that socks trap in the ooze that needs to naturally leak from the spider bites so they may heal properly. The Prince of Darkness laughed as I described the corn-colored hue of Shastacan's toenails. Fortunately,

Shastacan has accepted that our marriage is one of obligation, so there aren't any expectations we will carry on as a real couple. For the time being he's happy to be living a life free of persistent tiny attacks from spiders and the resulting ooze-filled boils they cause.

The Prince of Darkness respectfully asked if he could be allowed to break from his vegetarianism in order to eat Shastacan. I teased him for his jealousy, and we said goodbye with a kiss and went our separate ways. The pain of the distance between us is almost unbearable, but I know we will be together soon.

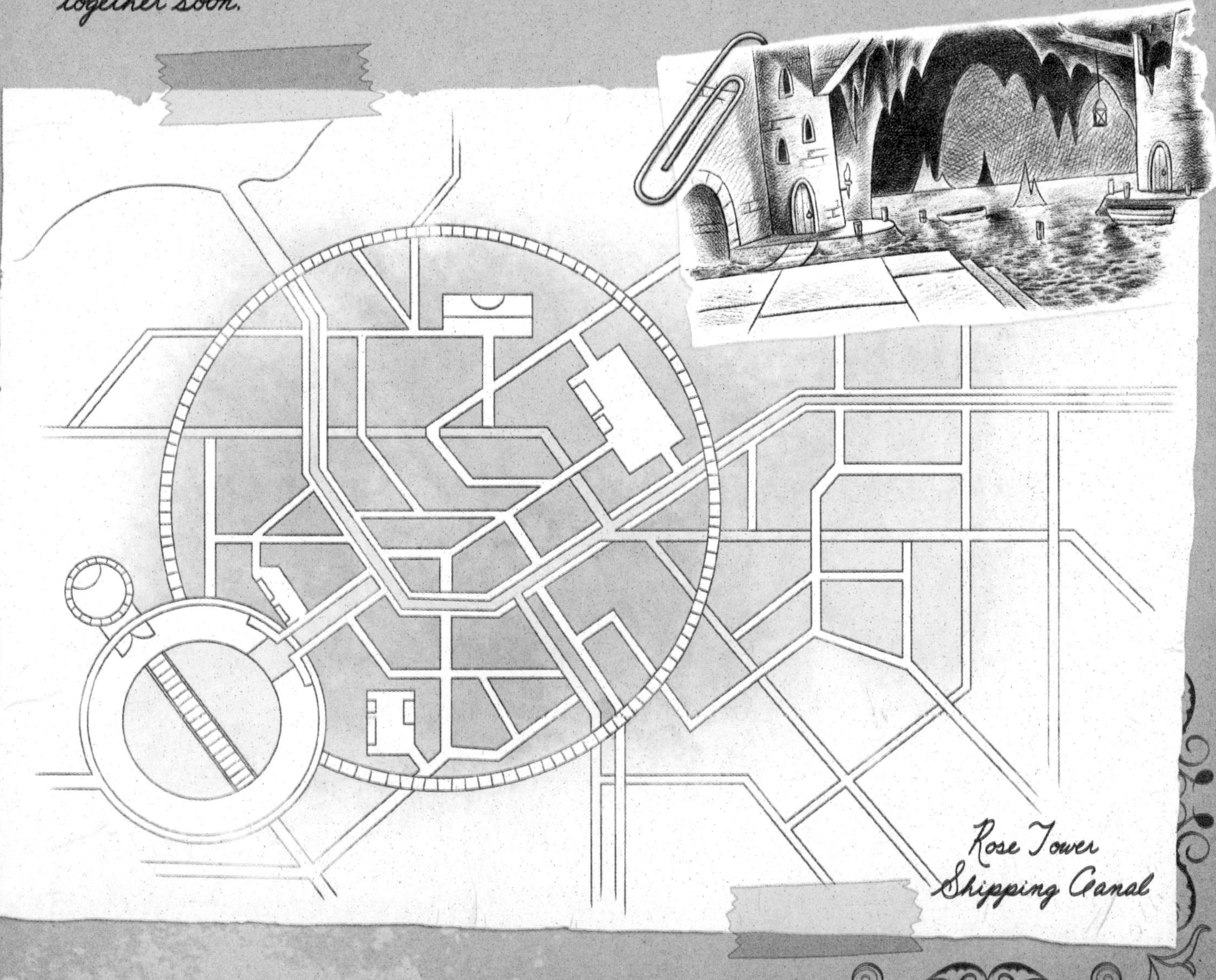
Rose Tower
Shipping Canal

240 ♠

What started as a mutually beneficial arrangement between Shastacan and me has become problematic. As a second-born son he'd be given no title in the Spider Bite court; the kingdom will go to his older brother. Taking him as my king has meant a lot as a show of solidarity and goodwill throughout all of Mewni. Being king of Mewni ought to have been the best he could have hoped for, but now he's feeling entitled, and he's starting to make demands.

He would like to have children.

I don't want to do that; not with him. I told him it's not too late to have our marriage annulled, and he told me that he felt he was falling in love with me.

I told him I love the Prince of Darkness.

He was shocked to learn this, but I told him I believed—and this is true—that the love the Prince of Darkness and I have for each other will be what creates lasting peace between the monsters and the Mewmans.

He laughed at me as though I were a foolish child.

The Prince of Darkness and I met tonight at our usual spot beneath the Rose Tower. Changes have been made in the ranks of the Monster Army and he has been put into a leadership role. The Solarian Warrior Army made significant advancements against the monsters, and he had a hard time not blaming me for this. I told him I was still advocating for armistice, but I had to lead the kingdom as well and the monsters must not trespass on our lands. He reminded me that, originally, all the lands of Mewni belonged to the monsters. He's right. "What do you want me to do?" I pleaded. "Leave with me," he said.

I was shocked to learn he was leaving. He is taking the army to a fortified monster sanctuary east of the Jaggies—a place for the monsters to regroup and plan for future movements against the Butterfly Kingdom.

I told him I couldn't betray my kingdom. "You've already done that by loving me," he said. He reminded me that his people don't blame me for the sins of my ancestors, and that I'd be welcome among them, at least for now. He warned that eventually I will have to pick sides, and even he won't be able to sway the monsters to accept me after a point.

He also warned that although what he and his group want is ultimately peaceful coexistence with the Mewmans, with a fair sharing of land and assets, there are other monster factions who feel they are superior to the Mewmans, and they want nothing but the destruction of our people and our magic.

One particular faction of some concern is the monsters of Septarsis. They're particularly cunning and full of righteous indignation, and our warfare will have to be rethought if there's ever proper conflict with them. They do not have the same weaknesses as the other monster hordes; they can't be killed properly. They seem to be ageless creatures with no ability to forgive or forget, carrying the grudges of their forefathers as if they were their own.

WANTED
WANTED IN ALL LANDS BY ORDER OF THE MAGIC HIGH COMMISSION
Seth
aka Seth of Septarsi

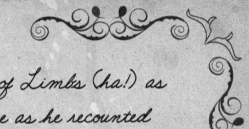

Even the Prince of Darkness, or the Plucker of Limbs (ha!) as he is known to my people, had fear in his voice as he recounted his dealings with the Septarians. He believes that he has some diplomatic sway with them, enough that he could quell their uprising, but he would need to know the Solarian Warrior Army would make no more aggressions toward the monsters.

I couldn't promise that to him.

"Then come with me and save both of our kingdoms," he finished.

300 ♠

Hello, Shastacan, my sweet king. I know that you found my key and have been leafing through this book, and you've likely read what I've written, though none of it ought to come as a surprise to you.

I have taken to learning Low-Mewnian, the ancient language of the Old Queens. Fortunately for me, its translation is a guarded secret passed between mother and daughter for generations, to be used only in times of crisis for transmitting information in secrecy. Well, this kingdom is in crisis, and so is this marriage. From this point forward, all of my entries will be in Low-Mewnian.

Bye, honey!

[illegible]

330 ♠

[illegible]

FESTIVIA
THE FUN

When the threat of monsters at the gate
has darkened out the sun,
let the kingdom find some peace and joy
in Festivia the Fun.

Festivia
@FestiviaTheFun

Got my wand today! #lovinglife #lovingmagic #feelingblessed

Era of year 1

39

Festivia
@FestiviaTheFun

My goblet wand is filled to the brim with cosmic importance! #tasty #cuptotallyfull

Era of year 1

97

Festivia
@FestiviaTheFun

I love the sparkly details! #gobletwand #goodtimes

Era of year 1

852

Wow! Party Grandma?
I LOVE IT!!!

Festivia
@FestiviaTheFun

My wand crystal is a little diamond right in the center! Oooh! #sparkly #blessed

Era of year 1

94

Festivia
@FestiviaTheFun

It's also surrounded by tiny diamonds! #extrasparkle #blingbling

Era of year 1

92

Festivia
@FestiviaTheFun

The face is the front of the goblet! I've never seen a wand with this design! #unique

Festivia the Fun
Aureole Sign: Pixie
Height: 6' 1"
Attributes
Strength: 12
Intelligence: 12
Wisdom: 8
Dexterity: 19
Constitution: 10
Charisma: 20

Festivia
@FestiviaTheFun

The grip is the base of the goblet. #nospillzone #getagrip

Era of year 1

115

Festivia
@FestiviaTheFun

My wand charger is hidden in the goblet base! It runs on sapphires! #verysparkly

Era of year 1

98

Festivia
@FestiviaTheFun

A new Millhorse has chosen to run my wand! Her name is Stephandipity! #thunderthighs

Era of year 1

352

Festivia
@FestiviaTheFun

Stephandipity said it was her destiny to be my wand horse! #cosmicimportance #grateful

Era of year 1

288

Festivia
@FestiviaTheFun

Glossaryck tells me I should write about my history, but I don't like living in the past! #neverlookback

Era of year 1

♥ 465

Festivia
@FestiviaTheFun

I will be the first queen in several years, my poor mother and father having been eaten by monsters. #Eclipsaforever #Shastacanforever #missyoumama #missyoupapa

Era of year 1

♥ 1,597

Festivia
@FestiviaTheFun

Since their deaths, the kingdom has been run by the MHC! They raised me. #lovingfamily #chosenfamily

Era of year 1

♥ 987

Festivia
@FestiviaTheFun

The MHC stands for the Magic High Commission: Glossaryck, Heckapoo, Lekmet, Rhombulus, Reynaldo the Bald Pate, and Omnitraxis Prime. #lifefulloflove

Era of year 1

♥ 1,231

Festivia
@FestiviaTheFun

Right now is an exciting time to be alive in Mewni! Magic mirrors now come in compacts! #magictechnology

Era of year 1

♥ 2,851

Festivia
@FestiviaTheFun

I can message my friends and my peasants and write in the Magic Book of Spells all at the same time! #productive #efficient

Era of year 1

♥ 2,067

Festivia
@FestiviaTheFun

The mirrors are made from mirror shards, mined by the pixies in Pixtopia! #thankyoupixies #pixielove #smallbutmighty

Era of year 1

♥ 2,014

Festivia
@FestiviaTheFun

I bought mine from Reflecta-corp, an amazing chain of compact-mirror stores! It looks like a clamshell! #Reflectacorp #takemymoney

Era of year 1

♥ 1,859

Festivia

ONLY 38 JEWELS!

Era of year 1

♥ 4,816

Festivia
@FestiviaTheFun

I LOVE pie!!!!! I don't even care if it's bad for you! #pieproblems #princesspie

Era of year 1

♥ 3,056

Festivia
@FestiviaTheFun

My favorites are rhubarb, lemon meringue, and pigeon. #givemepie

Era of year 1

♥ 3,014

Festivia
@FestiviaTheFun

PARTY AT PRINCE JAGS'S HOUSE TONIGHT!!! #jaggymountains #nopartylikejaggymountainsparty

Era of year 1

♥ 8,895

Festivia
@FestiviaTheFun

Wow. That was CRAZY FUN. Good night, Mewni and TMBOS! Xoxoxox #funnight #sunrise

Era of year 1

♥ 9,115

Festivia
@FestiviaTheFun

Party in my tower! VIP only! Heckapoo is going to be making her famous flaming mocktails! #coolaunt #princessparty

Era of year 1

♥ 10K

Festivia
@FestiviaTheFun

1 week!!!!!! #gonnadancewitheveryone #belleoftheball

Era of year 1

♥ 9,558

Festivia
@FestiviaTheFun

Beautiful and unforgettable night! Couldn't decide who was a better dancer, Prince Musty Mountains or Prince Jags. #princeproblems #dreamlife

Era of year 1

♥ 10K

Festivia
@FestiviaTheFun

Okay, I've been spending too much time on my compact! I need to unplug! #beinthemoment

Era of year 1

♥ 8,785

Festivia
@FestiviaTheFun

UPDATE! I'm back! I spent last year traveling to 16 different dimensions. I learned so much and really grew as a person. #livelearnlove #growth #skipyear

Era of year 3

♥ 12K

Festivia
@FestiviaTheFun

My top 4 visited dimensions: Pixtopia for the compacts, Spatatori for the pasta, Quest Buy for the shopping, Beachtropolis for the boys. #adventure #lovetravel

Era of year 3

♥ 9,896

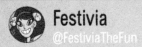

Festivia
@FestiviaTheFun

Also, NEWS FLASH, I'm going to be queen soon! The coronation is in just 3 weeks!!! #partyofthecentury #newqueenintown

Era of year 3

12K

Festivia
@FestiviaTheFun

I am so excited!!! People of Mewni, get ready for some fun!!! #letthegoodtimesroll #EraofSparkles

Era of year 3

9,899

Festivia
@FestiviaTheFun

I am now the queen! Best day of my life! I will do my best to be a good queen and make you happy! #gonnatr
#gonnaworkhard #loveMewni

Era of year 3

13K

Festivia
@FestiviaTheFun

Being a queen is hard work! JK!!! It is so much fun! #lovingthatqueenlife

Era of year 3

12K

Festivia
@FestiviaTheFun

After much consideration, please welcome the style of the Era of Sparkles! #soromantic #TheGreatBookofFashion

Era of year 3

10K

Festivia
@FestiviaTheFun

All citizens of Mewni! Please join me in the main castle square for the wildest toga party you have ever seen! #castleparty #EraofSparkles #sparklequeen

Era of year 3

15K

Festivia
@FestiviaTheFun

A scouting raven just informed me monsters have burned down a Mewman village in the Forest of Certain Death! #pleasebesafe #whydotheyhateus?

Era of year 3

10K

Festivia
@FestiviaTheFun

Monsters burned down another Mewman village we rightfully stole from them! #monstersareevil #somean

Era of year 3

♥ 18K

Festivia
@FestiviaTheFun

Having a meeting with the Magic High Commission in the War Room! #thisisserious

Era of year 3

♥ 9,879

Festivia
@FestiviaTheFun

No one can agree on what to do! Rhombulus thinks we should go to war. What do you think? Comment below. #warornot #youropinionmatters

Era of year 3

♥ 10K

Festivia
@FestiviaTheFun

Omnitraxis Prime doesn't think my magic is strong enough for war yet. #littleoffended

Era of year 3

♥ 8,995

Festivia
@FestiviaTheFun

Glossaryck isn't helping at all, and Heckapoo says she'll support me no matter what. #lovemyauntie #mommyanddaddyarefighting #beingqueenreallyishard

Era of year 3

♥ 9,990

Festivia
@FestiviaTheFun

I decided we should go to war! General Mina Loveberry has sent out the army! #goodluck

Era of year 3

♥ 12K

Festivia
@FestiviaTheFun

This may take a while. #Ihatewar #stopthefighting

Era of year 3

♥ 12K

Festivia
@FestiviaTheFun

The monster uprising continues! Some have invaded the castle! Don't worry, I am safe! #stopthemadness

Era of year 3

♥ 13K

Festivia
@FestiviaTheFun

Our army has successfully pushed the monsters out! But with many casualties. #momentofsilence

Era of year 3

♥ 14K

Festivia
@FestiviaTheFun

Omnitraxis Prime thinks I should try to make peace with the monsters. I say no way! #theystartedit

Era of year 3

♥ 14K

Festivia
@FestiviaTheFun

The war with the monsters still rages on! Please, everyone living in the forests, retreat to the castle! I will protect you! #queensorders

Era of year 3

♥ 13K

Festivia
@FestiviaTheFun

I have called the Mewman Army back home!!! #rejoice #celebrate

Era of year 3

♥ 315K

Festivia
@FestiviaTheFun

I am closing the castle gates! #wearesafeinside

Era of year 3

♥ 19K

Festivia
@FestiviaTheFun

The war will continue, but now only using my grandmother Solaria's magic army. #nomorelives lost

Era of year 3

♥ 11K

Festivia
@FestiviaTheFun

The Solarian warriors are very strong! The great general Mina Loveberry is leading them! #dontworry #magicarmy #MinaLoveberry #wegotthis

Era of year 3

♥ 20K

Festivia
@FestiviaTheFun

We will all live here in the castle together! No need to go beyond the gates! #noworries

Era of year 4

♥ 15K

Festivia
@FestiviaTheFun

People keep asking me about the safety of the Solarian warriors. They are fine! Almost invincible! They will keep the war going while we take it easy! #thankyouSolarianwarriors

Era of year 4

♥ 14K

Festivia
@FestiviaTheFun

Now let's celebrate!!! #partytime

Era of year 4

♥ 18K

Festivia
@FestiviaTheFun

The party goes on!!! Is everyone having a good time?! #goodtimes #nonstopparty

Era of year 5

♥ 16K

Festivia
@FestiviaTheFun

And on and on!!! How do you like my Never-Ending Fireworks Spell?! #partyforever

Era of year 6

♥ 9,889

Festivia
@FestiviaTheFun

I've filled the hallways with foam! #keepitgoing #partyofthecentury #slipandslide

Era of year 6

♥ 11K

Festivia
@FestiviaTheFun

I've learned how to turn the fountains into soda pop! Enjoy your sugar! #pickmeup

Era of year 6

♥ 8,995

Festivia
@FestiviaTheFun

I don't miss the world outside at all! #whoneedsit? #herewehaveeverythingweneed

Era of year 7

♥ 9,873

Festivia
@FestiviaTheFun

Yes, Mina and the soldiers are still fighting the monsters! #toasttoMina

Era of year 7

♥ 10K

Festivia
@FestiviaTheFun

Just magicked up an indoor swimming pool! #poolparty

Era of year 7

♥ 19K

Festivia
@FestiviaTheFun

Finally, the fighting has stopped! #finallypeace #lovenotwar

Era of year 8

♥ 16K

Festivia
@FestiviaTheFun

After 5 long years, Mina and the magic army have sent the monsters scurrying far into the dark forest where they belong. #wedidit #goMinaLoveberry #Minforthewin

Era of year 8

♥ 21K

Festivia
@FestiviaTheFun

I'm stopping the party, too. It's been fun, but after 5 years I really need to sleep. #beautyrest

Era of year 8

♥ 11K

Festivia
@FestiviaTheFun

The citizens of Mewni have given me the honor of "greatest queen to ever live"! #humbled

Era of year 8

♥ 13K

Festivia
@FestiviaTheFun

Thank you, everyone!!! I couldn't have done it without your love and support! How about an off-the-chains party to celebrate?!!! #theydontcallmeFestiviatheFunfornothing

Era of year 8

♥ 18K

Festivia
@FestiviaTheFun

Glossaryck tells me I should finally write down some of my spells, so I will! #Glossyknowsbest

Era of year 9

24K

Festivia
@FestiviaTheFun

I've just been so busy keeping the kingdom happy during the war and getting married to Prince Musty Mountains!!!! #excuses #sorrynotsorry

Era of year 9

35K

Festivia
@FestiviaTheFun

The Host-Me Spell: This spell will help turn you into the perfect hostess or host! I have done it to myself many times. #partylife4ever

Era of year 9

22K

FESTIVIA'S
MADHOSTING
SKILLS

Festivia
@FestiviaTheFun

It's not always advisable to do magic on your face, but in this case, point your wand directly at your face and say "Party hardy" and blast. #thismaysting #iwokeuplikethis

Era of year 9

25K

Festivia
@FestiviaTheFun

You will find yourself grinning from ear to ear, full of energy, and ready to make the party happen! #yourfacewillhurtfromsmiling

Era of year 9

27K

Festivia
@FestiviaTheFun

The Soda Fountain Spell: This spell will turn any boring old water into fun bubbly soda!

Era of year 9

♥ 35K

Festivia
@FestiviaTheFun

Take off your shoes and stand barefoot in the water (preferably a fountain) you wish to turn to soda. Dance about with your wand lit. #myfavoritespell

Era of year 9

♥ 28K

Festivia
@FestiviaTheFun

Dip your wand into the fountain and say "Bubbly wubbly," using your lit wand to mix up the water. You'll find it bubbling! #bubbletrouble

Era of year 9

Festivia
@FestiviaTheFun

You'll also find the water starting to heat up! Leap out quickly so you don't burn your toes! #ouchers #becareful

Era of year 9

♥ 31K

Festivia
@FestiviaTheFun

Once the water cools, you'll find you have made delicious soda! To speed up the process, throw some ice cubes in the water. #Ineverdidfigureoutagoodfreezespell

Era of year 9

♥ 25K

DON'T MISS
FESTIVIA'S FABULOUS
FOUNTAIN

Festivia
@FestiviaTheFun

The Fireless Rainbow Spell: Everyone knows rainbows are finicky and can easily catch on fire. #firesucks

Era of year 9

♥ 40K

Festivia
@FestiviaTheFun

Luckily, I created a spell that lets you make a beautiful rainbow minus the dangerous flames! #burnbabyburn

Era of year 9

♥ 37K

Festivia
@FestiviaTheFun

People love rainbows and ey're
don't cat

Era of

Festivia
@FestiviaTheFu

Just follow these simple directions. F
a spi rmelon
#refr

Era of ear

Festivia
@Festivi

Send a blas
Rainbur
olorful

Oops . . . I was playing around with glitter glue and accidentally dropped some here! I tried to clean it up, but I spread it all over the place. Would have been a useful spell to know. At least the glitter looks pretty!

Festivia's NO BURN
RAINBOW

Festivia
@FestiviaTheFun

The Never-Ending Fireworks Spell: A fan favorite! The one I did during the 5-year war is still going to this day! #impressive

Era of year 9

♥ 35K

Festivia
@FestiviaTheFun

This will already look like fireworks, so try to vary what blasts you do. These will repeat for eternity. #dontbeboring

Era of year 9

♥ 24K

Festivia
@FestiviaTheFun

You're going to need to be a master of a basic wand blast for this. Are you? Good! Start by blasting a basic blast into the air 100 times. #masterclass

Era of year 9

♥ 30K

Festivia
@FestiviaTheFun

As you blast, chant the words "Eternal Fireworks!" You need to say this 100 times, once with each blast. #trustmeitsworthit

Era of year 9

♥ 32K

Festivia
@FestiviaTheFun

Festivia
@FestiviaTheFun

fireworks go on for eternity!

FESTIVIA'S NEVER-ENDING
FIREWORKS!

The Heckapoo—A spicy watermelon agua fresca

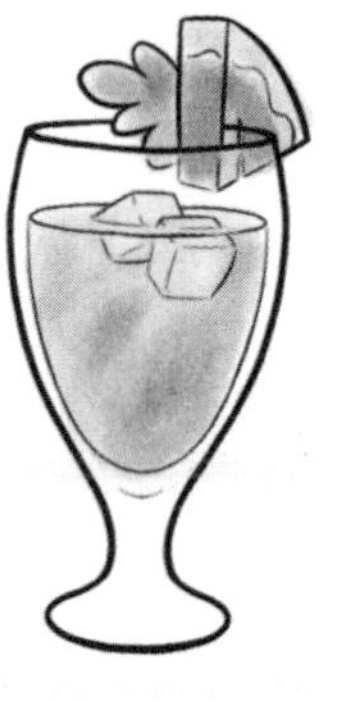
My fave party drinks!

2 cups cold water
2 cups watermelon, rind removed, seeded and chopped
1 tablespoon lime juice
2 tablespoons granulated sugar
½ jalapeño, roughly chopped

Combine all ingredients and puree until smooth.
Pour mixture through a strainer into a pitcher, forcing through most of the pulp.
Add some ice, chill, and serve.

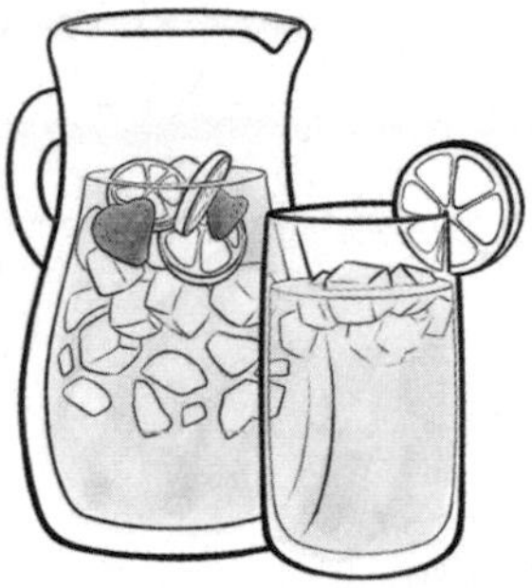

The Lekmet—A classic, refreshing strawberry lemonade

1 cup ginger ale
1 cup fresh lemonade
5 strawberries, chopped

In a glass, combine lemonade and ginger ale along with some ice.
Add the finely chopped strawberry pieces and serve.

The Omnitraxis Prime—A big, smart orange-colored juice

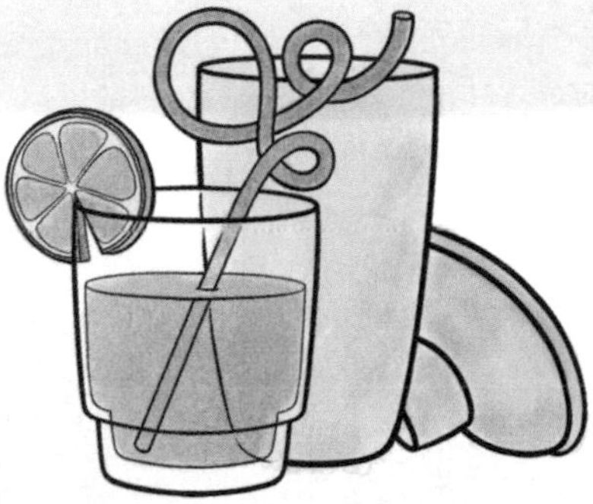

3 cups chilled carrot juice
2 cups chilled orange juice
2 tablespoons lemon juice
4 tablespoons honey
Crushed ice

Put orange juice, carrot juice, lemon juice, honey, and ice in a shaker and mix well. Pour the mixture into glasses and serve.

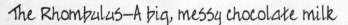

The Rhombulus—A big, messy chocolate milk

1 cup chocolate ice cream
A handful of crushed ice
½ cup half-and-half or almond milk
2 tablespoons chocolate syrup

Combine all ingredients in a pitcher and stir until smooth. Coat the rim of a glass with more chocolate syrup, pour mixture into glass, and serve.

The Reynaldo the Bald Pate—A boring glass of water

Poor some water into a glass. That's it.

Festivia
@FestiviaTheFun

Whether you are throwing a lavish ball or a bloodcurdling demoncism, these 9 steps will make sure your party is pure perfection! #expertadvice

Era of year 9

♥ 35K

Festivia
@FestiviaTheFun

Think about who this party is for. Like, if it is a party for ghosts, having tables of food they cannot eat would be very insensitive. #ghostsdonteat

Era of year 9

♥ 31K

Festivia
@FestiviaTheFun

Make sure you pick the right location. You may think a party inside a very large jelly mold sounds fun, but will your guests? #Ilikejelly #jellylife

Era of year 9

♥ 37K

Festivia
@FestiviaTheFun

Pick your guest list carefully. Make sure you are not inviting mortal enemies or predators and prey. I learned this one the hard way. #wolfbeastsandrabbitmicedontmix #oops

Era of year 9

♥ 39K

Festivia
@FestiviaTheFun

Always choose close friends first or they may feel left out. Like the time I forgot to invite Cloud the Barbarian and he cried for 6 days. #barbarianshavefeelingstoo

Era of year 9

♥ 41K

Festivia
@FestiviaTheFun

Pick a theme! This is so important that I've devoted a whole section to it on the next page. #themes

Era of year 9

♥ 38K

Festivia
@FestiviaTheFun

Decorate! The more the better! If you are throwing a Sandwich Dimension-themed party, you want your guests to really feel it! #cucumbercreamcheese

Era of year 9

♥ 42K

Festivia
@FestiviaTheFun

Get enough supplies! Nothing is worse than running out of pie at a party! #partyfoul

Era of year 9

♥ 45K

Festivia
@FestiviaTheFun

Make sure you have activities for your guests, such as flamethrower tennis, turtle races, bathtub surfing, air dancing, and grave digging. #underwaterrollercoaster #snakejuggling #lavasurfing #pieeating #theeyeofdeath

Era of year 9

♥ 48K

Festivia
@FestiviaTheFun

Make sure you have the right music or everyone will judge you. #musicsnob

Era of year 9

♥ 48K

Festivia
@FestiviaTheFun

Picking a theme helps your guests feel comfortable and know what to wear. This is the most important step to any party. #planahead

Era of year 9

45K

Festivia
@FestiviaTheFun

You could stick to a tried-and-true theme like scary masks or head cones, but I think it best to be original. #befun #beunique #beyou

Era of year 9

42K

Festivia
@FestiviaTheFun

Pick something that really screams YOU! This way everyone will know what a special, funny, interesting person you are! #dontbeboring #youdoyou

Era of year 9

46K

Festivia
@FestiviaTheFun

Remember, anything can be a theme. Look around you. A mirror? BOOM! Mirror maze theme. Cat litter box? Boom! Cats with human faces theme! #takefromlife

Era of year 9

48K

Festivia
@FestiviaTheFun

If you can't find anything from your life, just pick something you like! Rainbows? BOOM! That's a theme! Sausages? Boom! Also a theme! #keepitfun

Era of year 9

50K

Festivia
@FestiviaTheFun

Did you know a party doesn't need to have just one theme? It can have multiple! I refer to these as "Fun Zones." #funzone

Era of year 9

51K

Festivia
@FestiviaTheFun

You can have up to 4 Fun Zones per party. More than that and your guests just get overwhelmed. #dontoverdoit

Era of year 9

39K

Festivia
@FestiviaTheFun

These Fun Zones build up to form one unbelievably unforgettable party! Like Samarani-Neverzone-Barnacle-Duck-themed. #youknowthatsoundsfun

Era of year 9

49K

Festivia
@FestiviaTheFun

My top fav themes are: 1. Everyone is painted purple theme. 2. Sideways party on the side of building theme. 3. We are all bugs now theme. #feelfreetotake #gift

Era of year 9

52K

Festivia
@FestiviaTheFun

I have partied very, very, very hard. I must take a long nap. It may last for weeks. See you all at the next fiesta. #donteverstoppartying

Era of year 9

54K

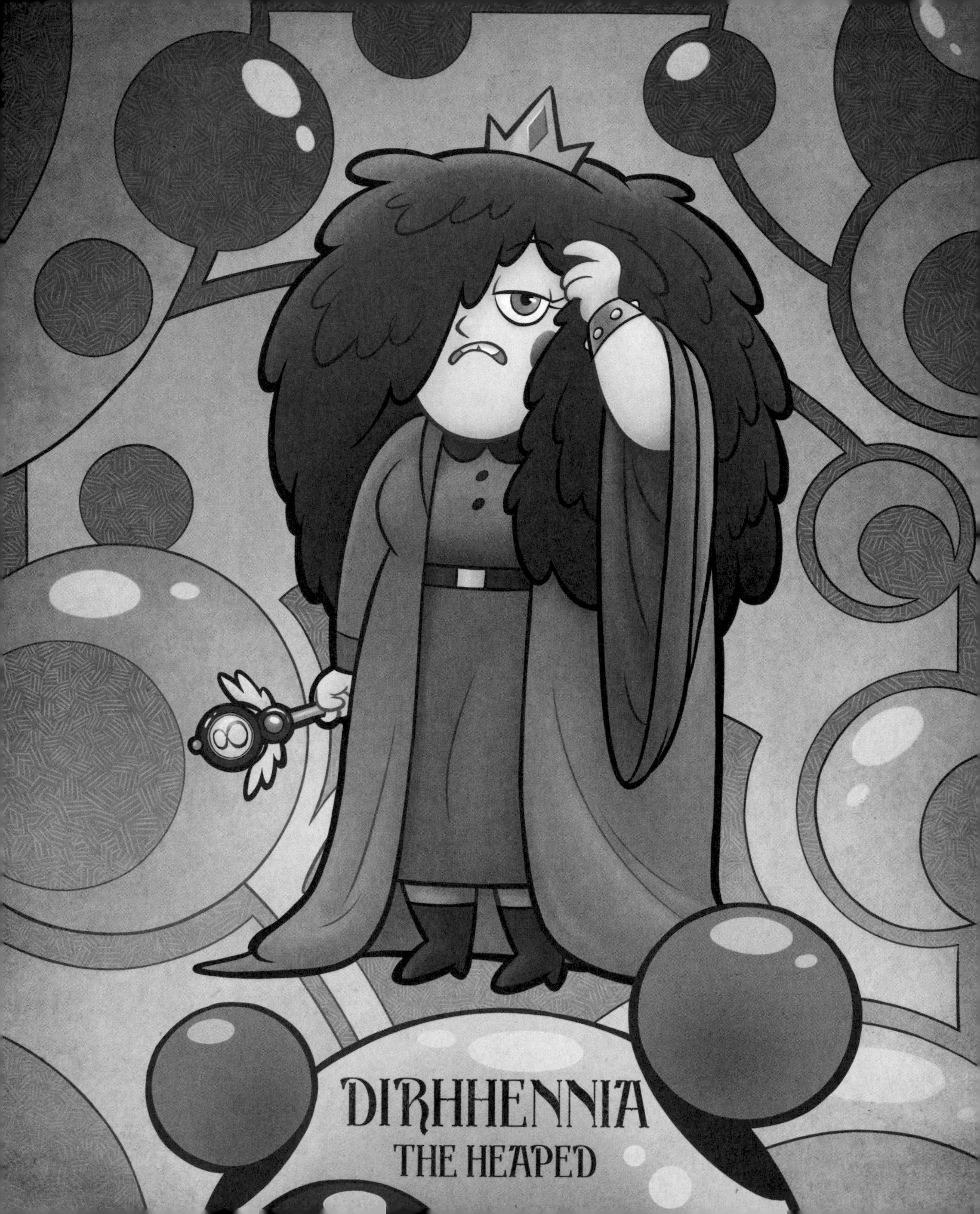
DIRHHENNIA
THE HEAPED

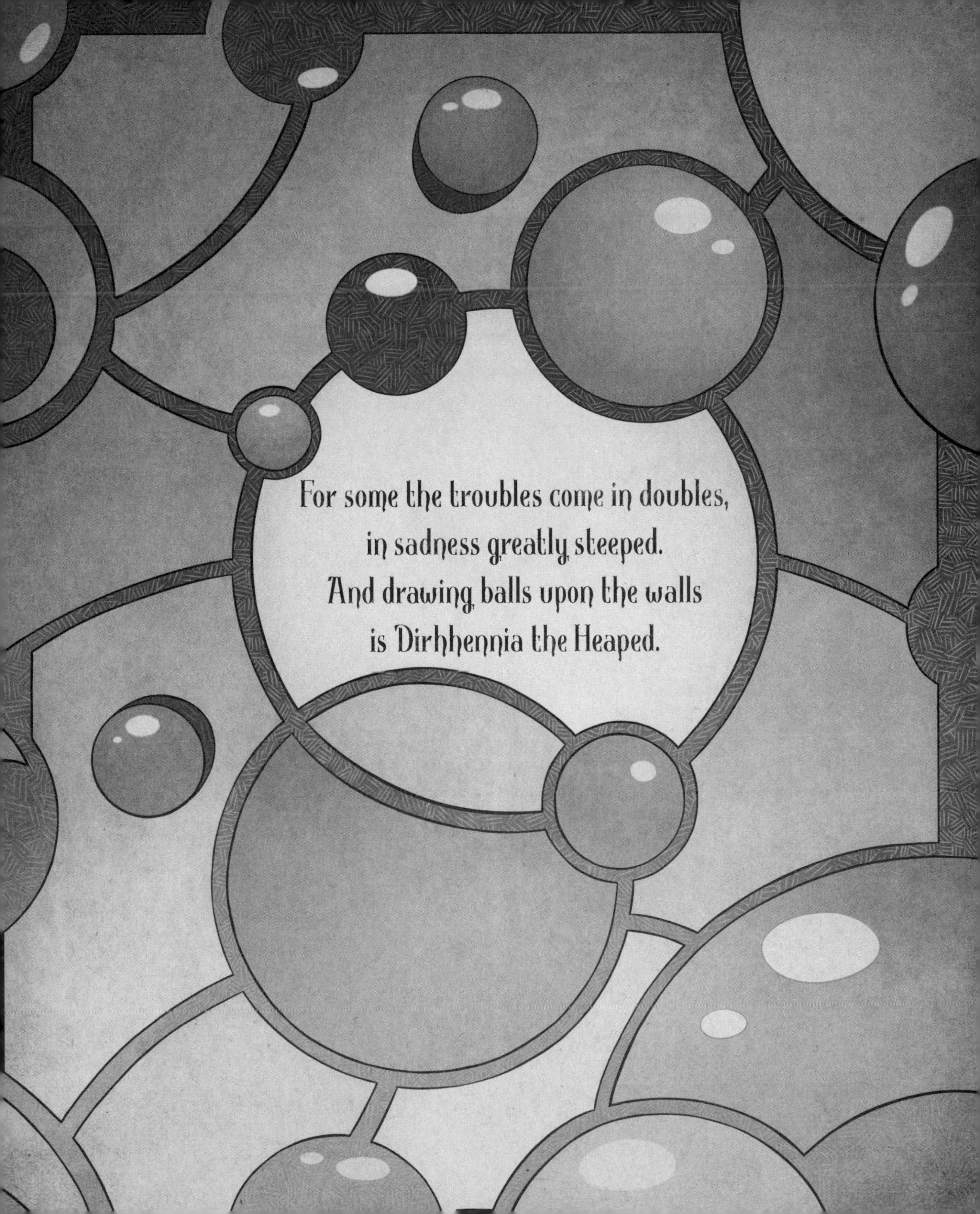

For some the troubles come in doubles,
in sadness greatly steeped.
And drawing balls upon the walls
is Dirhhennia the Heaped.

THE BELL—THE BELL OF MY WAND IS PROLLY MY FAVORITE PART. IT'S GOT A LITTLE WINDOW IN IT AND THERE'S A TRIANGLE DIE INSIDE THAT TELLS ME WHAT TO DO.
IT USUALLY LANDS ON "WHY GET OUT OF BED 2-DAY?" MAKES DECIDING EASY.
THE PORT AND CHARGER—MY WAND IS CHARGED WITH NUMBER 7 MUDSTONE.
TASTES JUST LIKE IT SOUNDS.

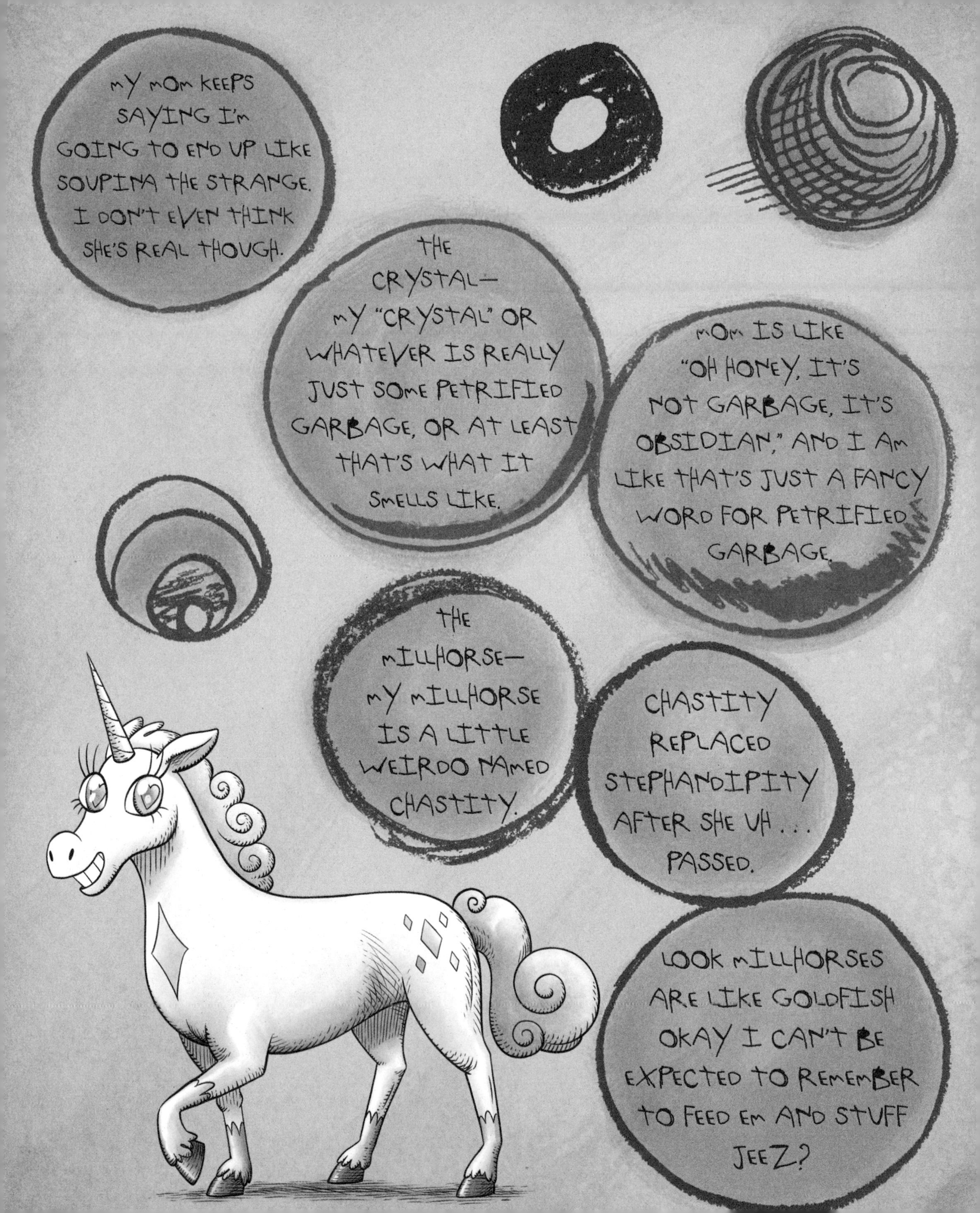
MY MOM KEEPS SAYING I'M GOING TO END UP LIKE SOUPINA THE STRANGE. I DON'T EVEN THINK SHE'S REAL THOUGH.
THE CRYSTAL— MY "CRYSTAL" OR WHATEVER IS REALLY JUST SOME PETRIFIED GARBAGE, OR AT LEAST THAT'S WHAT IT SMELLS LIKE.
MOM IS LIKE "OH HONEY, IT'S NOT GARBAGE, IT'S OBSIDIAN," AND I AM LIKE THAT'S JUST A FANCY WORD FOR PETRIFIED GARBAGE.
THE MILLHORSE— MY MILLHORSE IS A LITTLE WEIRDO NAMED CHASTITY.
CHASTITY REPLACED STEPHANDIPITY AFTER SHE UH . . . PASSED.
LOOK MILLHORSES ARE LIKE GOLDFISH OKAY I CAN'T BE EXPECTED TO REMEMBER TO FEED EM AND STUFF JEEZ?

YEAR ONE, ERA OF THE SHADE MOON

Skimmed this one; really liked her poem.

Dirhhennia the Heaped

Aureole Sign: Warnicorn
Height: 4' 2"

Attributes

Strength: NA
Intelligence: NA
Wisdom: NA
Dexterity: NA
Constitution: NA
Charisma: <3

MY MOM IS ALL LIKE "DIRHHENNIA, YOU GOTTA START TO WRITE IN THIS BOOK" AND I WAS LIKE I DON'T WANNA WRITE IN IT, CAN I JUST DRAW BALLS?

ANYWAY SHE WAS LIKE "NO."

BUT I WAS LIKE WHO ARE YOU TO TELL ME WHAT I CAN AND CAN'T WRITE IF IT'S MY BOOK AND SHE WAS ALL LIKE "YEAH, I GUESS YOU'RE RIGHT."

BUT SHE WAS ALL LIKE "YOU GOTTA WRITE SOMETHING, D." OKAY SO THEN I WAS LIKE ALRIGHT I'LL WRITE IT BUT LIKE WITH BALLS.

AND SHE WAS LIKE "I DON'T GET IT" AND I WAS LIKE OF COURSE YOU DON'T BECAUSE IT'S LIKE A SECRET LANGUAGE.

IF YOU'RE READING THIS NOW THEN YOU CAN READ BETWEEN THE BALLS. → LIKE ME, YOU TOO SEE THE DARKNESS.

WELCOME TO MY WORLD.

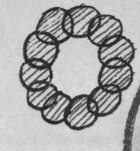

THIS IS THE JOURNAL AND LIFE OF DIRHHENNIA THE HEAPED AND THIS IS A JOURNAL ABOUT MY LIFE. IT'S NOT PRETTY INSIDE MY MIND, SO JUST BEWARE.

I MET THIS GUY CHAD IN THE GARDEN.

I FEEL LIKE I'VE KNOWN HIM FOR ETERNITY DO YOU KNOW WHAT I MEAN? LIKE SOMETHING WITH OUR SOULS OR WHATEVER.

BUT ANYWAY HE SHOULD STAY AWAY BECAUSE I WALK ALONE.

ALONE

BY DIRHHENNIA BUTTERFLY

OH
SWEET CHAD
STAY SWEET AND
STAY AWAY FROM
FALLING FOR ME
BECAUSE I AM LIKE A
LONE WANDERER IN
THIS PLACE
CHAD

IMAGINE
HOW A WOLF IS
ALONE
WITHOUT FRIENDS LIKE
A LONE WOLF
I KNOW I CAN SEE IN YOUR EYES
YOUR LOVE
BUT LOOK IT'S NOT GONNA
WORK OUT BECAUSE
I AM ALONE.
CHAD.

YEAR ONE SAME DAY,
ERA OF THE SHADE MOON

WHY BALLS?

I WAS BORN WITH BALLS ON MY CHEEKS.

LOTS OF QUEENS HAVE THESE AWESOME SHAPES LIKE CLOCKS AND DIAMONDS AND STUFF, BUT I GOT THESE BLACK BALLS.

WHAT A BUMMER.

MY MOM'S ALL LIKE "OH NO SWEETIE THEY ARE SHADE MOONS! A SHADE MOON IS WHAT HAPPENS WHEN THE MOON COMES BETWEEN THE SUN AND MEWNI" AND I'M LIKE NO IT LOOKS LIKE A I HAVE TWO GIANT MOLES ON MY FACE. THANKS, UNIVERSE >:(

YEAR ONE SAME DAY,
LIKE THE NEXT FRIGGIN DAY
OR WHATEVER
ERA OF THE
SHADE MOON

UGH MY MOM IS SO ANNOYING . . . ANYWAY SO I GOTTA PUT SPELLS IN HERE ACCORDING TO HER SO I TOLD HER FINE I WILL AND SHE'S LIKE "I'M GONNA CHECK, DIRHHENNIA."

OKAY, GOOD LUCK READING BALLS, MOM!

BLEND IN WITH BATHWATER SPELL

THIS IS A SPELL THAT YOU CAN CAST WHEN YOU'RE IN THE BATHTUB AND YOU WANNA BE INVISIBLE.

IT MAKES YOU THE SAME COLOR AS YOUR BATHWATER, SO PROBABLY CLEAR OR BUBBLY IF YOU'RE LIKE ME.

SOMETIMES I USE IT WHEN MY MOM IS LOOKING FOR ME AND SOMETIMES I USE IT JUST WHEN I WANNA BE INVISIBLE.

OKAY SO GET IN YOUR BATHTUB WITH YOUR WAND AND HOLD IT UP LIKE THIS:

8

Actually this is not true.

IT'S IMPORTANT YOU DON'T LET YOUR WAND GET IN THE BATHTUB CUZ YOU MIGHT GET ELECTROCUTED.

KEEPING YOUR ARM UP, SAY "BLEND IN WITH BATHWATER" AND YOU'LL INSTANTLY BLEND IN WITH YOUR BATHWATER.*

*THIS SPELL DOES NOT WORK IF YOU'RE CRYING.

Actually, this is true.

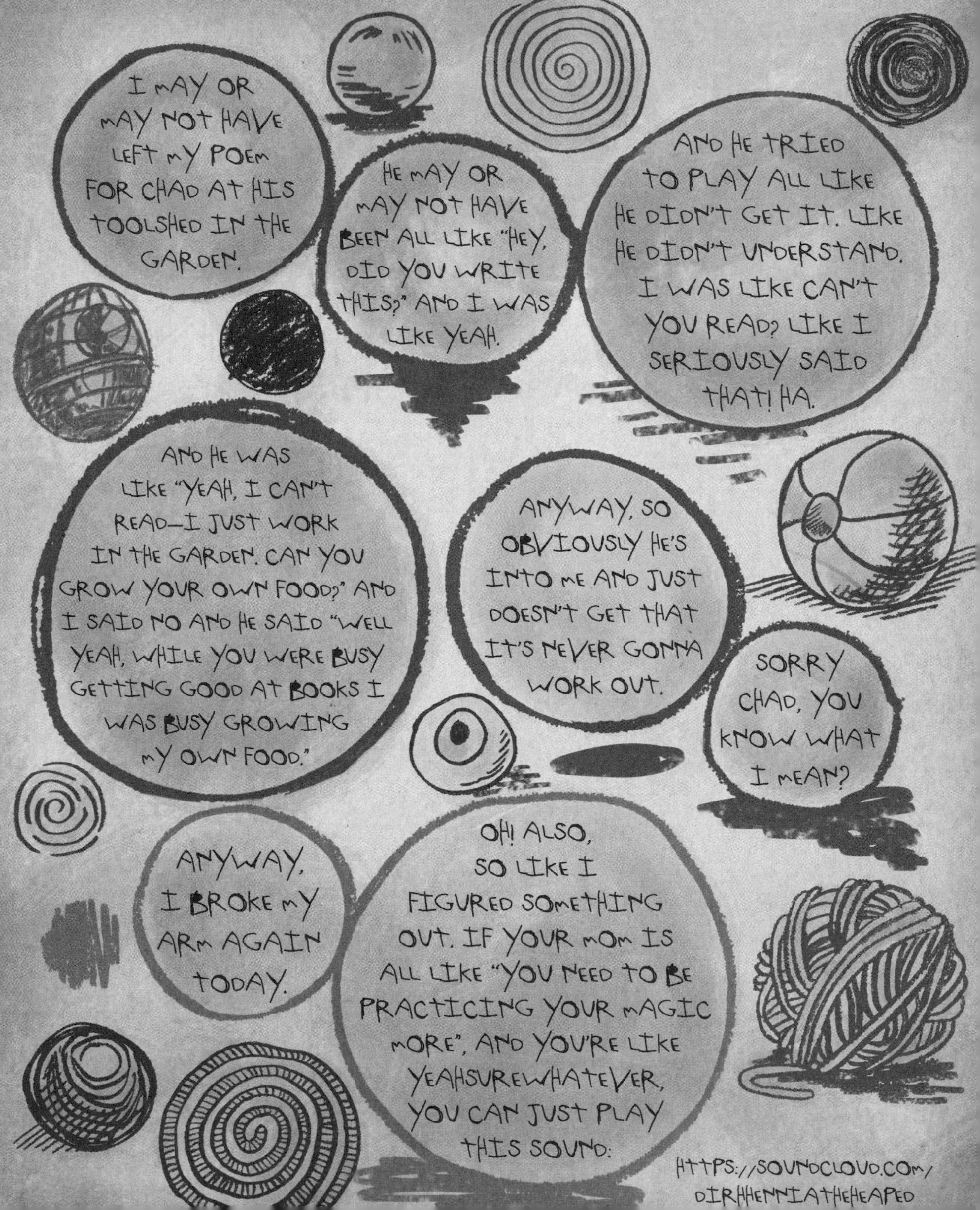
I MAY OR MAY NOT HAVE LEFT MY POEM FOR CHAD AT HIS TOOLSHED IN THE GARDEN.
HE MAY OR MAY NOT HAVE BEEN ALL LIKE "HEY, DID YOU WRITE THIS?" AND I WAS LIKE YEAH.
AND HE TRIED TO PLAY ALL LIKE HE DIDN'T GET IT. LIKE HE DIDN'T UNDERSTAND. I WAS LIKE CAN'T YOU READ? LIKE I SERIOUSLY SAID THAT! HA.
AND HE WAS LIKE "YEAH, I CAN'T READ—I JUST WORK IN THE GARDEN. CAN YOU GROW YOUR OWN FOOD?" AND I SAID NO AND HE SAID "WELL YEAH, WHILE YOU WERE BUSY GETTING GOOD AT BOOKS I WAS BUSY GROWING MY OWN FOOD."
ANYWAY, SO OBVIOUSLY HE'S INTO ME AND JUST DOESN'T GET THAT IT'S NEVER GONNA WORK OUT.
SORRY CHAD, YOU KNOW WHAT I MEAN?
ANYWAY, I BROKE MY ARM AGAIN TODAY.
OH! ALSO, SO LIKE I FIGURED SOMETHING OUT. IF YOUR MOM IS ALL LIKE "YOU NEED TO BE PRACTICING YOUR MAGIC MORE", AND YOU'RE LIKE YEAHSUREWHATEVER, YOU CAN JUST PLAY THIS SOUND:
HTTPS://SOUNDCLOUD.COM/DIRHHENNIATHEHEAPED

IT'S A BUNCH OF SOUNDS I RECORDED FROM MY FAVORITE MAGIC GIRL PLAY.

WHAT I DO IS I LEAVE THEM PLAYING REALLY LOUD IN MY ROOM AND THEN I CLIMB OUT THE WINDOW AND GO DO WHATEVER I REALLY WANT TO DO, LIKE SIT SOMEWHERE. OR STAND SOMEWHERE.

WANTED

WANTED IN ALL LANDS BY ORDER OF THE MAGIC HIGH COMMISSION

Bobipsa Magipsa of Mewni
aka Bobipsa the Barbarian,
aka Tonya

Wanted for general crimes of indiscriminate eating.
Approach with EXTREME CAUTION,
unless there are no babies present,
in which case she is otherwise harmless.

IT SOUNDS LIKE SOMEONE (NOT ME, OBVI) IS DOING REAL MAGIC!

FOUND THIS TACKED TO A WALL IN THE MEWNI MARKET.

I THOUGHT I WAS DARK, BUT THIS LADY TAKES IT TO A WHOLE OTHER LEVEL.

SOMETHING TO ASPIRE TO, I GUESS. . .

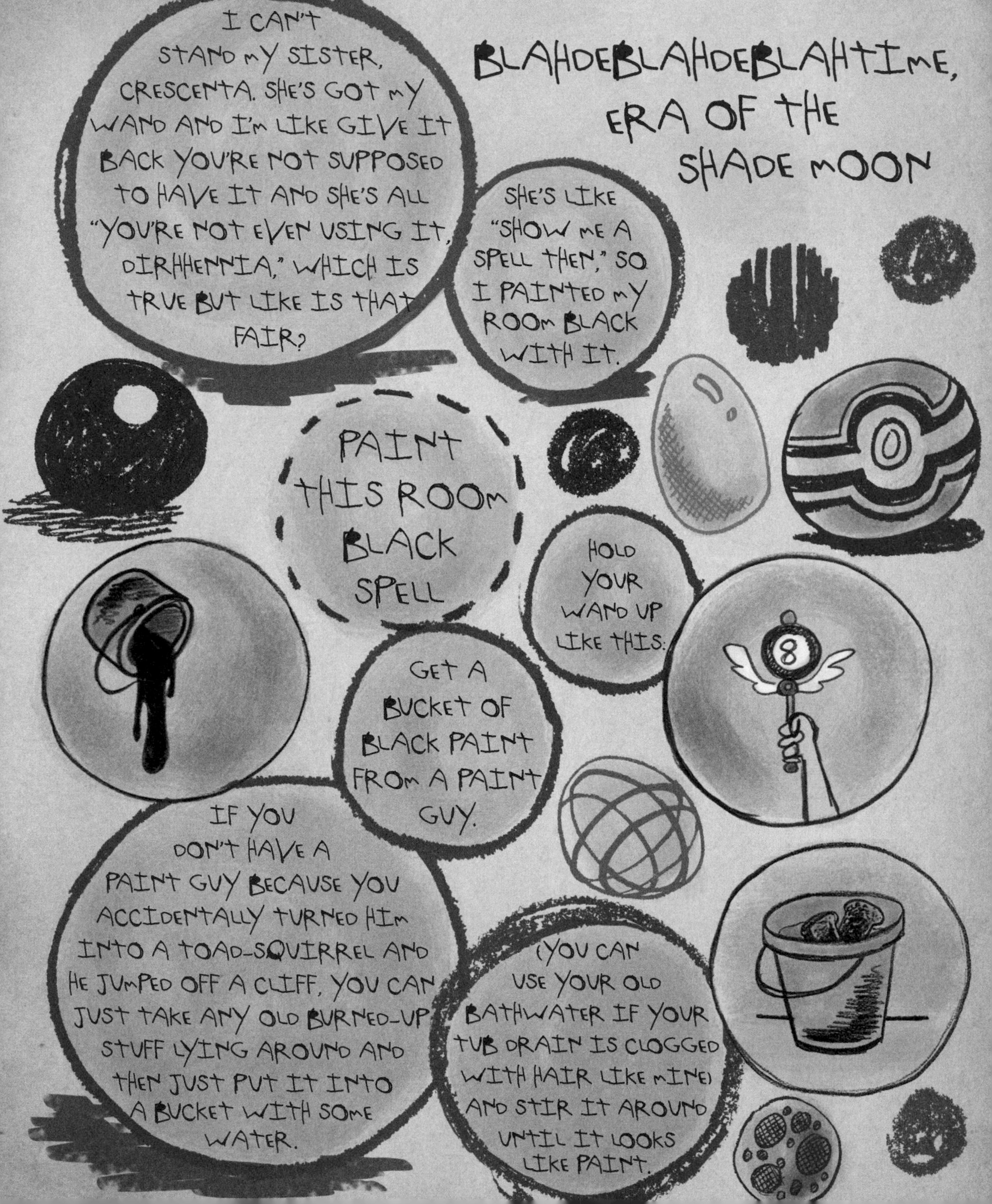
BLAHDEBLAHDEBLAHTIME, ERA OF THE SHADE MOON
I CAN'T STAND MY SISTER, CRESCENTA. SHE'S GOT MY WAND AND I'M LIKE GIVE IT BACK YOU'RE NOT SUPPOSED TO HAVE IT AND SHE'S ALL "YOU'RE NOT EVEN USING IT, DIRHHENNIA," WHICH IS TRUE BUT LIKE IS THAT FAIR?
SHE'S LIKE "SHOW ME A SPELL THEN," SO I PAINTED MY ROOM BLACK WITH IT.
PAINT THIS ROOM BLACK SPELL
HOLD YOUR WAND UP LIKE THIS:
8
GET A BUCKET OF BLACK PAINT FROM A PAINT GUY.
IF YOU DON'T HAVE A PAINT GUY BECAUSE YOU ACCIDENTALLY TURNED HIM INTO A TOAD-SQUIRREL AND HE JUMPED OFF A CLIFF, YOU CAN JUST TAKE ANY OLD BURNED-UP STUFF LYING AROUND AND THEN JUST PUT IT INTO A BUCKET WITH SOME WATER.
(YOU CAN USE YOUR OLD BATHWATER IF YOUR TUB DRAIN IS CLOGGED WITH HAIR LIKE MINE) AND STIR IT AROUND UNTIL IT LOOKS LIKE PAINT.

DIP YOUR WAND IN THE PAINT OR WET BURNED STUFF AND PAINT THE WALLS WITH IT.
IF YOUR MOM IS ALL "OH MY WORD, WHAT DID YOU DO TO YOUR WAND?" YOU CAN JUST BE LIKE "WHOSE WAND, MOM?" AND SHE'LL BE LIKE "YOUR WAND, DIRHHENNIA," AND YOU CAN JUST BE LIKE YEAH THAT'S WHAT I THOUGHT. MY WAND! I DO WHATEVER I WANT TO IT!
WHAT ARE YOU GONNA DO, MOM, GIVE MY WAND TO CRESCENTA?
FINAL YEAR, ERA OF THE SHADE MOON
YEAH SO MY MOM GAVE THE WAND TO CRESCENTA.
I GUESS SHE'S GONNA BE THE QUEEN SOMEDAY, NOT ME.
BUT IT'S COOL BECAUSE IT'LL BE HARD FOR ME TO BE QUEEN WHEN I'M LIKE OUT IN THE WORLD LIKE A LONE WOLF.
MY MOM IS SAYING I HAVE TO GO NOW AND I CAN'T WRITE IN THIS BOOK ANYMORE.
I'M LIKE IT'S NOT WRITING IT'S JUST DRAWINGS OF BALLS ;)
Sounds like she did you a favor.

CRESCENTA
THE EAGER

When the one before her proved unfit,
Crescenta the Eager took the role,
and along with her gal pal, Emily
kept the monsters under Mewman control.

Welcome to the Era of Bunnies!

Personally, I find them much more charming than Shade moons.

I know my dear, sweet, simpleminded sister, Dirhhennia, is upset, and I feel for her. I truly do. I mean, what a disappointment to be over-sparkled by your little sister at just about everything! It must be so hard to be her! The only thing I can say she's better at than me is drawing balls. I'll give her that, Dir draws a great ball!!! And really, none of this is her fault. I mean, you can't mess with destiny. You can try, but you'll just make yourself miserable, and the thing you are trying to stop from happening will just happen anyway.

I am exceedingly excited to write in the magic Book of Spells! I also love scrapbooking and plan on pasting some personal photos in here!

me and my big sis, Dirhhennia, ages 6 and 3.

I knew it must be my destiny to be queen the moment I snuck into my sister Dir's room and took her wand. It transformed into this beautiful, perfect little object you are looking at now. Much lovelier than her ball wand. Very special.

I haven't read her chapter yet but I'm getting weird vibes.

Personally, I always preferred her sister, the heaped one.

Crescenta the Eager
Aureole Sign: Hydra
Height: 5' 2"
Attributes
Strength: 13
Intelligence: 16
Wisdom: 10
Dexterity: 20
Constitution: 20
Charisma: 4

The Crystal—
My crystal is a radiant, glowing quartz in the shape of a heart. I am very bighearted and wish more than anything to serve my people and help others!!!

The Bell—
Another pure golden heart surrounding the first with a small pink ruby heart on top! Altogether, my wand has three hearts! More than any queen in history! I am very proud of this fact; not to brag, but it is a tremendous accomplishment to have three hearts.

The Wings—
Glowing, graceful swan feathers. Some have said I am very graceful, which must be why my wand has taken this form.

The Bow—
A remarkably different quality to my wand! It represents my uniqueness.

The Charge Port and Wand Charger—My wand drinks nothing but the purest pearls taken from the most beautiful clams.

The Millhorse—
I am happy to say I saved my millhorse from my sister. Her name is Chastity! She's a dream!

The Era of Bunnies, year 1

most queens get everything handed to them on a golden platter. Well, not me. I had to work hard to get where I am! As the younger sister, it wasn't a given I'd be queen, even though it was so obvious that Dirhhennia wasn't meant to be queen. I hate to say it, but the truth is some people are just shining stars, and others are sad, endless black holes of nothingness. You see, I knew I was special, but I had to prove it. So, one day I borrowed Dir's wand and started creating spells. I needed to show my mother my true potential. That is how I created the great Levitato Spell at age 12. I am one of the youngest princesses ever to have created spells! And I didn't stop there! In the time of exactly one moon cycle, I created 37 spells! I'm pretty sure that's the most spells created by any queen in one moon cycle! So, through a combination of destiny, inherent specialness, and hard work, I will soon be queen!

The Era of Bunnies, year 2

I have been very busy! Not only have I been creating lots of useful spells, but I have been going to Magic High Commission meetings with my mom, writing a play, and learning how to play the trumpet. I started the Future Leaders of Mewni club with the other princes and princesses of the minor kingdoms. I also joined the Junior Castle Guard and help keep watch over the castle during the night. I do volunteer work for the poor, and in my spare time I sew socks for the kingdom's poverty-ridden snakes so they don't freeze in winter. I know some say I am an overachiever, but I think they are just jealous. You might wonder how one can get so much done in a day; well, these days I need very little sleep! I have created a spell that enables you to get 8 hours of rest in just 4 minutes! I used to believe you can't make your days longer, just better—but now I have found a way to make them longer, too! This is the kind of brilliant thinking that separates simpleminded monsters from strong Mew-women.

Speaking of simple, I saw my sister, Dir, in the rose garden today hanging out with Chad. Just sitting there, doing absolutely nothing, like rocks. I had a purpose in the rose garden. I was with the Mewni Junior Gardeners, working tirelessly in the sun to plant petunias. What was Dir doing? Nothing, just giggling with that dummy Chad. What do they even have to giggle about?! Fine. I'll be honest. Sometimes being so special can be isolating. I don't have many people, if anyone, I can talk to. Everyone my age is so immature. I thought all my great accomplishments would bring real friends, that people would want to orbit my shining star. It turns out the road to greatness is a lonely one.

The Era of Bunnies, year 3

Still busy! And things have been going well! Especially in my Future Leaders of Mewni club. I think we have made the most of our time and achieved much. For example, we noticed there was a real problem in the Kingdom when Princess Johansen was coming to a meeting and slipped in pig-goat dung. She didn't care much, but her smell during the meeting was a constant reminder of what a mess our streets are.

We had to do something! I drafted some proposed rules right away. The other future leaders got involved and had some great suggestions! Especially Princess Kelpbottom—she's a big believer in ethics—and we've been having some intelligent conversations. All in all, we created 110 public conduct rules for the citizens of Mewni to abide by.

FLOM CHARTER

Me with the Future Leaders of Mewni club

For example, all pig-goats in an open space must wear diapers; all raven scouts must fly at least 7 feet off the ground to avoid flying into anyone; if you spit on the street, you will be thrown in jail; etc. I was hoping my mother would help me implement them, but she thought they were "not fun." So I took it upon myself, pasted the rules around the Kingdom, and got my fellow members of the Junior Castle Guard to help me patrol the streets. At first, the rules were quite despised. It amazes me how ungrateful people can be when you are trying to help them! But over time, and with all the rule breakers locked up in the castle dungeon, people started following the rules. The streets were a much safer and, more importantly, cleaner place. And the citizens of Mewni mostly appreciated it.

The Era of Bunnies, year 4

Been having some fantastic talks with Princess Kelpbottom, or as I call her, Emily. She just really understands what it's like to be exceptional and the loneliness that sometimes comes with it. She is a true friend, someone ambitious and mature upon whom I can depend. Unlike my deadbeat sister, Dir, whom I haven't seen much of lately. Dir and Chad ran off into the Forest of Certain Death together to be a pack of two lone wolves or something. I would say it is too bad that I won't have a sister around to love and support me as I become queen, but as Emily and I always say—you can only rely on yourself!!!! No matter what you do, the dwarves will always try to sabotage the giants.

I finally went through Mewberty! I was starting to get worried it wouldn't happen for me, but of course, it did. It is a unique Butterfly family trait. Prolonged exposure to magic eventually hits a peak where it can't be contained any longer. It surges through your body, causing you to make a cocoon, and when you emerge, you get a quick peek of your ultimate magic form: your butterfly.

You will not see that butterfly again until you master the art of dipping down, which brings that surge of magic to the surface again. It is a beautiful, very natural thing, and it doesn't happen to all princesses. My sister, Dir, for example, has never been through Mewberty and probably never will. Most princesses go completely boy crazy when it hits! I managed to keep total calm and composure. Emily happened to be over at the time, and she said my ultimate magic form looked magnificent.

The Era of Bunnies, year 5

Never give up on your dreams. My dream is to be queen, and one day that dream will be a reality. Emily and I spend a lot of time discussing the kind of queen I will become. I will be strong, but fair. In control at all times, unlike my mother, Festivia. The people will respect me but love me. Emily has been studying medicine and hopes to be a nurse queen under the sea. I think she will be an excellent nurse queen, but I wish she didn't need to do it so far away.

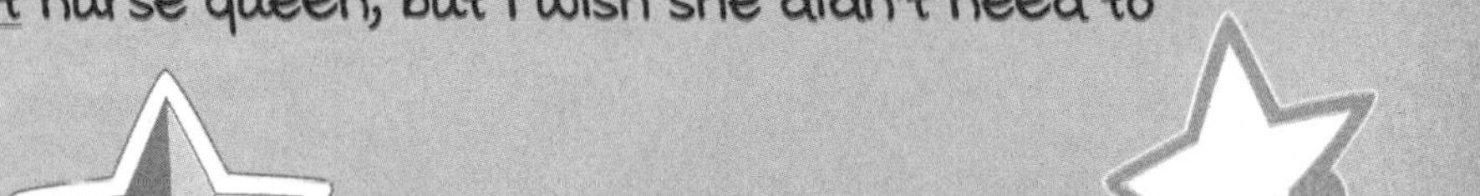
Big Sis
Levitato master

On the next page is the very first spell I ever created, at age 12! I still use it just about every day. You can bring any object to you or away from you. I created it so I could get more done. You save on average 20 seconds just levitating your daily to-do list to you. That might not seem like much, but that's nearly 2 and a half minutes a week, 10 minutes a month, 120 minutes a year! Think about how much you can accomplish in 120 minutes!!! I use Levitato to feed myself, make the bed, travel down stairs, and carry heavy objects. I save lots of time.

You may wonder what all that unusual writing is. Well, It's the secret ancient language of the mewni queens, Low-Mewnian. I'm fluent in English, Mer-Bubble, Demon-Tongue, and Low-Mewnian! When I was 5, I taught myself using flash cards while Dirhhennia was, per usual, sleeping.

my first spell!!!

Levitato

How to Levitato:

1. Simply point your wand at the object you wish to move and clearly say "Levitato."

2. You will find you now have the object trapped in a force field connected to your wand.

3. From here, use your wand like a baton. Where you point, that's where the object goes. The quicker you point, the farther it goes. Point your wand toward yourself to have it come to you.

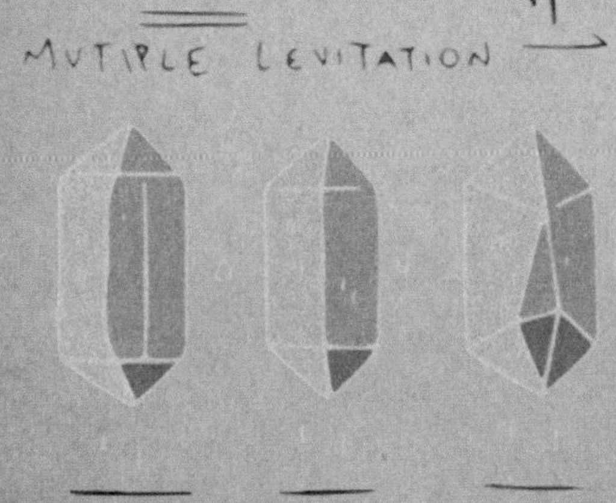
MUTIPLE LEVITATION

The theory behind the spell is fascinating. It's all about the magnetic crystals that exist inside every object. No matter what form your wand takes, it will always have a crystal. Crystals with unlike poles naturally want to be together, so even without a blast, inanimate objects will be attracted to your wand. This spell simply gives them the chance to connect magnetically. When you send objects away from you, it is like flipping the magnet over. Now you have two like poles facing each other, and they will repel.

The Era of Bunnies, year 6

The monsters are at it again. They don't think they are treated fairly, but that's ridiculous. If they weren't so lazy and bloodthirsty, of course they could have everything we have. What they want is a bunch of handouts! Don't they understand you have to work hard to get ahead? They say they're at a disadvantage because they don't have magic. Well, cry me a river. I had to work very hard to be any good at magic. No one handed anything to me. To date, I have created 4,700 extremely beneficial spells.

The Era of Bunnies, year 7

Finally, I have the crown! I am queen! My mother threw me the most beautiful coronation ceremony. Parties are her only specialty, after all. I am so happy I have been jumping up and down all day! Emily told me I looked lovely in my coronation dress. I had sent a raven scout to deliver an invitation to Dir, and in response all I got was a pile of mud tightly packed in a ball. Typical, but I let negative thoughts slide off me like bog water off a log.

As queen, I have been getting right to work! Of course I have. I am so excited to make my mark. As Emily always says, the first spider catches the fly, and I'm catching a lot of flies! From the bottom of my heart, I love my mother, but I always found her style of ruling to be a bit lax. She doesn't believe in strict rules, or really any rules. But I love rules! How will the sheep-cows know how to behave unless you tell them?

Without rules, all you have is chaos, anarchy, and uncertainty. What you need is someone in charge who really cares about her people, someone with strong ethics and a good sense of what is right and wrong. Someone like me!!!!!!!!!!

The Era of Bunnies, year 8

Being queen has been excellent! My days are full of meetings. I love meetings! When I tell someone to do something, they have to listen to me! This kind of leadership has made my ruling very efficient.

My main project has been working on the monster problem. You see, they have been led as of late by a scaly gecko-like monster named Seth. He's been convincing them that the fact they are living in filth is somehow our fault instead of their own doing! The monster situation is already bad, but we have been living in relative peace for my whole life. I'm worried this new bad leadership will bring us back into a time of warring like when my mother was a young queen. Luckily, Emily and I have a plan! Emily has decided not to be queen of the Waterfolk! The Waterfolk are really a more minor kingdom, just like the Pony Heads, Spider Bites, and Lucitors. The Butterflys rule them all, and Emily thought she could do more good for the kingdom as a whole staying by my side and helping me rule. She's just exceptionally thoughtful like that.

The Era of Bunnies, year 9

What a productive year! I'm jumping up and down again!!! Emily's and my genius plan for the monsters has almost worked!!! You know how I explained about minor kingdoms? Well, you see, the monsters are so uncivilized they've never had one. Oh, sure, they've tried; many years ago they had a Mewman-eating giant of a monster they wanted to make their king! Of course, we never let that happen, but it got me thinking. . . . What if they did have a queen and king? Someone dependable and Mewman-friendly. Someone who would keep the monsters in check. Someone Butterfly-controlled.

Not having clear, responsible leadership opens up a path for losers like Seth, but if they had a queen and king, it might squash the current civil unrest. Now, of course, this kind of thing can be tricky; you can't just put someone in charge, or the monsters will feel they have been cheated. You need to make them believe they have gotten to pick their leader. So we are having an election! Emily and I searched through monster camps in the Forest of Certain Death for months until we found the right candidate. Her name is Pemma Avarius, and her husband, Sudo Avarius. They will do whatever we say, and are happy to do so, as long as we supply them with a castle, gold, and power. Perfect! The monsters have put up for election, no surprise, that disgusting Seth.

The Era of Bunnies, year 10

And the winner is . . . Pemma Avarius! Were you worried? Well, I wasn't. I happen to be supremely good at campaigning. The secret to any plan is believing in it, and we did. We spent the year, and tons of gold, smearing Seth's name and reputation. By contrast, we got Pemma the best speechwriters. We staged her saving a baby monster from a burning mud hut. We gave her whole cornfields to give to the monsters! Despite all that, the vote was still close; but, thank the Stump, Pemma is the winner, fair and square! She's currently enjoying her new castle and helping us implement lots of new and exciting rules for the monsters. We did it!!!

The Era of Bunnies, year 11

As always, very busy! Everything is going wonderfully! Queen Pemma Avarius is doing a great job keeping the monsters in check, and they haven't given us any trouble. Emily has been attending my meetings with the Magic High Commission, and they just think she's wonderful. Glossaryck even likes her! A surprise, because you know who Glossy spends more time with than me?

my lazy sister, Dirhhennia, that's who! She and Chad are back from being lone wolves and have decided to live in a tent in the garden. Great. Luckily, I'm creating some new restrictions on where and for how long you can have a tent set up in a public space.

The Era of Bunnies, year 12

I'm excited to announce that I am making Emily my chief advisor and partner in ruling Mewni. I have given it a lot of thought, and although I am more than capable of ruling on my own, it is nice to have someone by my side when I make big decisions. Plus, we are compatible in every way. Isn't that great?! The first decision we made together was to take a vacation in the Waterfolk Kingdom!

me and Emily on vacation

Now, at this point, I have literally written over 5,000 spells. Far too many to put in this one book!!! For all my spells, please go to the castle library and reference Crescenta's Spells volumes 1–26.

Emily and I believe I should write a few of my most special spells in this book to give you, the future generations, a taste of my abilities. I've picked a few unique ones for your enjoyment. You see, I've created so many, sometimes I get creative! I like this one because it shows both my genius and imagination.

Releaseo Demonius Infestica

To be cast in the rare instance when you need to heal a broken bone AND infect the host with a demonic tentacle virus.

Part 1

1. Simply power up your wand.
2. Lift it above your head.
3. Shoot it toward the person you wish to both heal and infect and say "Releaseo Demonius Infestica."

Part 2

1. Bone heals.
2. Virus braids itself into the host's skeletal system.
3. Healed bone "hatches" into a sentient tentacle being.
4. Tentacle being turns evil, implanting negative and disparaging thoughts in host.

Yes . . . creative. This is the spell I used to try to heal Marco's broken arm. I used the Echo Creek reading technique of skimming. If you skim, it does LOOK LIKE a bone-healing spell! I see zero use for this spell.

You're wrong, Star; this spell is beneficial. I've used it exactly twice, both on Rhombulus. How do you think he got those nifty snake hands? Very useful. Crescenta was pretty obnoxious, but she did know how to make a spell! Also, remember, Star: always be a dipper, not a skimmer.

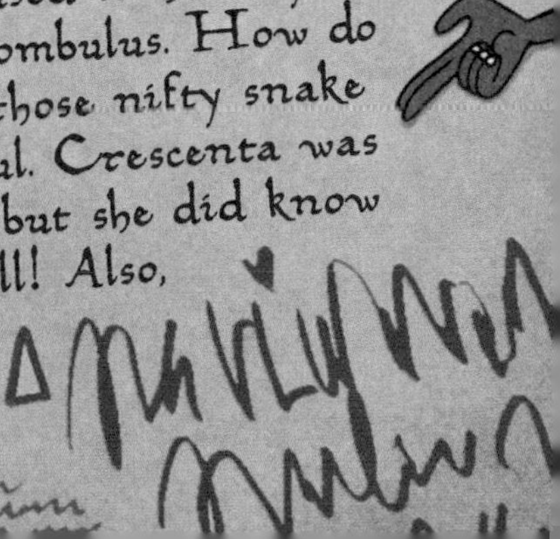

Annexus Ignis Idem

To be cast in the rare instance when you need to tie your shoes and set a building on fire.

Part 1

1. Put your shoes on your feet. Don't be lazy. This spell won't do that for you.
2. Point your wand at your shoes.
3. Blast your shoes and say "Annexus Ignis Idem."

Part 2

1. Shoelaces tie into perfectly symmetrical bunny ears.
2. You will be surrounded by fire.
3. Get out of building quickly.

Warning!
Don't skim this one!

Lux Locus Scabrosus

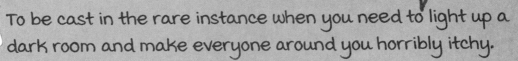

To be cast in the rare instance when you need to light up a dark room and make everyone around you horribly itchy.

Part 1

1. Go into the dark room you wish to light up.
2. Hold your wand out into the dark.
3. Quietly say "Lux Locus Scabrosus Falsus."

You can find this spell in volume 19!

19

Part 2

1. Room will be lit from within by a beautiful golden light.
2. If anyone is with you in the room, they will start with a small itch on the ankle.
3. The itch will quickly spread all over their body until they are writhing on the ground in horrible itchiness.

ugh, no!!!!

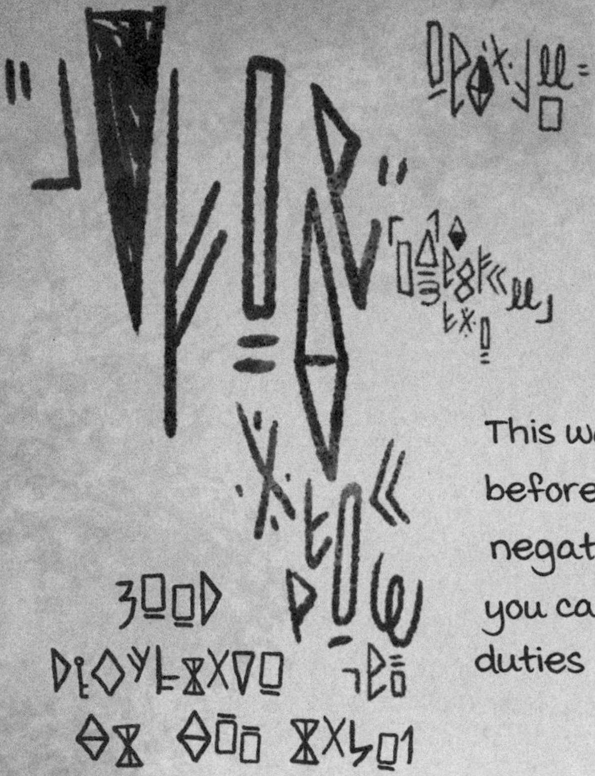

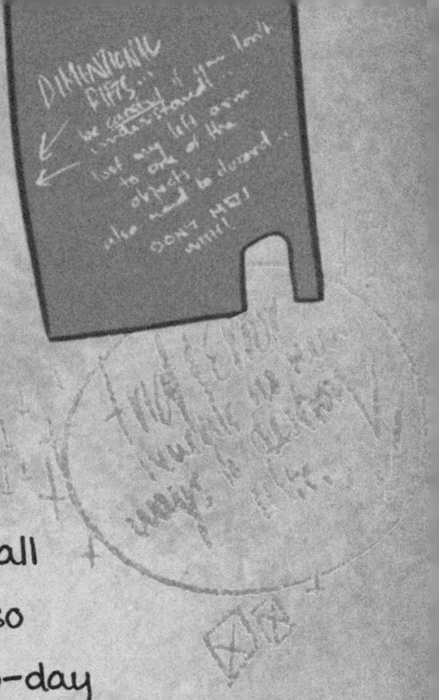

Regiis Solum Lacrimae

Takes away feelings of loneliness so you can get to work!

This was a spell I used a lot before I met Emily. It takes away all negative thoughts and feelings so you can just go on with the day-to-day duties of being princess or queen!

1) Point your wand to your temple.

2) Say "Regiis Solum Lacrimae!"

3) Pull the negative thoughts out of your brain like little threads.

4) Enjoy the rest of your productive workday!!!

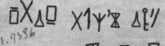

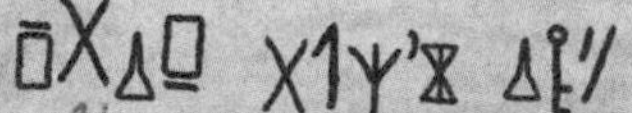

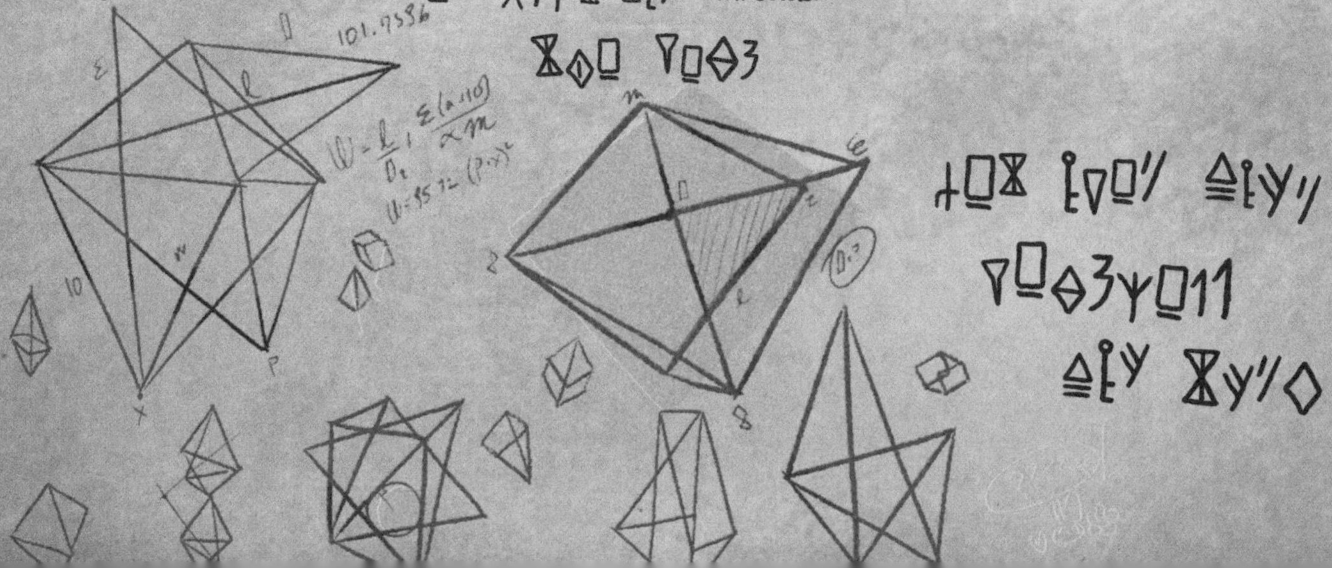

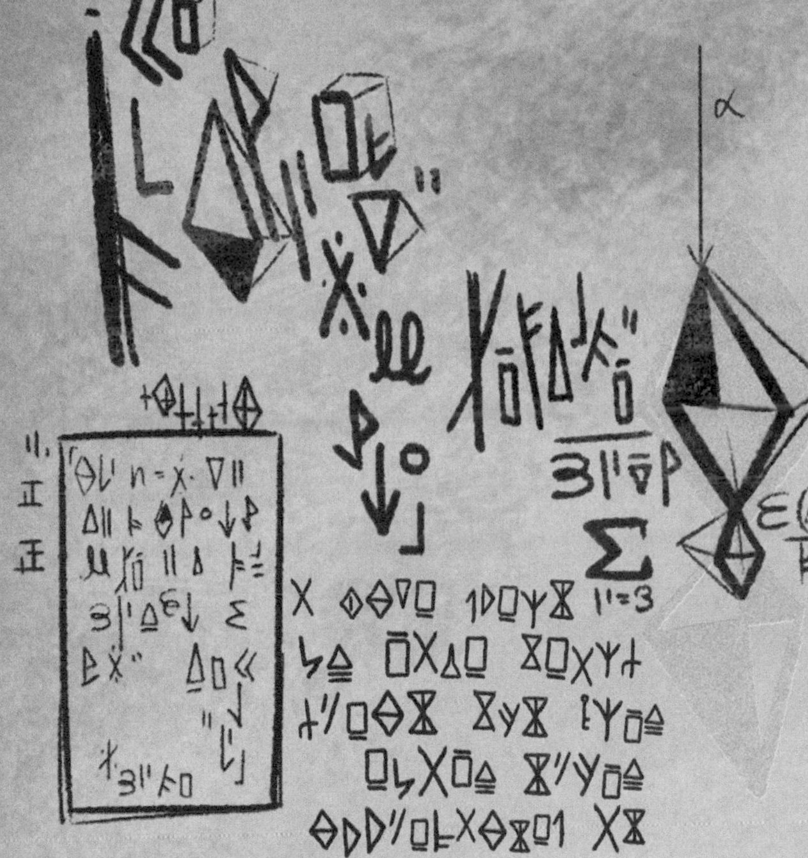

A list of some of the other spells you can find by me, Crescenta Butterfly, in the Royal Library.

Avium Canticum—Makes you hear lovely bird sounds in your ears wherever you go.

Brutum Fulmen—Makes thunderbolts.

Bulla Spiro—Will encase you in a bubble so you can breath underwater. I used this when I was on my vacation in the Waterfolk Kingdom.

Fiduciam Speculo—Will give you loads of confidence!

Digitus Pygmy—Will paint your nails and give you webbed fingers at the same time!

Frumentum Delectamenti—Makes bland corn taste delicious.

Habitu Auxilium—Will pick out an outfit for you in the morning so you don't waste precious time thinking about it.

Industria Capulus—Will give you loads of energy!

Labyrinthus—Makes an endless maze in which you can trap your enemies.

Lupus Mutatis Soror—Will turn your sister into a real wolf so she shuts up about being a lone wolf.

Magis Armis—Will give you extra arms for getting more things done at once!

Nihil Fuga Mannulus—Will take away a Flying Pony Head's ability to fly.

Novis Inamabilis Sciurus Cornu—Will turn a squirrelicorn inside out.

Papilio Multa Caput—Will make any butterfly have multiple heads and tongues. Helpful for pollinating the Kingdom's rose gardens.

Somnum Nihil Magis—Makes it so you get 8 hours' worth of sleep in just 4 minutes!!!

You can find this spell in volume 22!

YOU ARE HERE

THIS WAY . . .

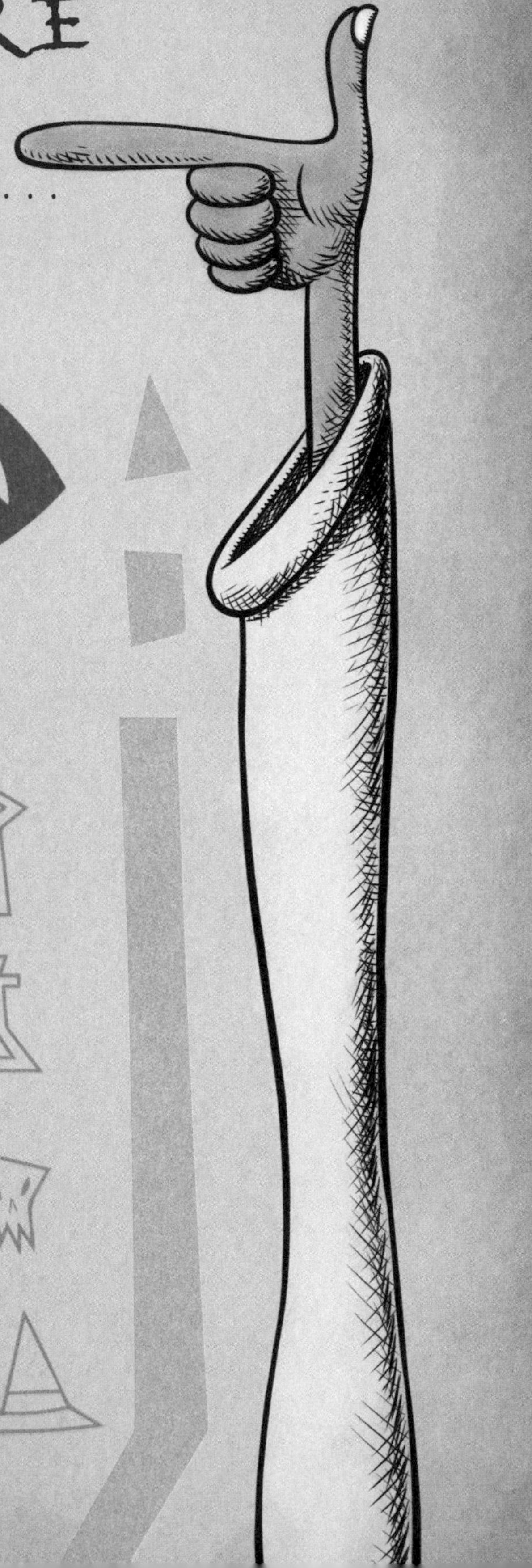

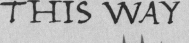

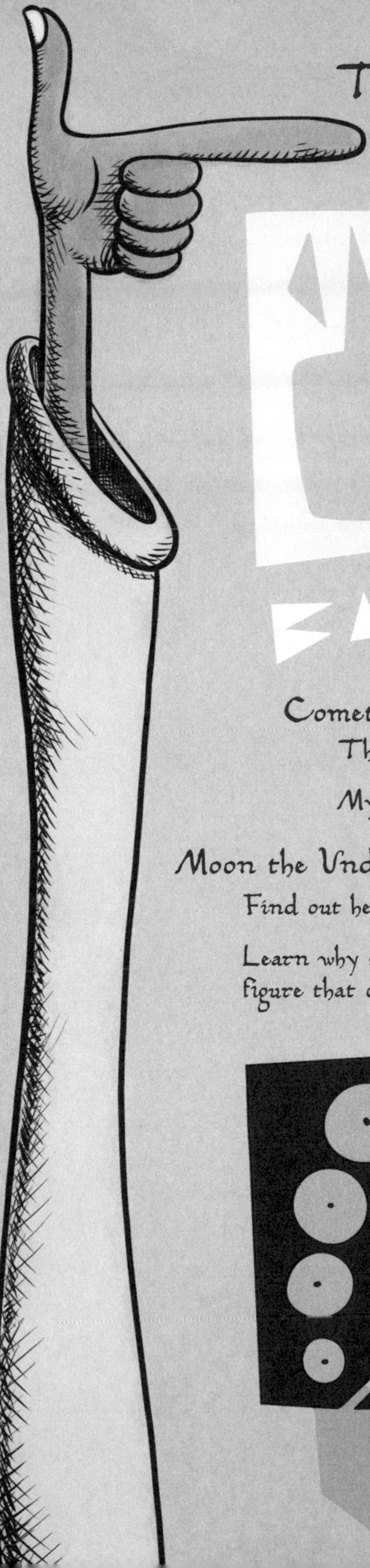

THIS WAY . . .

Glossaryck's Guide to Dipping Down for Idiots

Okay, it's not nice to call you an idiot. We're already starting off on the wrong foot. I'm gonna have Sally or Sassafras come in here and paint over that. I'll have them call you something else, or maybe we will just put some simple wallpaper over it.

Anyway, ignore it for now and don't think that I actually think you're an idiot. I always get myself into these situations. It's just like my sister Tableaucontenta always used to say: "Glossaryck, don't always say what you're thinking. Also, you don't have a sister."

What a way to find out you don't have a sister, ya know? And here you are all mad I called you an idiot. You probably feel bad getting all upset at a sisterless guy like that.

Let's start over.

Glossaryck's Guide to Dipping Down for

____

(your name here)

Let's talk Mewberty. I know, I know. Gross. But, hey, the reality is this: your first "dip" into magic is Mewberty. Before that moment you're willy-nilly blasting woodland creatures with your wand. But once you're Mewbertized, you will forever be changed, and you've essentially opened the gateway to more dips.

Why?

That's what everyone wants to know. To be honest, I don't even know. Or it could be I'm just too lazy to explain it all to you—what's the difference, really? Anyway, one thing is for sure: Mewberty equips you with tools you may find useful later in life as a magic user. Unlocking them and controlling them is the trick. The form you take in Mewberty, when evoked later in life, is called your Ultimate Magic Form, or your "Butterfly."

You can pop into this form when your emotions are heightened—when you're in love, angry, hungry, exhausted, etc. Usually the following phenomena occur:

Mewberty Wings

Mewberty wings appear in your first breakout and they'll grow throughout your life. Your Mewberty wings will only show when they are needed. It's not necessarily up to you when that happens. If you get to where you can control it, then congratulations. You're amazing.

Once you reach adulthood, your wings will be strong enough to carry you away from danger when you are in your Ultimate Magic Form.

Keep them clean, but don't machine wash them. If you spill chili all over your Mewberty wings, eat off the chunks and then wipe the soupy gunk off with a moist towelette.

Omatidia Eyes

You won't be able to see it, but man, do these eyes make you look goofy! The Omatidia Eyes are faceted, allowing you to see more than one dimension at a time. You probably won't be able to comprehend it as it's happening, unless you get really good at using them.

One of the ancient queens, Soupina of the Old Book, actually got stuck viewing the overlapping dimensions, and she never returned to her own. She went mad. Be careful you don't get lost in your new power to see all dimensions at once. Or, if you prefer, disappear forever.

Fun fact: if you are ever having trouble reading a Mewni newspaper in Low-Mewnian, pop into your Ultimate Magic Form and read it—your Omatidia Eyes can read any language. Trick is, you probably won't retain anything you've read.

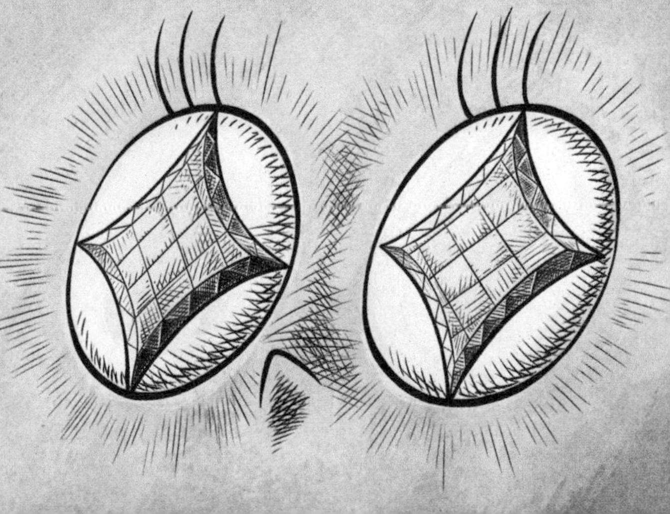

Density Changes

Depending on your emotions, your density could decrease to the point that you become lighter than air and float off the ground. Ideally, your wings will pop out to hold you aloft, but if they don't you'll eat it hard and crash. Dirhhennia, who never really went through Mewberty, would nonetheless occasionally wake up on the ceiling, only to come crashing down onto her bed. She went through a lot of beds.

Hexapoda Arms

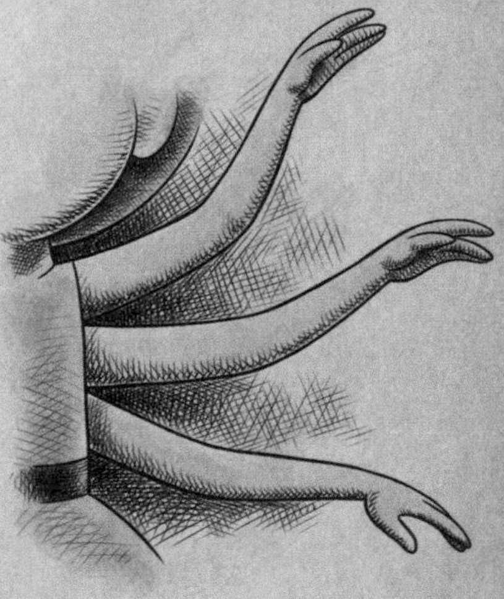

You're gonna get some more arms. Don't worry, they are only going to pop out when you need them. I've only heard of 5 or 18 times when a queen has not been able to get them to go away after a battle.

Once you can do magic without your wand, you'll be able to use all six of your arms in your Ultimate Magic Form for firing off spells.

Glottalimous Voice

Your Mewberty or Glottalimous Voice will also change throughout your lifetime. At first it's a raspy growl, but later it advances and separates, sounding almost like several voices speaking at once. Just as you have multidimensional vision, you also have a multidimensional voice, causing a layered, slightly offset sound. You want to try and keep talking until the offset voices become one. Hopefully, the one voice you end up with is actually yours.

Other Effects

This is where it gets weird. Every queen will have her own unique signifiers in her Ultimate Magic Form. Crescenta would grow one giant eyebrow every time she dipped down. It looked like a caterpillar trying to mate with her face! Ha. Then it turned into an actual caterpillar named Thteven, and he ran off into the Forest of Certain Death.

Getting There from Here

Every princess wants to know the quickest way to dipping down. Here is a list of dip-evoking emotions.

- Envy—An envy dip can be a nasty one. There's a tendency to not become fully formed, i.e., you may not get all of the traits of your Butterfly.
- Anger—Like the envy dip, an anger dip can be volatile and unpredictable.
- Frustration—These dips offer a bit more control but are hard to come by. Careful, though; these transition quickly to anger.
- Betrayal—This is probably the surest way to make a good dip happen. You can test this one by having a loved one betray your trust. You're most likely to experience a change in density and float off the ground.
- Love—Perhaps the most powerful dip down comes from love or a combination of love and protection. A love dip is usually full-featured (full wings, Hexapoda Arms, Omatidia Eyes, etc.), but magic blasts can be weak or labored.
- Protection (of another)—This is the Grand Poobah of dips. The combo of protection and love is quite intense for you and dangerous for your adversaries. Your magic blasts will be at their most powerful, but volatility may make them difficult to control. You'll likely dip into your full Ultimate Magic Form.

If you don't dip down after Mewberty, don't worry—a lot of queens can't get there. Honestly, it might not actually be that healthy with all the magical radiation and whatnot, so maybe you're better off not being able to do it?

- Take on the form of someone else
- Spend a day in the body of a cat with a human face
- Spend a day in the body of a human
- Build a nest
- Lick your elbow
- Spend a day in the body of a centipede ✓
- Teach a non-queen how to use magic ✓
- Live in the Sandwich Dimension for one year
- Pick nose with toe ✓
- Perfect the ukulele
- Ride a tornado
- ~~Don't eat pudding for one month~~
- Surf on Lava Lake Beach
- Swim in shark-infested waters
- Say nothing but "Globgor" for a whole year
- Reconnect with an old friend ✓
- Be in two places at once ✓
- Send yourself mushrooms
- Be in three places at once ✓
- Be in four places at once ✓
- Live a day in reverse ✓
- ~~Bathe in pudding~~
- Send yourself flowers
- Fire the Magic High Commission
- Be in five places at once
- Be immersed in pudding
- ~~Do nothing for a day~~
- Do nothing for 5 days ✓
- Learn to paint with pudding
- Roast pudding
- Learn to stop thinking ✓
- Attend a pig-goat toast
- Hypnotize a hawk ✓
- Eat 100 Goblin Dogs in one day
- ~~Learn to sing~~
- Learn to sing opera
- Replace teeth with gold
- ~~Hypnotize a chicken~~
- ~~Talk to that judgmental cat, Baby~~
- Get a fish pedicure ✓
- Sleep on hot coals ✓
- Find long-lost brother
- Perfect sensory deprivation ✓
- Make new flavor of toothpaste
- Live in a book ✓
- ~~Be a best man~~
- Publish book of haiku
- Die in a book
- Be a bridesmaid ✓
- Be a tourist in your own book
- Learn to belly dance
- Create a new language ✓
- Adopt a monkey
- Learn to tap dance
- Eat pickled dragon feet ✓
- Write a musical
- Learn to tango ✓
- Stay awake for 72 hours
- Learn self-photosynthesis
- Learn to meditate ✓
- Learn how to make lasagna
- Create life from nothing ✓
- Cruise in a low-rider
- Create competent life from nothing
- Eat nothing but burgers for one month ✓
- Toboggan
- Know the meaning of cosmic importance ✓
- Befriend a ghost ✓
- Travel through space-time ✓
- Go without shaving for one year
- Make peace with an adversary ✓

Own a dimension

Make sacrifice to a volcano

Make own kimchi

Learn to speak in two voices at once

Be on reality TV

Write a pudding-themed cookbook

Eat own weight in pancakes in one day ✓

Learn ventriloquism

Travel to the bottom layer of the Underworld

Grow extra fingers ✓

~~Learn how to apologize~~

~~Rule the multiverse~~

~~Save the multiverse~~

Get fashionable head crystal ✓

~~Help mortals find the meaning of life~~

Throw away all pants ✓

Read 10 books in 10 days ✓

Eat leaves

Learn to make cheese

Host a lovely dinner for friends ✓

Floss

Use a donut for a flotation device ✓

Spend a year living underground

Use a donut for a flying device ✓

Spend a summer in Oregon

~~Say sorry to that judgmental cat, Baby~~

Name a pet Mr. Panda Pants

Live in donut box for a full day ✓

Pop out of a birthday cake ✓

Experience time backward ✓

Go to high school reunion

Create evil clone

Get a degree in medicine

Grow a tail

Tell a stranger you love them

Learn anatomy of a Pony Head

Put together a 5,000-piece jigsaw puzzle

Buy a haunted bus

Fall in love ✓

Find buried treasure ✓

Buy a haunted houseboat ✓

Direct a movie ✓

Bury treasure

Reanimate a squirrelicorn

Make a time capsule and hide it at bottom of ocean

Travel to Pie Island ✓

~~Wear two taco shells as shoes~~

Everything on this list, probably

Wear a taco shell as a hat ✓

Change my voice

Set a rainbow on fire ✓

Use goldfish as skis

Walk on water

Become invisible ✓

~~Apologize to Reynaldo~~

Die and be reborn

Have the ultimate beach day

Make a leaf hat

~~Apologize to Father Time~~

See if you can survive without a heart

Win staring contest ✓

Stand still long enough to be mistaken for statue

Crochet your own socks

Lie still long enough to be mistaken for dead

Crochet your own underwear

Buy a unicorn

Travel to the beginning of creation and watch the multiverse get made

Teach a unicorn dressage

Create new flavor of ice cream

Find a cure for spider bites

Go to grad school ✓

Create a new flavor

Buy a magic bell

Start a small business

Teach a spider sign language

Make mediocre beach art

Travel to every dimension in the multiverse

It's good to have pets. I love coming home to a group of little idiots who love me no matter what and have no idea what is going on in the multiverse. It's comforting. I am the proud papa to three silkworms, a centipede, a beetle, and an earwig.

Silky—My sweet babycakes. Always quiet and careful, a perfect angel. My favorite darling who can do no wrong. I call her my Sweet Silky-T, or Silly Silks.

Stinky—My little troublemaker. I can't sit down to a nice meal of pudding without this little bug trying to get a taste! It's cute, though. My Stinky-Dinks.

Sassafras—She's my tiny ball of sass. I call her Sassa-Sassy-Pants or just Sassa. She only wants affection on her terms, and at about 3pm every day she will come sit on my lap.

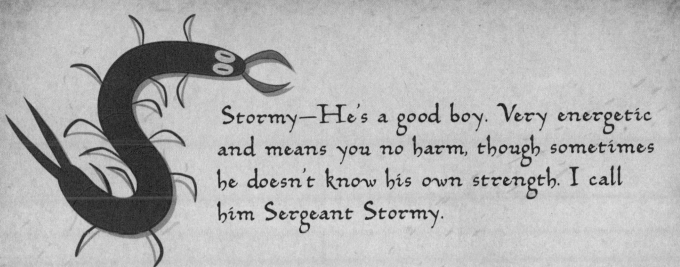

Stormy—He's a good boy. Very energetic and means you no harm, though sometimes he doesn't know his own strength. I call him Sergeant Stormy.

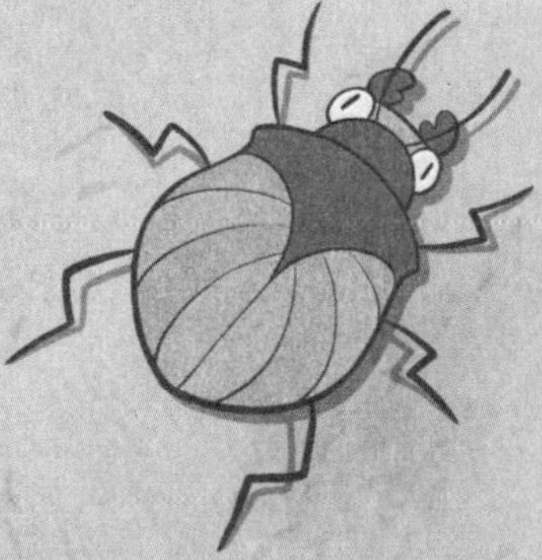

Simone—She's gorgeous and she knows it. I call her my Tiny Snooty-Toots. Or Snooty-Tooty Don't Be Rooty. She is a nice girl, though, and likes to sleep next to my head.

Sally—My shy Sally-Pally. She's really a very smart and helpful little earwig. She fetches items I need from around the book and trims my toenails. She will hide under the bed from strangers, so don't expect to see her around.

By the way, what you are smelling is not my babies, it's my room. It's on the next page! I'd appreciate you skipping past it because it's private, thank you very much.

GLOSSARYCK'S ROOM!
HOW TO DRAW MEWMANS

COSMIC IMPORTANCE
FRAGILE

RHINA
THE RIDDLED

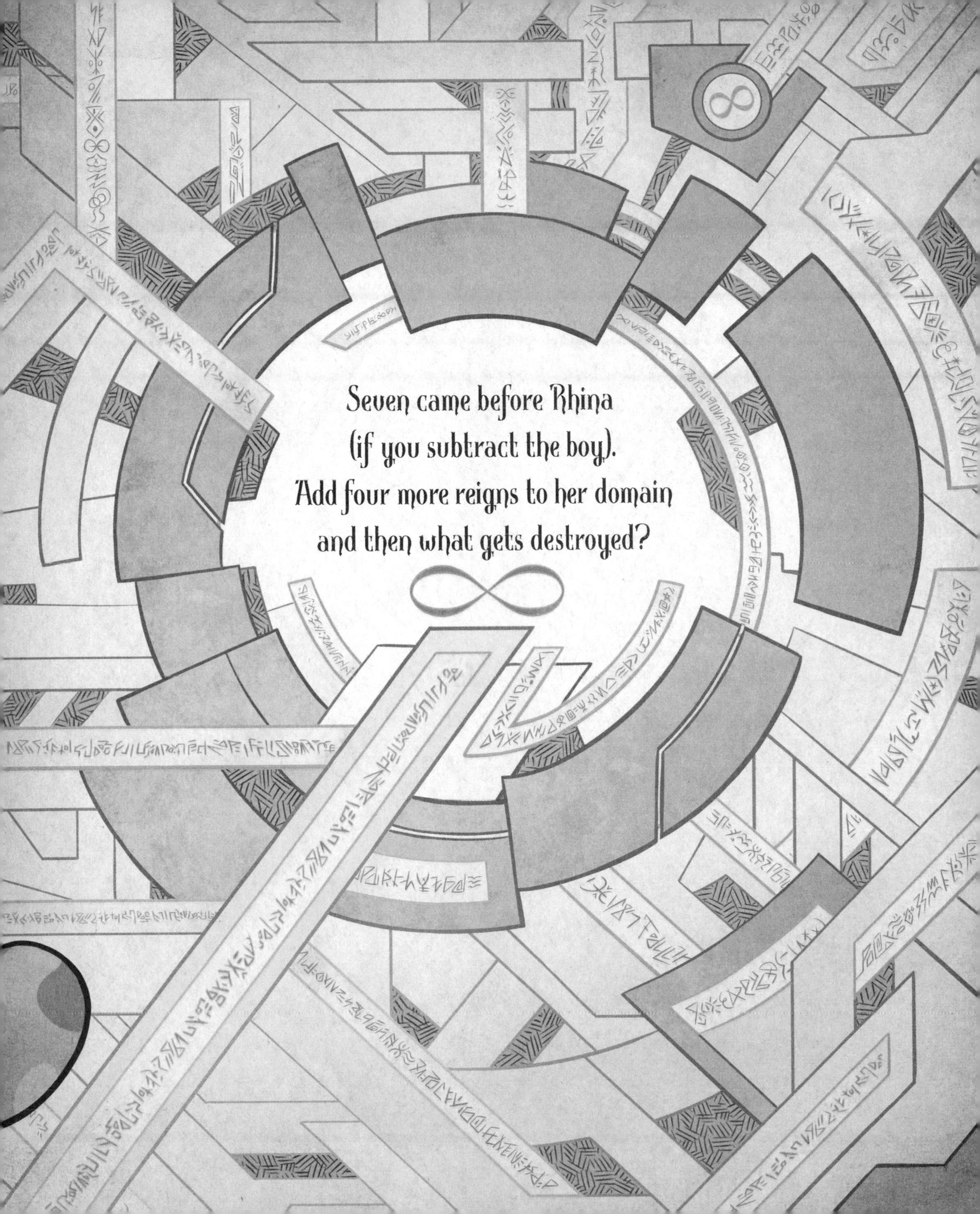
Seven came before Rhina
(if you subtract the boy).
Add four more reigns to her domain
and then what gets destroyed?

A rubrikian spinning cube—there are only seven of them in existence in all the universes.

The cubes must be rearranged before every spell.

Don't stare at the cubes for very long; their hypnotic effect is outrageously strong.

*Note to me: You have to remember to write down spell for spoiled porridge army, k?

A heart made from painite, the rarest of rare, is perfect for riddle craft, if you dare.

I make magic out of mist.
I am strong like a fist.
When you are in my presence,
time is of the essence.
Best make haste
if you see me pointed at your face.

What am I?

The base of the wand can also cut glass . . .

or be used as a crystal cudgel.

A: My wand

Note to me: Tell Glossaryck no. Not now. Not ever. No way. I don't eat algae on principle. Also: Ask Lady Gyoza to feed Turtle Hopkins while I'm away for post-coronation retreat week. And my mother should probably be told that Turtle Hopkins is going to be living in my chambers now that I am queen. I know she feels like a turtle's place is in the royal gardens, but I miss him dreadfully when he is not there beside me in the mornings, asleep on my other pillow.

Because of the intricacy of my wand, there are five Millhorses at work inside.

Ghost

Ogilvie the Third

Chastity

Torento

Blossom

Note to me: Remember red ribbon tied around your wrist since visit with Lady Gyoza to Dimension of Cats with Human Faces . . . really . . . don't forget it's there. Important.

Note to me: What were you supposed to remember?!?

Re: red ribbon. See prev. note.

My Nine-Step Stairway to Riddle Magic Mastery

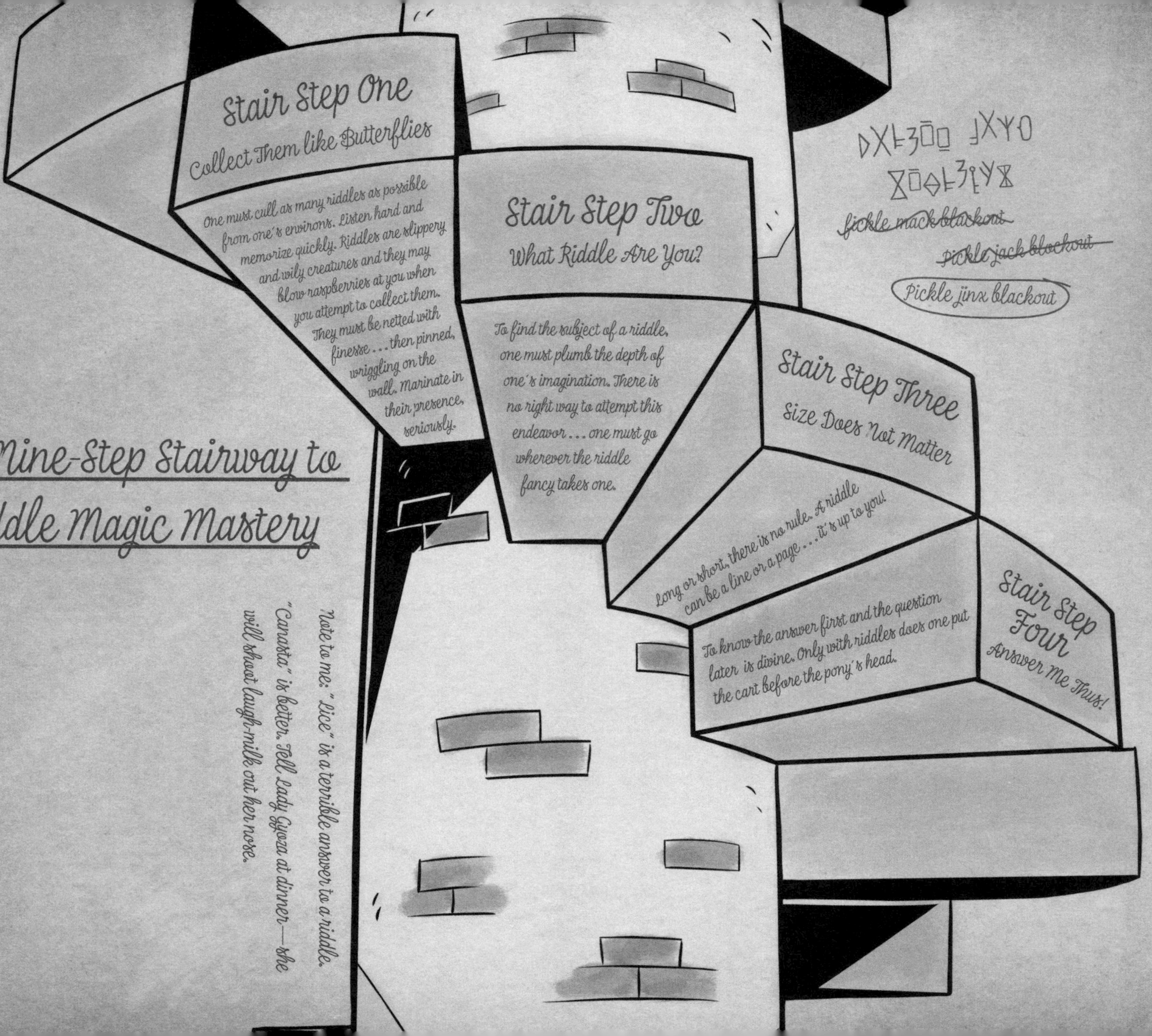

Stair Step One
Collect Them like Butterflies
One must cull as many riddles as possible from one's environs. Listen hard and memorize quickly. Riddles are slippery and wily creatures and they may blow raspberries at you when you attempt to collect them. They must be netted with finesse . . . then pinned, wriggling on the wall. Marinate in their presence, seriously.
Stair Step Two
What Riddle Are You?
To find the subject of a riddle, one must plumb the depth of one's imagination. There is no right way to attempt this endeavor . . . one must go wherever the riddle fancy takes one.
Stair Step Three
Size Does Not Matter
Long or short, there is no rule. A riddle can be a line or a page . . . it's up to you!
Stair Step Four
Answer Me Thus!
To know the answer first and the question later is divine. Only with riddles does one put the cart before the pony's head.
~~pickle mack blackout~~
~~Pickle jack blockout~~
Pickle jinx blackout

Note to me: "Lice" is a terrible answer to a riddle. "Canasta" is better. Tell Lady Gyoza at dinner—she will shoot laugh-milk out her nose.

Stair Step Five
Proper Drafting Tools for Success
For the best attempts at Riddle Craft, one should possess a wand with a rubrikian spinning cube—but a #2 pencil, sharpened and sporting a rubbery new eraser, will do in a pinch.
Stair Step Six
Metaphor This, Metaphor That
A metaphor can describe an object in a flowery way so that in your mind's eye all the words come together in a picturesque play. Imagine this: "The clock was like a ticking heartbeat of hourly measure." Or "The road was as curved as a ribbon of caramel in a scoop of melting ice cream."
Stair Step Seven
Alliterationally, My Dear, I Don't Give a Rhyme
Alliteration (picking words that possess the same sound), or making your words rhyme . . . use these two tricks if you can, then let your riddles overflow with razzmatazz!
Stair Step Eight
Riddles Can Be People, Too
Use "I" and then add a verb. Let the answer speak about itself in a Mewmanly way. Imagine thusly: "I am black as night, but add a little cow to the mix and I turn beige in fright!"
answer: coffee
Stair Step Nine
Lend Me an Ear!
Share your riddles with lots of friends, be they Pony Heads, monsters, humans, part-owls, or Mewmans. They will let you know if you are on the right track.

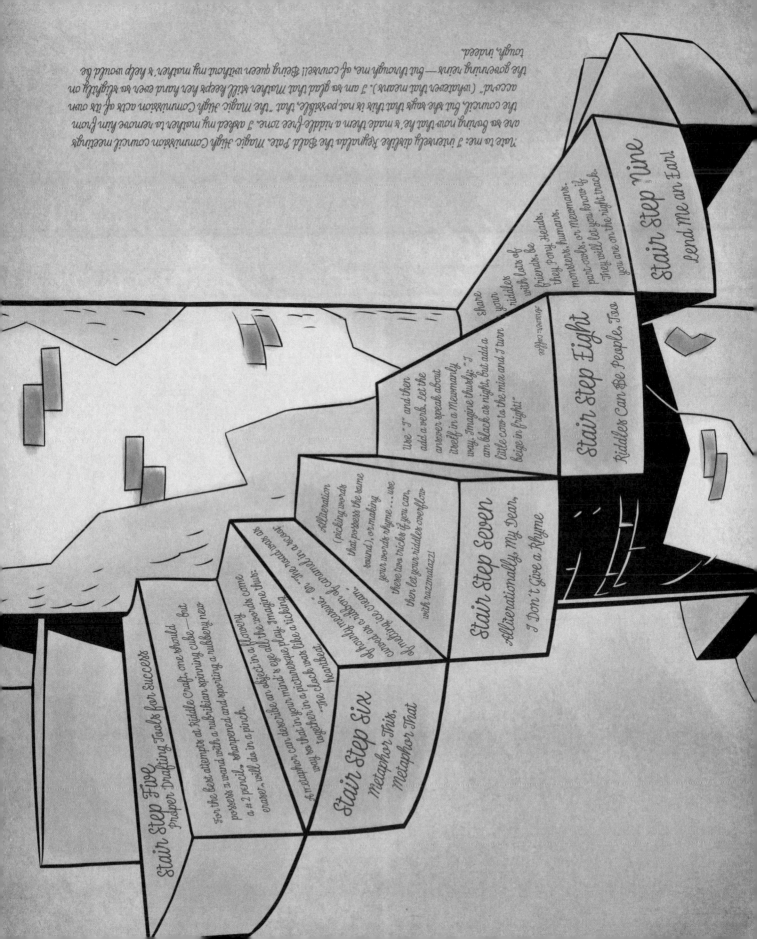

Note to me: I intensely dislike Reynaldo the Bald Pate. Magic High Commission council meetings are so boring now that he's made them a riddle-free zone. I asked my mother to remove him from the council, but she says that this is not possible, that "the Magic High Commission acts of its own accord" (whatever that means). I am so glad that Mother still keeps her hand ever so slightly on the governing reins—but through me, of course!! Being queen without my mother's help would be tough, indeed.

Historical Record/Journal Entry #1:

There is a little man of blue in my Magic Book of Spells who is called Glossaryck. He is very opinionated and he leaves crumbs wherever he goes. I was given the book when I became queen—something I hoped would not happen for a very long time. Maybe forever? I was fine to let my mother be queen forever, but she wanted to spend more time cataloguing her massive library of spell books. Anywho . . . Glossaryck is messy and he is bossy—but he appreciates a well-crafted riddle and for that I am extremely grateful! To be saddled with a mentor/bossy book nanny/spell driller/new friend that didn't like riddles would be a Catastrophe of Epic Proportions!

Rhina, a riddler after my own heart.

Historical Record/Journal Entry #2:

My best friend is called Lady Gyoza. She came to stay with my family when I was five and we have been inseparable ever since. We love to go on long walks through Mewni and pick flowers—daisies—that we braid together and put in our hair.

Historical Record/Journal Entry #3:

I have a pet turtle named Turtle Hopkins. Lady Gyoza brought him from the Dimension of Cats with Human Faces, where he was a prized possession of a cat prince. Lady Gyoza won him in a whist game and gave him to me as a "Hello" present when she came to Butterfly Castle. He was already a fan of top hats before he came to live with me. My great-great—oh, fiddlesticks, I can't remember how many greats right now—grandmother Skywynne knew Lady Gyoza's grandfather and it is through their acquaintanceship that Lady Gyoza came to join my family. Sort of a family friendship/exchange program.

Historical Record/Journal Entry #4:

My first order of business as queen was to declare National Riddle Day on my birthday. From henceforth there will be a big fête on this day and every one of my loyal subjects will be tasked with gifting me a new riddle of their own devising. It will be a day of much celebration.

Historical Record/Journal Entry #5:

Being a queen is as difficult as I believed it would be. Thank the Stump for my mother.

Historical Record/Journal Entry #6:

I have taken a meeting with the Magic High Commission about the state of monster and Mewni relations. It was very boring. *yawn*

Note to me: National Riddle Day is not the success that I would have anticipated it to be. Lady Gyoza says the ones who hate will always hate. *sigh*

Make Magic Happen, Yay!

Glossaryck says to tell you that I use riddle magic to make my spells, which is why I put all the previous stuff (about crafting riddles) in this book. It's just basic stuff. The hard part is making the spells actually work. For a long time, I could only riddle, but after lots of practice with Glossaryck—I only burned off the bottom of his beard a couple of times . . . okay, like five times . . . but that's not that bad—I learned that a lot of the trick to riddle magic is how you do the spinning of your rubrikian spinning cubes. They are really tetchy . . . I mean, super-duper finicky. Like my best friend, Lady Gyoza, if you wake her up before 7 a.m. She's a night owl. Like, seriously, she is fully part owl—at least a quarter.

Note to me: Buy lifetime's supply of Liquid Crystal Clean-Clean Roux . . . my wand eats that stuff like no one's business. It does make it smell like gladiolas and look real shiny, though. It does not charge my wand, obviously—I have a wand charger for that—but it makes the cubes spin way better.

- It smells like yellow bun-blossom gladiolas from Septarsis.

- Glossaryck might be allergic to yellow bun-blossom gladiolas from Septarsis—he sneezes a lot when I clean my wand.

Note to me: I hope Glossaryck is happy with this new title because he has officially made me rename this section seven times. Seriously, it has to be punishment for my porridge army spell.

Wrist/Hand/Arm Exercises to Bolster Your Magic Happening Faster And Better*

*Disclaimer: Consult a doctor (or witch doctor) before attempting any of these exercises. Getting hurt isn't fun.

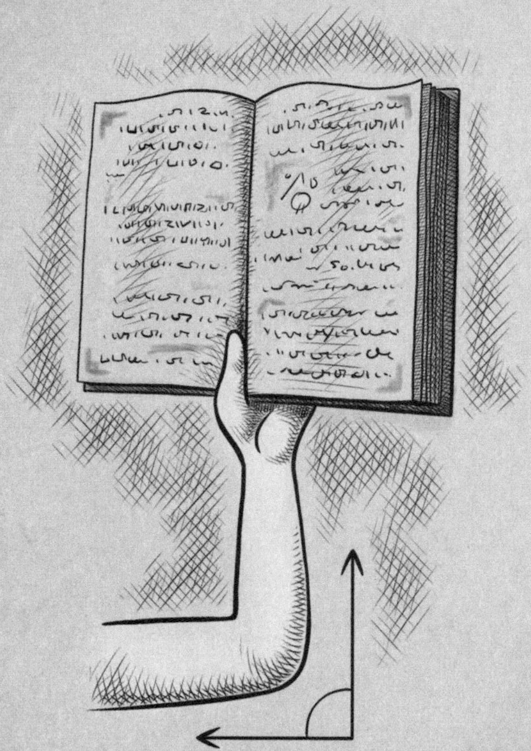

Lift Spell Book Growl

(Perfect for strengthening forearms)

1. Hold up spell book so that your arm makes a 90-degree angle
2. Extend arm so that it straightens out, but remains at shoulder level
3. Growl really loud
4. Lift book back up so that it forms a 90-degree angle again
5. Repeat steps 2, 3 & 4

Caution alert: Don't forget to tell anyone living inside your spell book that you are doing this exercise, because it can cause motion sickness and/or if you open to the wrong page, someone could fall out.

Squeeze Crystal Ball Shout

1. Hold crystal ball in your hand
2. Squeeze crystal ball for ten seconds, then relax
3. Shout "I am a crystal ball!" (really loudly)
4. Repeat steps 2 & 3

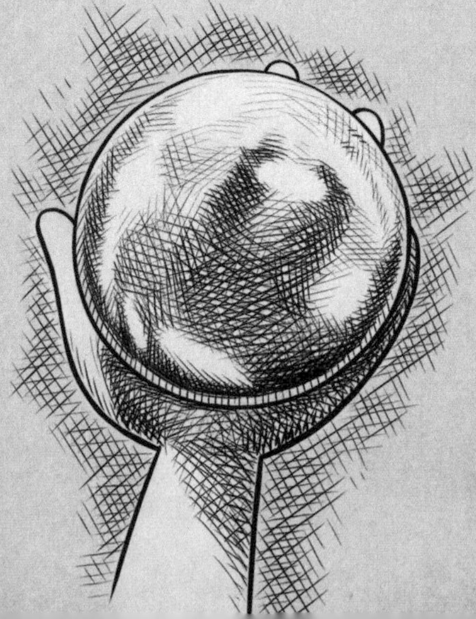

Note to me: There are exercises to build up your wits . . . I should include them in this book!

Historical Record/Journal Entry #7:

I refuse to make any more "entries" —from henceforth, I will call these "Thoughts from a Queen." This time I will tell you about my last evening's adventure: Lady Gyoza and I attended a demon ball. We wore masks that looked like black cat faces replete with whiskers. Lady Gyoza danced every dance.

No one knew who I was behind my mask. It was very pleasurable to be so obscured from view. I would like to wear a mask every day. We came home in time to watch the sunrise from the castle ramparts.

A perfect night.

Thoughts from a Queen #1: A perfect morning as envisioned by me.

~~puny frizzy~~ ? ?? ~~punk flizzy~~ very quizzy!!

1. Wake up at 6:45 a.m. on the dot and sit up in bed and stretch.

2. Wash face with flower-scented water from a white marble bowl.

3. Go downstairs for breakfast:
    a. Tea
    b. Juice of one horned melon
    c. Three ladyfingers made with love and care by a retired Millhorse turned artisanal baker

4. Get dressed and spend the day at work on my book of magical riddles, some of which I have travelled through dangerous dimensions to collect.

5. Have dinner with my mother. . . . She is encouraging me to settle down and find a king. I, personally, have no inclination toward anyone at all. I can hardly participate when Lady Gyoza whispers about her love adventures—I just find the whole subject BO-RING.

Note to me: Have cat mask dry-cleaned for later reuse.

Rubrikian Cube Revolution Moves (*RCRM*)
a.k.a. "Finger Tricks"

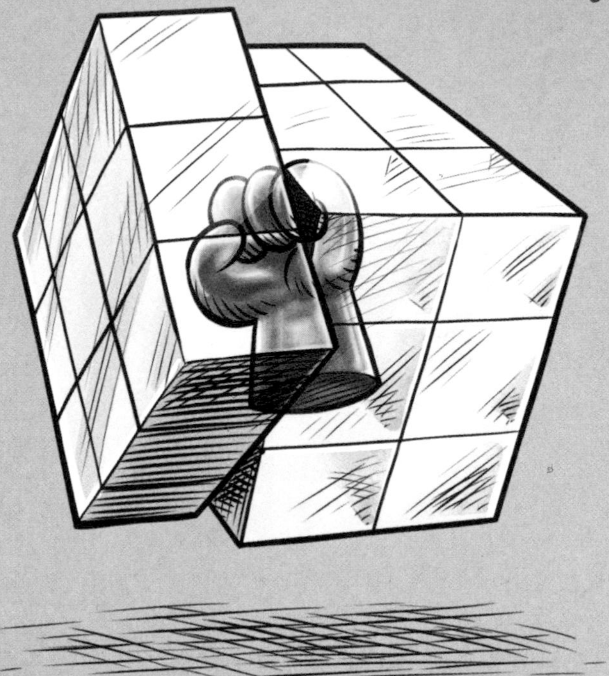

Left-Hand Turn

I spent a lot of time on this one. I know it looks super easy because it's basic. But if you don't master this trick then you will never make riddle magic happen in your life.

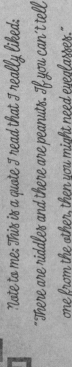

Note to me: This is a quote I read that I really liked: "There are riddles and there are peanuts. If you can't tell one from the other, then you might need eyeglasses."

Retro-Redo Spin

This is the prettiest cube pose. (I think.) Medium difficulty.

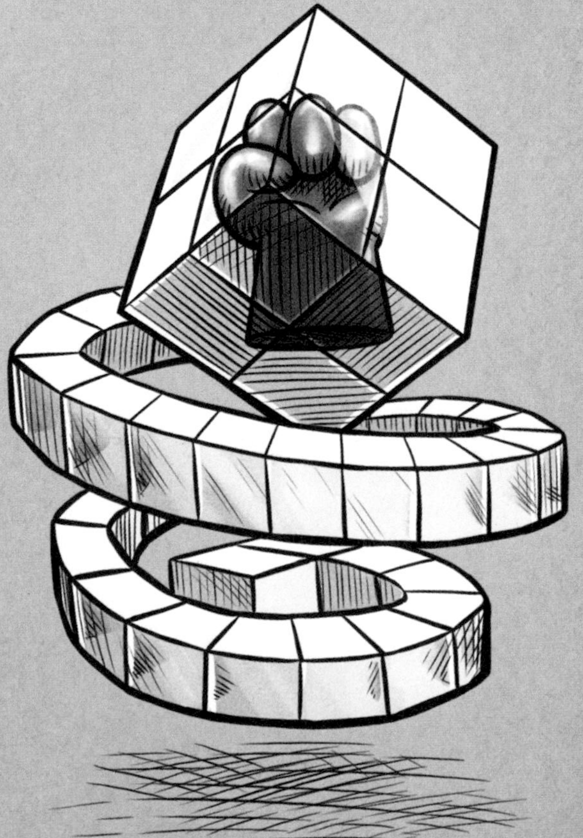

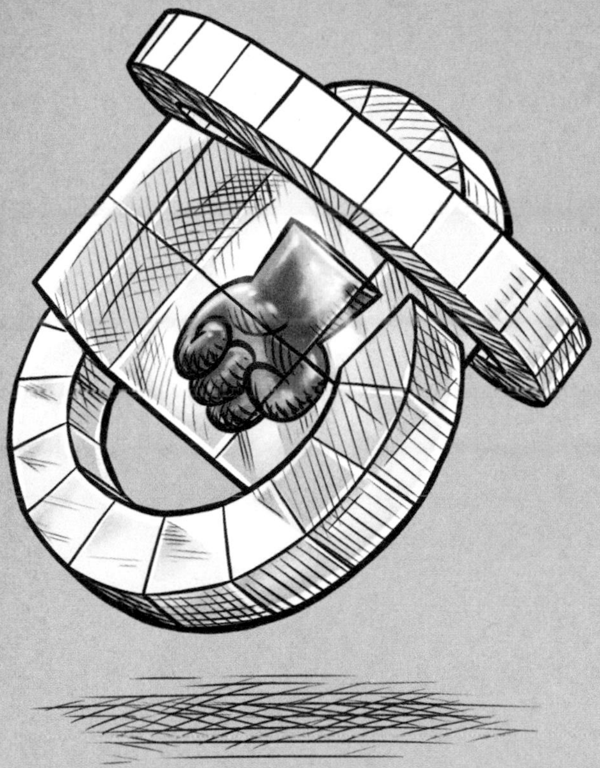

Sweep-d' Loops

You need nimble baby fingers to do this one . . . but if you don't have baby fingers then you can just use the tips of your nails. Unless you bite your nails (like I do) and then you might have to use your toenails (like I do). . . . So the lesson here is that you can't pick your nose with bitten toes.

Chihuahua Stamp Spin

It looks like a cute little Earth chihuahua! If you do it right, it will bark after each spin.

Note to me: Six ha bag dhorts. Coo? Coo!

Spell to Make Someone Who Did Not Like Riddles Before Having a Spell Put on Them Like Riddles

(Special Spell for Reynaldo the Bald Pate)

RCRM

4 clockwise left-hand turns—2 clockwise swoop-d'loops—1 clockwise retro-redo spin

Then you answer this riddle:

I am closest to a buzz.
I am lonely without fuzz.
Even a doll
has a more luxuriant fall.
What am I?

4
2
1

A: Reynaldo's bald head

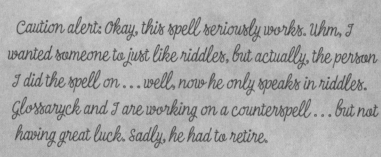

Caution alert: Okay, this spell seriously works. Uhm, I wanted someone to just like riddles, but actually, the person I did the spell on . . . well, now he only speaks in riddles. Glossaryck and I are working on a counterspell . . . but not having great luck. Sadly, he had to retire.

Note to me: Buy flowers for Lady Gyoza's going-away party. *sob*

Note to me: What in the world is this red ribbon for? It's been on my wrist forever and I still can't remember why.

Spell to Disarm Any Monster by Dazzling Them with Your Inner Beauty (Unless You Aren't Feeling Your Inner Beauty That Day, and in That Case the Spell Is Called: Spell to Disarm Any Monster by Dazzling Them with Your Inner Bad Attitude)

RCRM

1 clockwise left-hand turn—for inner beauty

1 widdershins left-hand turn—for inner bad attitude

1
1

Then you answer this riddle:

I am often round,
but you can't bounce me.
I like to shine,
but not in the dark.
Sometimes I show you what you want to see
and sometimes I don't—
but I am always honest
to a fault.
What am I?

A: a mirror

Caution alert: If you don't want to make those flower monsters (the ones that live in the Forest of Certain Death and have the green glowing eyes . . . you know the ones I mean) cry, then maybe using this spell isn't a good idea. It made them cry . . . a lot . . . a lot lot . . . and then I felt really bad. But they were disarmed . . . so that part was good. . . . I think maybe my inner beauty was just too beautiful for them.

Note to me: Need to do more wrist exercises. . . . The faster you are with the rub-ikian cubes, the less chance you have of accidentally dying.

Spell to Make Yourself Fall in Love with Someone When You Don't Want to Fall in Love with Anyone, Period

RCRM

5 clockwise Chihuahua stamp spins

5 widdershins retro-redo spins

5
5

Then you answer this riddle:

I pump my hardest to keep you alive,

but if you fall in or out of love, I might not survive.

Caution alert: Be mindful that when you do this spell (because you are forced to because you are queen and queens have to toe the line) your heart will grow two sizes—and this hurts. But you will be interested in falling in love and that's kinda nice. I guess. (Not.)

A: A heart

Rhina the Riddled
Aureole Sign: Tadpole
Height: 5' 5"
Attributes
Strength: 14
Intelligence: 11
Wisdom: 10
Wrist Power: 20
Constitution: 17
Charisma: 3

Note to me: Blind date tonight. He's a demon, a second cousin to the Lucitors. He's called Lord John Roachley. I was told that he is very tall, plays seven different monster-gut-stringed instruments, speaks twenty dead languages, and enjoys making up limericks in his spare time. Sounds like a match made in Mewni. Sigh. Time to do the spell . . . see me on the other side.

I'm not even touching this.
I hate riddles.

Spell to Break a Demon's Heart

RCRM

1 widdershins swoop-d'loop — 1 clockwise swoop-d'loop

1 widdershins swoop-d'loop — 1 clockwise swoop-d'loop

1 widdershins swoop-d'loop — 1 clockwise swoop-d'loop

1
1
x3

Then you answer this riddle:

I make up dumb limericks.

I speak twenty dead languages.

I pluck the monster-gut-strings of seven instruments.

I'm tall.

I'm a demon.

What am I?

A: A cruel husband

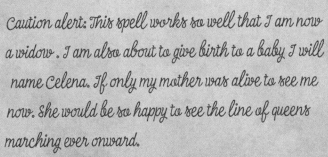

Caution alert: This spell works so well that I am now a widow. I am also about to give birth to a baby I will name Celena. If only my mother was alive to see me now. She would be so happy to see the line of queens marching ever onward.

Note to me: Lady Gyoza has returned from the Dimension of Cats with Human Faces to console me!!! Turtle Hopkins and I are beside ourselves with excitement to have the old gang back together.

Note to me: Procure poultice for wrist aches.

Lady Gyoza and I have always been great fans of the Great Book of Fashion. As young girls, we would peruse the pages and giggle over all the amazing finery held within the book's pages. Together, we drooled over the foppery of the Renfairyite ensembles we saw inside the book and—upon my rise to queen—we made this fashion our own.

The High-Necked Flouncer

The Breestal Areaview

The Double Caper

Thoughts from a Queen #2:

I have learned over the years that to do what you want is Mewman—to do what you MUST is divine and queenly. Today I was part of a contingency—along with King Pony Head and his eldest daughter—to speak with a faction of demons who are still, all these years later, upset with me because of the "incident" surrounding my husband's untimely demise. I believe that a meeting between us would be a lovely idea and that it will succeed to make us all happy and companionable again! Lady Gyoza is not convinced.

Thoughts from a Queen #3:

Turtle Hopkins went to the great beyond in his sleep last night. *sob*

Thoughts from a Queen #4:

Today we return to meet with the demons. The pain in my wrists has been making spell-casting more difficult these days, but there is so little cause for me to do riddle magic as of late, I hardly worry. Now I think I am going to have to use my riddle magic to impress upon the demons that there is no bone of contention between us. Wish us luck! Lady Gyoza still does not believe the demons can be swayed. She does not trust them, but I will show her the error of her ways. I tried to invite my daughter, Celena, to come with us—she will be queen soon and must learn the queenly ways—but she hid in her room behind the hanging drapes of her canopy bed. She thought I could not see her . . . but the outline of her face was quite prominent behind the drape.I am turning over ownership of this book as soon as I return. . . . This, I hope, will force her to finally come into her own.

An Easy Riddle

I am not the beginning
because that is too soon.
I am not in the middle
like a dipped-down spoon.
I am . . . ?

A: The end

Note to me: After all these years, I have finally remembered what the red ribbon on my wrist is for.

CELENA
THE SHY

What lies behind the golden fan
the hand does sweetly hold?
A trove of cosmic secrets
that never will be told.

UNINU

A Cicada Comes Privileged

Upon Young Coda Row

Doltish Countermen

Painful Shyness Shall Be the Curse

on Those Who Try to Sneak a Peek

at Celena's Magic Wand

Millhorse Ghost

He is special because he is shy like me . . . and a real ghost. That's not just his name, it's his state of being.

I started reading this chapter, but there weren't as many secrets as I thought there'd be. :(

Celena the Shy

Aureole Sign: Pony Head
Height: 5'

Attributes

Strength: 2
Potion Crafting: 20
Wisdom: 14
Dexterity: 3
Constitution: 4
Shyness: 20

The Apple of a Love's Eye

If you seek the eye of a love-to-be
This spell will set that new love free.

Pick an apple in the dead of night
Make sure the moon is shining bright
Say these words as you peel its skin
In one long loop, unbroken:

"My love, my love, I see your heart
When you see mine, our love shall start
My love, my love, I know your heart
When you know mine, we shall never part"

Put the peel under your bed
And sleep the sleep of the newly dead
You will soon catch your love's eye
Of this I promise, I make no lie

Living with Shyness

As a shy person, I spend most of my time with my eyes on the ground. That way I don't have to look at anyone. I apologize to inanimate things (like footstools and stone fences) if I accidentally bump into them (they have feelings, too) and I never, ever speak in public. My mother dislikes that I apologize to inanimate things . . . unless I do it in a riddle. Sigh.

Adorable.

To Call a Spirit to Your Side

Call up a spirit to super-power your magic
when a spell requires something tragic.

Lemon and Calendula Oil for Spirit Attraction

When working a spell that calls for a sad or tragic ingredient, the thoughtful witch can call up a spirit to take the ingredient's place.

The spirit has already passed over—a sad and tragic event in itself—and is, therefore, the perfect substitute.

SPIRIT
ATTRACTION
POTION

What is needed:

One mason jar with lid

Dried calendula flowers

Dried lemon peel from two lemons

Almond oil

One potions bottle

Fill the mason jar half full of dried lemon peel and calendula flowers. Cover herbs with almond oil by an inch or more. Stir to release bubbles. Cover with lid and set in a sunny spot. Shake your jar daily. In 2 to 3 weeks, your oil will be ready. Strain and then put in potions bottle. For use in spells or as a magical perfume only—never for drinking or eating . . . it will turn the magic-wielder into a spirit herself!

THE CORN

Aureole Sign Guide

I'm a Pig-Goat

Dec 22 - Jan 20

Pig-Goat

Torax 1–Norvath 66

Hyper, Fun-Loving, Brave, Stubborn, Impulsive, Hates Rules

Mar 20 - Apr 19

Warnicorn

Gravnogk 45–Spleenax 1

Creative, Eccentric, Deep Thinker, Distant, Complicated Love Life

Silkworm

Jan 21 - Feb 18

Norvath 67–Sagnog 2

Intelligent, Independent, Innovative, Impulsive, Powerful, Secretive

Apr 20 - May 21

Demon

Spleenax 2–Zameranor 8

Enjoyment-Seeking, Loyal, Dynamic, Mischievous, Too Much Pride

Rafael is a Tadpole

Feb 19 - Mar 19

Tadpole

Sagnog 3–Gravnogk 44

Eccentric, Free Spirit, Joker, Likes Games, Clever

May 22 - June 21

Hydra

Zameranor 9–Qork 19

Many Talents, Hardworking, Achiever, Two-Faced, Self-Reliant, Likes to Please

CASTLE

Blowhole June 22 - July 22

Qork 20–Thurq 81

Artistic, Down to Earth, Faithful, Quiet, Sensitive, Good Taste

Lion Dragon July 23 - Aug 22

Thurq 82–Grevanz 30

Strong, Self-Righteous, Adventurous, Hates to Be Restricted, Dominating

Pony Head Aug 23 - Sep 23

Grevanz 31–Dartuk 25

Alluring, Mysterious, Admired, Forgives but Doesn't Forget, Lavish

Pixie Sep 24 - Oct 22

Dartuk 26–Squartuk 62

Life of the Party, Sets Trends, Loving, Can't Function Alone, Popular, Vapid

Angie is a Narwhal

Narwhal Oct 23 - Nov 22

Squartuk 63–Ooag 2

Open-Minded, Bighearted, Practical, Many Talents, Can Lead Others

Deadhorse Nov 23 - Dec 20

Ooag 3–Skweg 7

Straightforward, Faithful, Leader, Rule Follower, Wise, Cold

Marco is a Deadhorse

Bog Slug Dec 21

Mondarn 1

Charming, Relatable, Kind, Timid, Indecisive, Unlucky

Spell to Mend a Broken Friendship

When a friendship is cleaved apart
this spell rekindles the friendship's heart.

A candle's light must flame bright
Illuminating a photo of the severed friends
Then write down these words with a long-feathered quill
Onto a slip of paper . . . make the sentiment feel real:

"Our friendship was strong
But something went wrong
And now it has fractured in two
These words that I write
Signal my fight
To give this old friendship its due"

Place the paper and photo in a wooden box
Bury it deep under the roots of an oak
Wait three weeks for the spell to congeal
Then your friendship will return to its friendly ideal

Shyness Is a Gift

Because you only have to talk to who you want to talk to . . . oh, and you can always talk to Glossy. I like him because he's small. And silly.

So precious.

Spices of Protection

Cinnamon and anise to protect your soul

In a velvet sachet to keep them whole.

Cinnamon and Anise Charm for Protection

When someone has put the evil eye on you, this charm will work hard to keep you safe. A velvet sachet filled with cinnamon, anise, and a cat's-eye crystal—all the good things for an extra dose of protection. Keep it under your pillow or in your bag or pocket . . . or even slip it on some string and wear it as an amulet around your neck.

What is needed:

Charm Bag

One tiny velvet drawstring bag in black, purple, or blue

Dried cinnamon sticks broken into halves or thirds

Cinnamon Sticks

Star Anise Seed Pod

Dried star anise seed pods

One small cat's-eye crystal

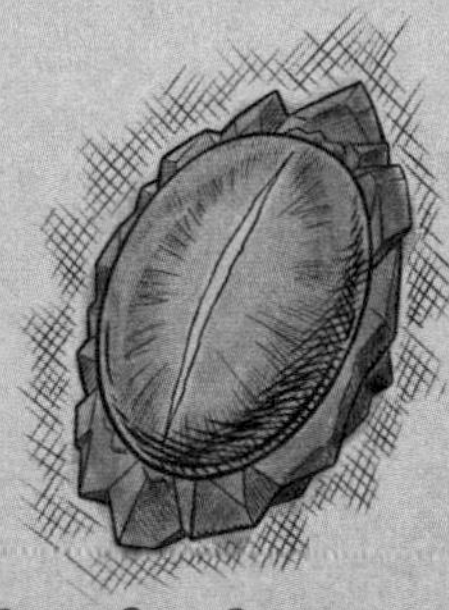

Cat's-Eye Crystal

Put all ingredients in the velvet bag.
Cinch tightly. Wear daily for protection.

Ode to a Pumpkin I Grew

A lit - tle or - ange globe Full of ripe seeds How ma - ny tas - ty things
Can we make of thee? Yum - my pie Or heart - y gourd - ish stew A lit - tle cur - ry dish Or a
sweet - ling bread? All these rec - i - pes Sweet and sa - var - ies I can see in my head
Lit - tle or - ange ball On a green vine How ma - ny tas - ty things We can make of thee!

The Tarot

Celena had many ways to read the cards, but my favorite is the Mewberry Tarot Spread.

Death

An ending, but also a beginning. Going forward with nothing to fear. Letting go of the old.

The Queen

Personal power, confidence, and skill. Leadership, decision-making.

The Princess

A loving friend, a female influence. An ally who has advice.

The Hungry One

Knowledge that you are provided for. Enough to go around. Love, support, and safety.

The Shooting Star

A connection with nature. Reflection and quiet contemplation. Freedom to be your truest self.

The King

Kindness, compassion, and forgiveness. Healing, and giving credit where credit is due.

THE MEWNI TAROT

DEATH

THE QUEEN

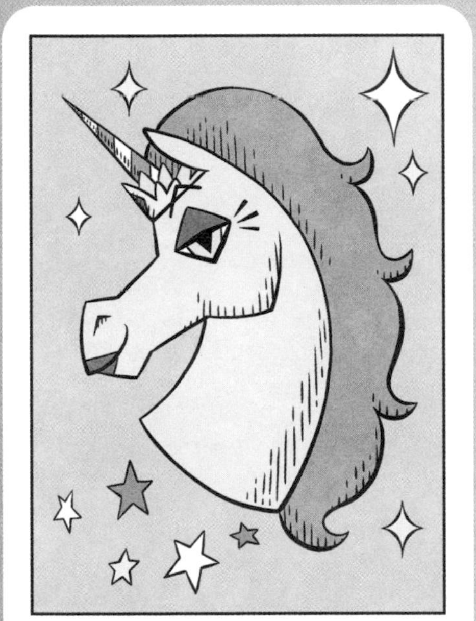
THE PRINCESS

THE HUNGRY ONE

THE SHOOTING STAR

THE KING

THE MASTER OF THE BOOK

TRUE LOVE

THE SEPTARIAN

THE FULL MOON

BATTLE STRENGTH

THE RISING SUN

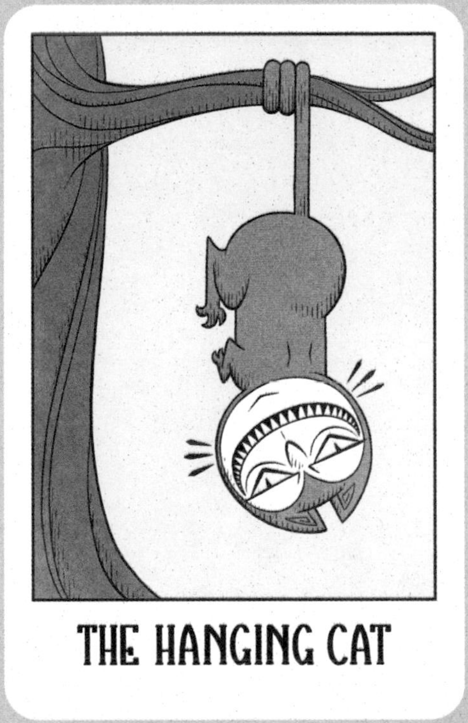
THE HANGING CAT

Get some scissors and cut all the tarot cards out. Try and do a neater job than I would. Unless you like jagged edges. You might! To each her own.

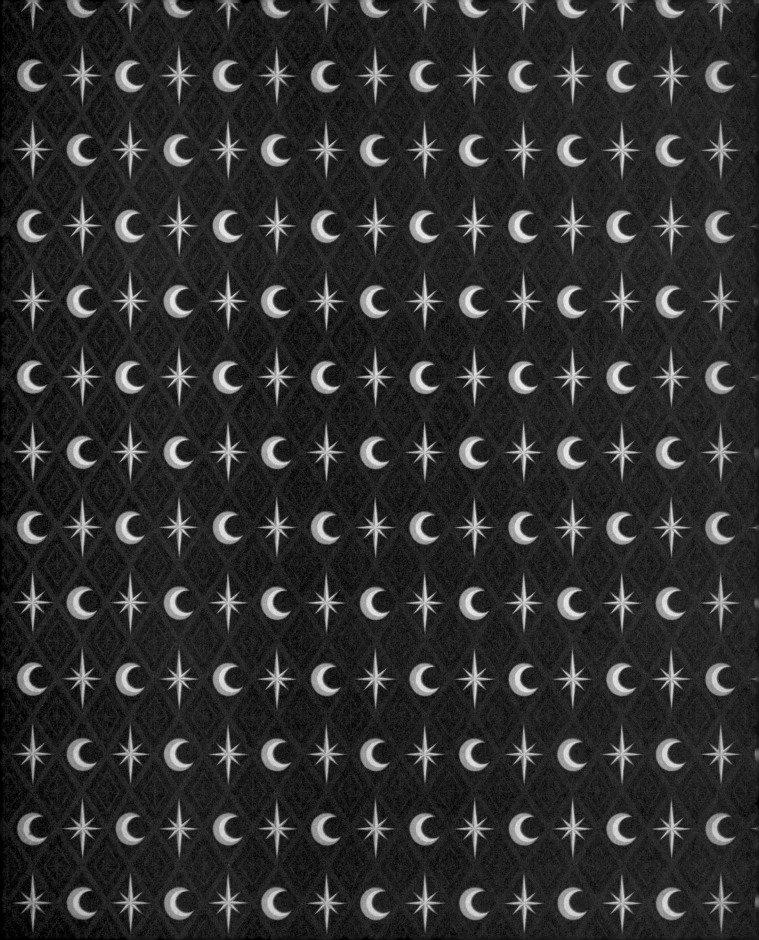

The Master of the Book

Challenges, sacrifices, consequences. Facing reality.

True Love

A crossroads. A reminder to remember who you are. Togetherness, a union.

The Septarian

Expression of emotions, even anger. Passion, the unknown, all that is taboo.

The Full Moon

Actions make for potential. Conflicts can be beautiful. Consider your perceptions.

Battle Strength

Victory, strength of purpose, and achievement. Recognition and acclaim versus shame and defeat.

The Rising Sun

Personal gain and success. Taking advantage of opportunities.

The Hanging Cat

Decisions that carry weight. Letting go of the past. Things that are out of your control.

ESTRELLA
THE DRAFTED

She cannot write, she cannot sing,
But she can draw, her only thing.
Sketching late until the night . . .
But will she ever draw it right?

Estrella hated writing, so I'll explain her wand for her. It was a pen. It probably had some magic abilities, but who knows? She never used them. She mostly used her wand for her drawings, which were okay, but art is subjective, so you be the judge. Below is the drawing that inspired her to devote her life to art: It's a pig-goat.

Estrella Age 9

Millhorse—still Ghost

I like books with pictures. Or books that are all pictures. :)

Estrella the Drafted

Aureole Sign: Blowhole
Height: 5' 5"

Attributes

Strength: 4
Intelligence: 16
Wisdom: 16
Dexterity: 10
Constitution: 8
Charisma: 12

Estrella was a quiet one. She didn't talk a lot, and she didn't do much as queen, either . . . which made her a popular queen, because nothing changed. Mewmans hate change; they are extremely boring. She spent most of her time sketching by herself around Mewni, where she discovered many interesting plants. These plants were later used by her daughter to make delicious food!

Recipes are thataway. Make me a little something when you get there, will ya?

While sketching out in the forest today, I came upon the most delightful smell. I've named it the Unflowered Sprig of the Creeping Scentgrass. I've gathered a bunch to take home to the castle.
Unflowered Sprig of the Creeping Scentgrass
Found some lovely Red Solanaceae today. My mother's favorite. It was growing red and plump on some vines as I was sketching near the bog. I took a bite and it was both juicy and delicious. Bringing some home.

Castle Avarius. The home of the former monster king and queen who sadly sank their fortunes in the corrupt scratch-and-sniff trade.
Red Solanaceae

Hill of Flags, where the traditional Game of Flags is played with our closest allies, the Johansens. Whoever wins gets to look down on the other family for a whole year.
Found some green sprigs sticking out of the ground today while I was sketching. I pulled at one and found a very smelly plant. I've named it Crying Dirt Pearl.

While sitting out by the Mewni River, I found some interesting white rocks. I chipped at the rocks a little and the prettiest sand fell out. I sprinkled a little on my potato salad and it tasted amazing. I have named it Frown Sand and am bringing some back to the castle.

Frown Sand

I don't like this Seth—he's a Septarian. You know what that means: indestructible!
He's got a group of rebels wrapped around his slimy finger. Luckily, it's a small group.
Hisss

The monsters like Archduke Batwin. They won't go for this extremist. I say we wait it out.
Baaaaaa!!!!...
Estrella often sketched during the Magic High Commission meetings. Omnitraxis Prime thought it was rude, but it was the only way Estrella could stay awake.

Estrella also liked to sketch her family. Below are some drawings of her mother, Celena; her husband, Azul Saint (a songstrel); and her baby, Comet.

Celena looks happy there because she has a belly full of corn casserole. I, on the other hand, am extremely hangry. Get to the next chapter and make me a pie!

All of my loves.

COMET
THE CHEF

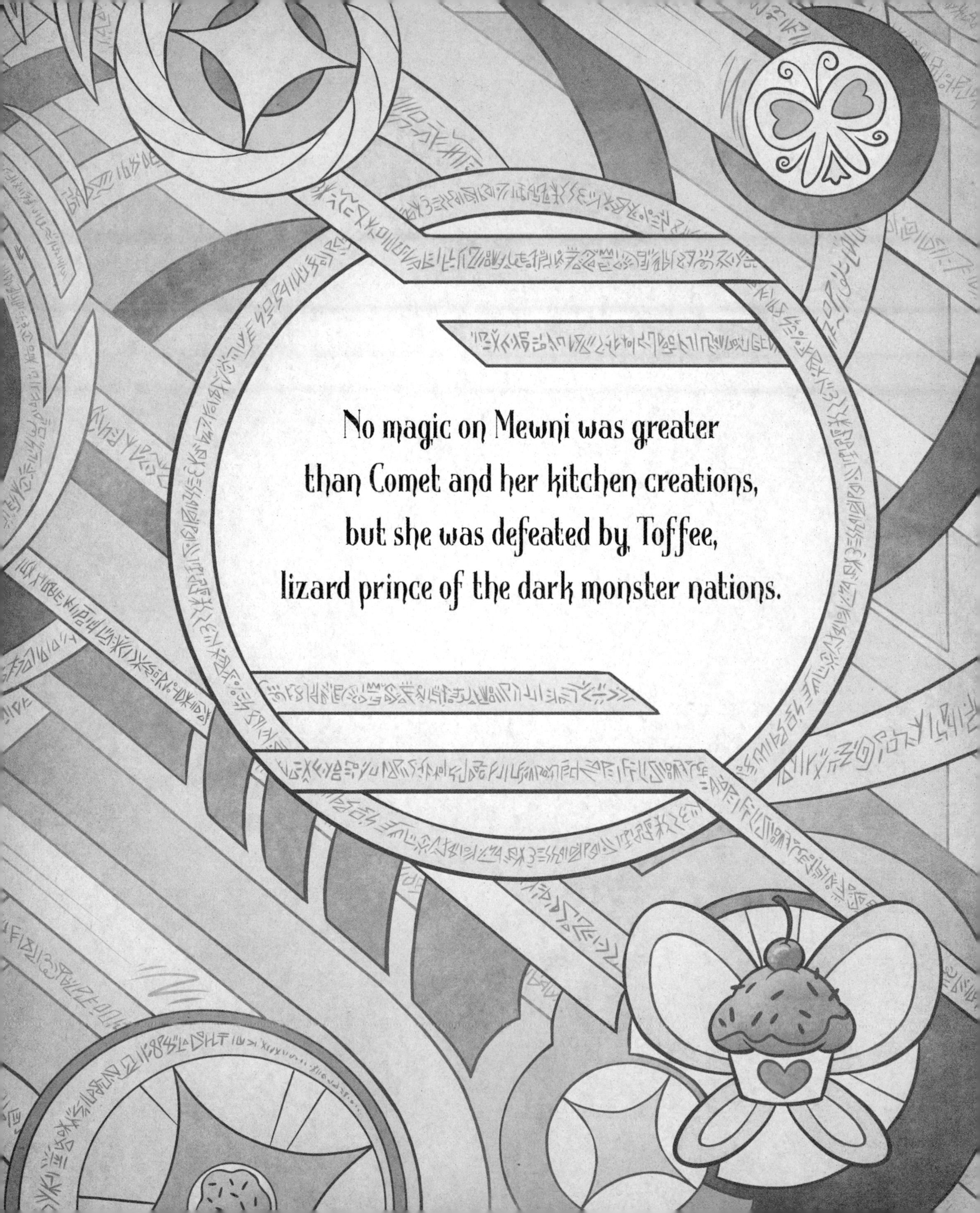

No magic on Mewni was greater
than Comet and her kitchen creations,
but she was defeated by Toffee,
lizard prince of the dark monster nations.

Crystal—My wand crystal is Baker's Quartz. It's called this because it's impervious to high temperatures.
Comet a.k.a. My Favorite
You're not supposed to have favorites!
Handle—My wand handle is a rolling dowel from petrified Neverzonian Oak.
Wand Charger—My wand is recharged with Pantry Crystals, pink or lavender.

Millhorse—Little Pumpkin. Ghost retired, so Pumpkin has big horseshoes to fill. I have high hopes.

Comet the Chef

Aureole Sign: Narwhal
Height: 5'

Attributes

Strength: 13
Intelligence: 18
Wisdom: 18
Dexterity: 12
Constitution: 17
Charisma: 17

My grandma grandma! I haven't met her, though, because she lives on a grandma farm with other grandmas. Mom says it's nice.

First Year, the Era of the Comet

I have put off receiving this book and my Wand Passing ceremony as long as possible. It's with reluctance and boredom that I make my first entry in this book.

It goes without saying that there are many raised eyebrows throughout the kingdom about my mother, me, my choices, etc.

I'm going to write this in a way that would be helpful to a princess/queen-to-be, and less as a matter of historical record. Hopefully, my daughter will get to read this one day and find some comfort in my experiences.

Speaking of my daughter, you've likely heard that I am the first princess ever to have married and had a daughter before my coronation. Maybe you are my daughter reading this now. If so, hello, sweet baby Princess Moon!

So if you want to know how this came to be, I'll put it simply: My mother is an artist.

Okay, that's not fair. Here's the truth: I chased food, love, and happiness across the dimensions, and I relished every minute of it. I got a little overfed, a little married, and a little pregnant, and I had a little baby, my sweet Princess Moon (hello again, sweetie!). Soon after, I got a little divorced. Oh well. Baloo-Balee Baloo-Balow, I let you go, I let you go.

Anyway, I am back on Mewni now to accept my fate; I am going to be queen of Mewni once Mother decides I'm ready. However, I am going to do it my way: I'm going to rule from the kitchen.

About Mewmans and Monsters

I'd rather not be burdened with the problems between Mewmans and monsters, but the only thing that really separates us from the beasts in the forest is that we savor food. It's either a curse or a blessing, depending on who you ask. If you're critical of the monsters but you don't sit down to enjoy a meal, then how are you any different from them?

First Year, 17 moons, the Era of the Comet

Imagine the situation room on the eve of a battle: Generals from all of Mewni along with the Magic High Commission stand around a chairless table, with maps and charts and little wooden figurines pointing tiny swords at one another. Each general has his or her own plan or idea for how the battle ought to go, where to expect losses and advancements, etc.

The queen watchfully presides over the sometimes passionate banter of the generals, and ultimately she decides what is to be done.

Today, Mother invited me to witness this in preparation for when I am queen. Twice I caught her nodding off, and once I fell asleep myself, standing straight up in the middle of the room. When I woke, I found that the hoop on my dress was holding me upright, and I was slouched over it like a rag doll.

Upon waking, having the lack of clarity one often does after accidentally falling asleep, I noticed the arguing was still going on. I went off to the kitchen and returned with 7 Red Solanaceae pies. Wordlessly, I slid plates of the sliced pie in front of all the generals and the Magic High Commission.

The room slowly quieted as the smell wafted to their noses, and they quickly devoured their slices. I had the attendant keep their plates filled, and before long, the entire group was passed out on the floor of the situation room. They slept for 4 days.

Needless to say, Mewni didn't show up for the battle and it was never fought. The monsters simply waited at the battlefront for half a day and then went back to their lives in the forest.

Officially, my mother acted disappointed in my actions, but behind the scenes she praised my artful thinking and vowed to never allow the generals and Magic High Commission to argue war plans on an empty stomach.

So, before I pass down melee tactics and magic strategies as implements for combat, I recommend first making sure everyone is fed.

Start with pie.

Why Pie?

My many-greats-ago-grandmother Skywynne thought that her raining food spell was enough to conquer hunger. While it certainly feeds people, it certainly does not feed their need for a satisfying meal shared with others.

As long as I can remember, I've had a gift for making pies. Mother says it's in our blood, but that doesn't seem too scientific. It makes more sense that I am just good at it. Here you'll find my Red Solanaceae pie recipe. Try this before any magic or swords.

Crust

You can put just about anything inside a pie as long as you have a good crust. Rats, rotted dates, nightshades, bad marriages—they all come out better once they've been cooked into a decent pie. And a decent pie has to have a stellar crust.

- 2 cups milled wart-corn sand You can use flour.
- 6 tablespoons cold, unsalted pig-goat fat cut into ½-inch bits butter
- 1 teaspoon Smile Sand sugar
- ½ teaspoon Frown Sand salt
- 2 tablespoons ice water

Whisk the dry ingredients together in a bowl. Toss the cubed fat into the dry ingredients to coat, then squish each coated cube with your fingers so they become disks. Add the cold water and quickly knead this mixture into a loose dough. From this point forward, you want to handle the dough as little as possible to assure maximum flakiness. Leave this dough in a covered bowl in a cool place; if you don't have any prisoners, you can leave it in the ice dungeon overnight.

It's okay to just use the refrigerator.

To blind-bake the crust:

Roll the crust until it's flat and roundish. I use a run-of-the-mill monster-bashing club and that works just fine. Lay the rolled crust in a greased glass pie dish. Cover the crust with parchment paper and fill with Smile Sand or beans; this acts as a weight to keep the crust from rising too much during blind-baking. Cook at low heat, 350 degrees, for 40 minutes to 1 hour.

rolling pin

Decorations

It's very important that the top of your pie is beautiful. If there's a famine, the inside of the pie may be filled with . . . interesting things. One year after the monsters ate all of our food, we filled pies with a custard of sawdust and sandal straps. Nevertheless, the tops of the pies were decorated as though the pies themselves were filled with fresh creamed zuberries.

I always decorate my pies with the symbol of our family: a small braided butterfly. It's a simple shape to tie from the dough once you've figured it out, but here's a little poem for remembering how to tie the crust decorations:

This is also how I learned to tie my shoes!

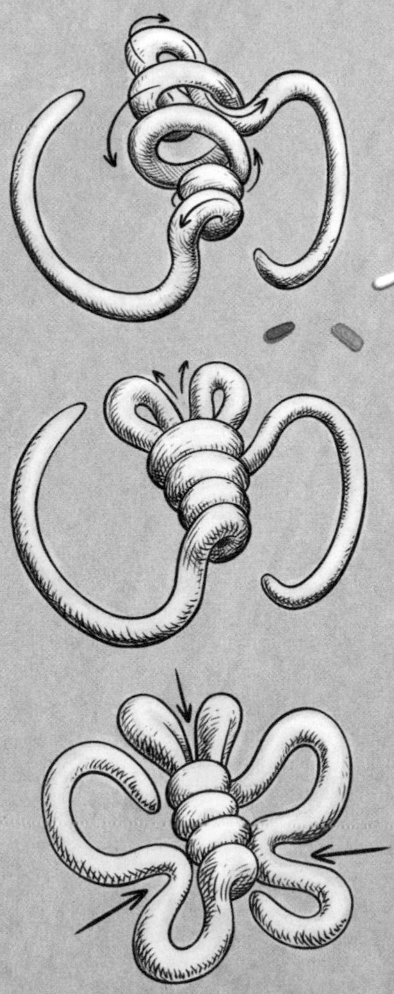

Over

Under

Around and through

Grab the little Mewni rabbit

Pull him through

Pinch it

And fold it

And tie it in a bow

Like two little bunny ears

Made out of dough

She always baked the crust scraps for me and left them on the counter for when I got back from my morning stroll.

First Year, 150 moons, the Era of the Comet

This is my first official entry as queen of Mewni. We had a quiet, unremarkable turnover from Mother to me—it was as she wanted it. She doesn't like a lot of attention, and is pleased to have some more time to go on a drawing retreat.

She probably won't come back!

Anyway, in my first act as queen, I am making perhaps the boldest move imaginable.

After many strained negotiations—and to the disdain of all of my generals and the Magic High Commission—I have arranged for a banquet hosting the monster king, Archduke Batwin. The banquet will be as grand as it would be if we were hosting diplomats from the Forest of Unlikely Spider Bites or the Underworld.

I commissioned the court portraitist to paint this picture of Archduke Batwin and me, and I've had it distributed throughout the Mewni Groundlands.

I've even commissioned the Songstrel Guild to write a song about the potential for a more peaceful union, and the winning songstrel will have his piece performed by Moon on the night of the banquet!

It goes without saying that this type of meeting is unprecedented. Throughout the entire history of the Butterfly family, no queen has attempted this type of negotiation. As an added point of aggravation to the entire kingdom, I will be serving Mewnipendence Day Pie, a treat we serve once a year to celebrate our reign over the monsters. For this banquet I am renaming it Peace Day Pie, and it will forever be named that so long as we are able to establish an accord with the monsters.

The Magic High Commission is particularly concerned with Seth. They are worried any accord with Batwin will put us in bed with the rebel Septarian factions and could potentially lead to our collapse.

I am not afraid of crusty old Seth. The Septarian rebellion is a war of old men, and my accord is the path to the future. Well, if Seth wants to come to the banquet, I may even send him an invite! Ha! I say let them eat pie!

Pie of the Red Solanaceae

I adapted this pie from a recipe I learned from my grandma Celena. It uses the fruit of the Red Solanaceae because there was a corn famine in her time and the Solanaceae was all that was available.

One pie crust, blind-baked (see earlier)

Filling

1 pound Fruit of the Red Solanaceae [On earth they call these tomatoes!]
1 Unflowered Sprig of the Creeping Scentgrass [Thyme works just fine.]
1 Crying Dirt Pearl, sworded [1 onion, diced]
2 tablespoons cold, unsalted pig-goat fat [butter]
1/4 cup milled wart-corn sand [flour]
2 cups plant soup [vegetable stock or any old broth]
Frown Sand and Sneeze Sand [salt and pepper]

Topping

1 block of curdled pig-goat fat, [Gruyere cheese]
coarsely frightened [shredded]
1/4 Bread Sand [bread crumbs]

Preparation

Dry-cook the Red Solanaceae in a pan. Mash them as they cook until they take on the texture of porridge. Once the Red Solanaceae is broken down, add the sworded Crying Dirt Pearl. After the Crying Dirt Pearl has become translucent, in a separate pan or a scorching knight's helmet, prepare the milled wart-corn sand, unsalted pig-goat fat, and plant soup as a roux. Add the cooked Red Solanaceae mixture and the Creeping Scentgrass, then add Frown Sand and Sneeze Sand to taste. Cook on a low frolic for 25 minutes.

Ladle 1/4-inch layer of this mixture into the blind-baked pie crust. Mix the curdled pig-goat fat with Bread Sand and cover the pie with it. Decorate the pie top with slices of Solanaceae and bits of the leftover dough. I always use a butterfly shape for the decoration (see directions on previous page). Bake at 400 degrees for 30 minutes or until pig-goat fat is golden and bubbling. Remove from the oven, sprinkle with some loose Creeping Scentgrass leaves, and let cool before slicing.

Okay, so perhaps you've tried these pies as a peace offering to your enemy, and though they're delicious, you didn't have any success.

It's time to leave the kitchen.

You're now headed for the battlefield. Here are some spells that may be useful:

NIGHTSHADE DISARM

This spell will disarm up to 12 marauding adversaries.

Say "Nightshade" as you tilt your wand down with the tip almost touching the ground.

Raise your arm with your wrist bent, and rapidly "whisk" the air in front of your adversaries as you say "Disarm."

Your adversaries will fall into a pile atop one another, at which point you can have a flock of Razor Cranes drag them from the battlefield.

SKYWYNNE

SUMMONING RAZOR CRANE CHARM

Lifting your arm up above your head, say "Summoning Razor—"

And finish with "Crane Charm!" as your wand face touches the ground.

Provided you've summoned a quality flock of Razor Cranes, they should know to pick up the disarmed horde and carry them off.

Once you've returned from the battlefield, treat your armies to a meal of Red Solanaceae pie and plenty of ale tea.

Mewnipendence Day Pie

One pie crust, blind-baked
(see earlier)

I tried making this for my Mewnipendence Day party. I thought droop sacks were garlic and also I accidentally added 14. Marco ate it anyway, to be nice.

Filling

2 Razor Crane ovules — eggs

¼ cup pig-goat fat — butter

1½ cups tarred Smile Sand — brown sugar

1 teaspoon scentstick — vanilla

1½ cups diced meat of tree stones — nuts

4 droop sacks, sliced into bite-sized pieces — figs!!!

Marco after he ate the pie

Whip pig-goat fat and tarred Smile Sand together in a mixing bowl. Whisk in the ovules, scentstick, droop sacks, and tree stone meats. Pour mixture into blind-baked crust. Bake at 350 degrees for 20-25 minutes or until droop sacks become golden and caramelized.

First Year, 160 moons, the Era of the Comet

I just got off the mirror phone with Archduke Batwin, and he and his . . . erm . . . wife (?) are quite excited to be the first monsters invited to the Grand Banquet Hall in Butterfly Castle this weekend.

I quite like Batwin. We chuckled about how my invitation to Seth went unanswered. Batwin is just so much more gentle than the strange and bankrupt Guido Avarius before him. In fact, I worry he may be too soft for his role. Even though Seth is a dried-up, crusty old gecko, Batwin is still going to have to have some grit to stand up to him. Despite my conviction that Seth's position is an old, decaying one, it has become attractive to some of the younger Septarians, which I suppose is some cause for concern.

Welp, this is the final entry. She never wrote down her recipe for pudding pie, my favorite. Sorry about the tears. . . The nice thing about tears is that they dry . . . eventually.

MOON
THE UNDAUNTED

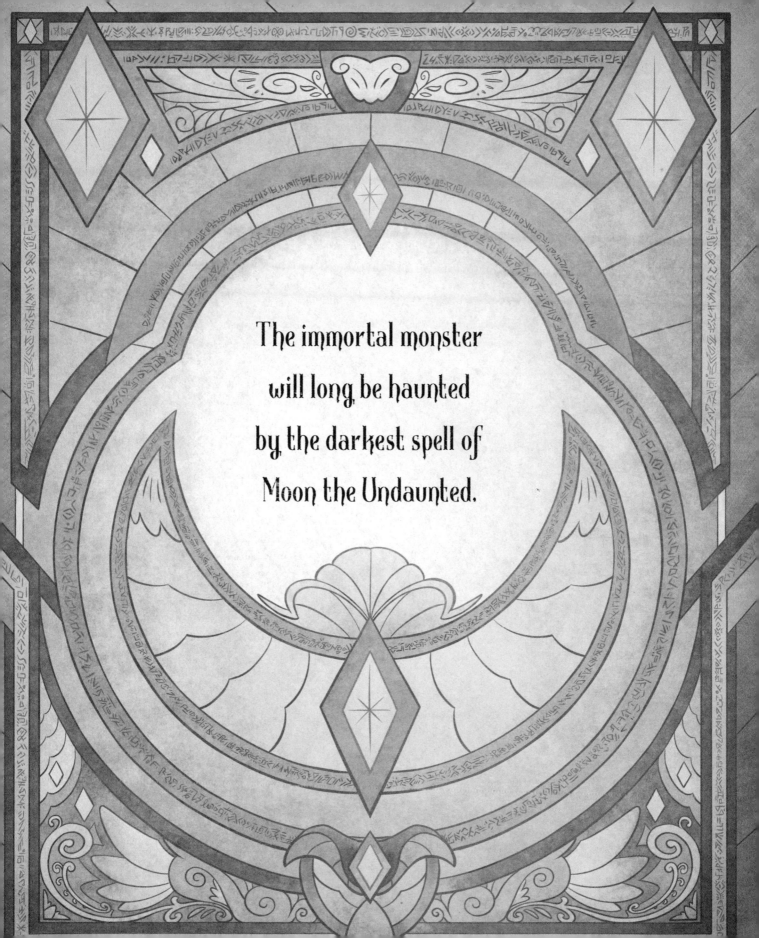

The immortal monster
will long be haunted
by the darkest spell of
Moon the Undaunted.

Columbrian Crystal Bulb

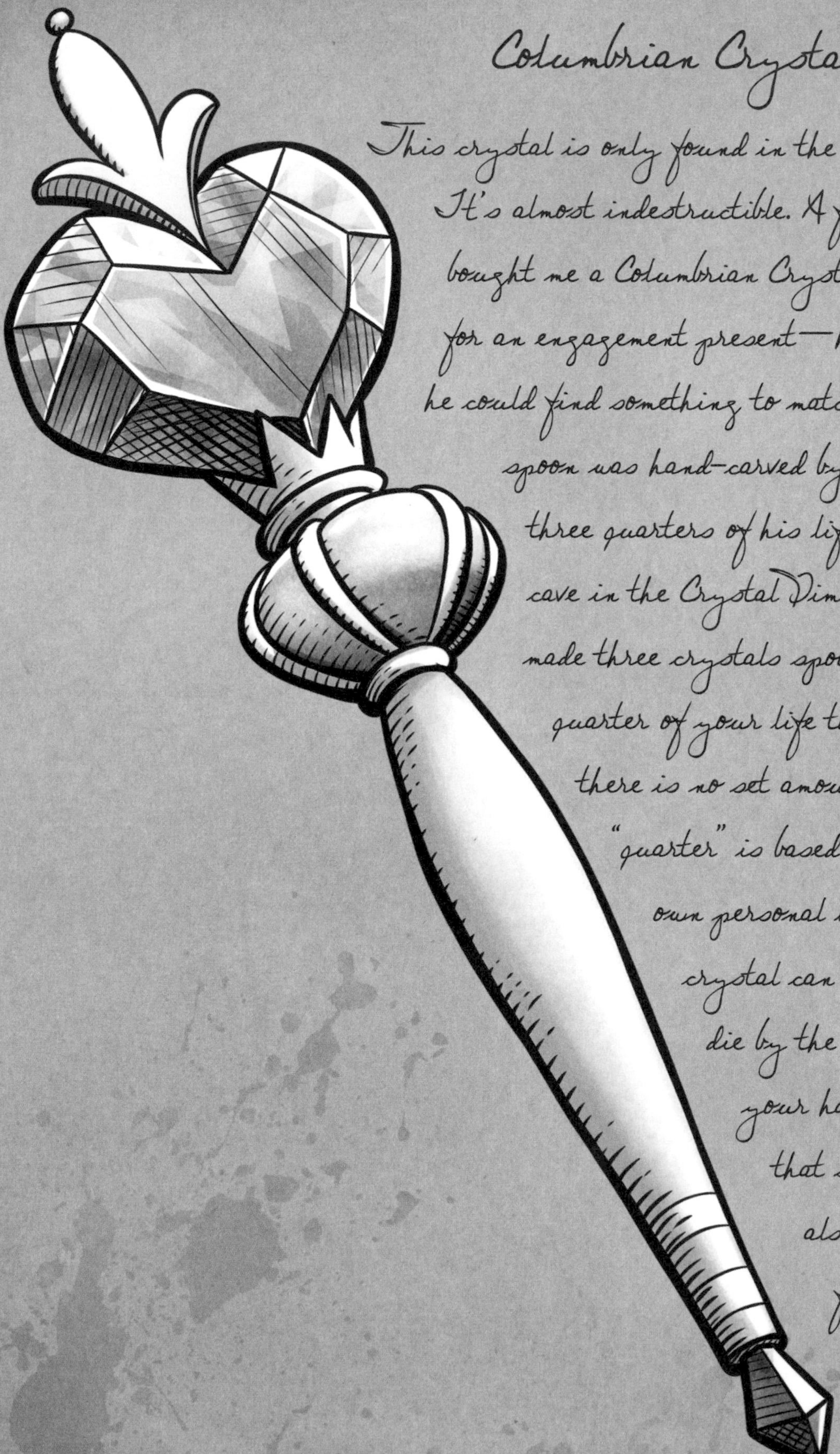

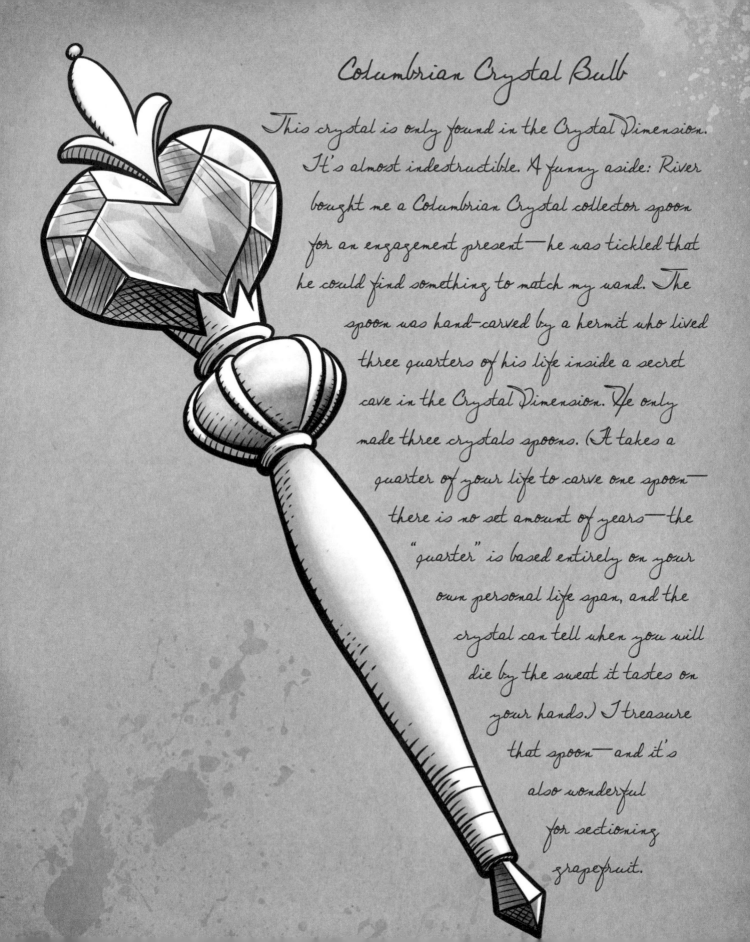

This crystal is only found in the Crystal Dimension. It's almost indestructible. A funny aside: River bought me a Columbrian Crystal collector spoon for an engagement present—he was tickled that he could find something to match my wand. The spoon was hand-carved by a hermit who lived three quarters of his life inside a secret cave in the Crystal Dimension. He only made three crystals spoons. (It takes a quarter of your life to carve one spoon—there is no set amount of years—the "quarter" is based entirely on your own personal life span, and the crystal can tell when you will die by the sweat it tastes on your hands.) I treasure that spoon—and it's also wonderful for sectioning grapefruit.

Pumpkin

This is Pumpkin, my Millhorse. He was sired by a brother of Stephandipity—Festivia the Fun's Millhorse. He has a special relationship with my pig-goat, Lil' Chauncey. Millhorses are truly magical creatures—and without them, we queens would be at a severe disadvantage.

Snakewood Handle

A little-known fact about Snakewood: it is not found in our dimension. The only recorded instance of it being in Mewni (other than on my wand handle) was when two pixies from Pixtopia found a stick of it when they visited the Neverzone and took it home with them as a souvenir. While trying to fix a defective pair of dimensional scissors, Heckapoo accidentally visited these pixie travellers while they were having a baby shower for their neighbor. They were so taken with her that they gave her the stick as a gift.

THIS BOOK
BELONGS TO
Princess Moon Butterfly
PLEASE RETURN WITH CARE

Moon the Undaunted ✖✖✖✖✖

Aureole Sign: Deadhorse
Height: 5' 7"

Attributes

Strength: 15	Common Sense: 19
Intelligence: 17	Constitution: 13
Wisdom: 17	Charisma: 16

Knowing stuff about your teenage mom and dad is just TMI. Think I'm gonna skip this chapter for now.

An Addendum

I have gone through the beginning of my chapter and marked everything BD (before death) so that there is a clear deliniation between the pages written before my mother died and after (AD). There is also a section marked Grieving.

Please do not judge me for the choices I made during those first dark days. Those were rather difficult times and I was barely seventeen. I was not prepared to be queen—and royal responsibility proved a hefty mantle upon such innocent, adolescent shoulders.

I must also say that were it not for my betrothed, River, I do not know what would have become of me. It is his eternal optimism and good cheer that have made my reign, well . . . survivable.

To River, I dedicate this addendum.

Hello, Whoever You Are That Is Reading This!

This has been quite a morning for me! My mother summoned me to the battlefield to have a breakfast of hard tack and canned meat with her in her tent. She handed me this Magic Book of Spells, and told me she thought I was ready to begin writing in it, now that I am fourteen years old! I was alarmed at first; I asked if something was wrong—was she going away? She assured me no, absolutely all is well . . . this is a normal step forward for all princesses.

She led me on a tour through the military encampment. It was quite a sight, seeing the armies of Mewni assembled, and a bit of a concern I must say. Mummy assures me that I need not be concerned; these are just exercises to impress our might upon our foes. I was quite surprised to see that the Johansens, a rogue's gallery of hardscrabble warriors, were called to provide us with reinforcements. I met their General, Lord Bloxq Johansen, and his son, River. River seems to be very sweet, and a bit lacking in the gruffness of the other Johansens. Anyway, Mummy says the most important thing I can do for the kingdom is write my thoughts and spells in this book (this is my own chapter!), and one day other queens will read my words just like I now read the words of all the other Butterflys before me. For example, I spent the first evening after Mummy gave me this book reading all of Queen Skywynne's chapter . . . and I must say, it was thrilling and rather informative.

I cannot wait to dive into the other chapters! It was lovely speaking to you and I hope that these pages will one day be filled with all of my amazing spells-to-be.

Yours truly,

Princess Moon Butterfly

Hello, Whoever You Are That Is Reading This!

Today was an incredibly special day. I have added a new member to our family and it fills me with such joy to be able to introduce you to Lil' Chauncey.

Carrying Lil' Chauncey home

Isn't he just divine? I love him so much already and he has barely been in the castle for an hour. Mummy has promised to make pies for the whole castle in celebration of his arrival—she's so good like that, always thinking of others and how to feed them.

Lil' Chauncey is a pig-goat, with all the best qualities of each animal. He's very smart and well mannered and he eats everything and he's also extremely loyal. Did I say that he's ridiculously sweet and loves to cuddle? I didn't!? Well, consider that omission remedied now.

How, you ask me, did I choose Lil' Chauncey out of all the other pig-goats at the royal bestiary? Well, I will tell you: he came over to me and nuzzled my hand. When I looked into his incredibly beautiful eyes, I just knew. It was kismet. Mummy knew immediately that I had made my choice. So I carried him all the way home! What a wonderful birthday surprise. . . Oh, did I neglect to say it's my birthday? Yes, today is my seventeenth birthday—and Lil' Chauncey is the best birthday present ever from Mummy!

Yours truly,

Princess Moon Butterfly

Lil' Chauncey is the best friend a princess could have.
He makes me very happy!

LIL'
CHAUNCEY
Lil' Chauncey's beautiful pink diamond collar, which was a gift from Mummy

Me and Lil' Chauncey at the fair

Lil' Chauncey eating everything!

Eating Mummy's shoe

Pumpkin & Lil' Chauncey: A Friendship That Transcends Space and Time

Best
Friends

From the moment we brought Lil' Chauncey home, it was clear that there was something special about him. I quickly became convinced that he could use his brainpower to nonverbally communicate with other animals. But even I was shocked when I realized he could speak telepathically with my Millhorse, Pumpkin. They quickly became the best of friends—even though they were separated by the magic and space of my wand—and for a while, I actually found myself a little jealous of their connection. But I am so busy helping my mom run the kingdom that I cannot devote the time I once did to Lil' Chauncey—so who am I to be unsupportive of his need to find connection with others? He is still my favorite confidant and I trust him with my life . . . as I do Pumpkin.

~~Row Upon Young Corder~~
Down can
~~Dottish Countermen~~
Unicorns me
?!?

An Addendum

Here begins the grieving part of my chapter . . . a time in my life that I consider to be the darkest. When my mother was killed and my sadness was strongest. As I said before, do not judge me for the action I took and the choices I made . . . especially where a particular former queen is concerned.

Written before I pass this book on to my daughter, Star Butterfly

The Chapter of Grieving

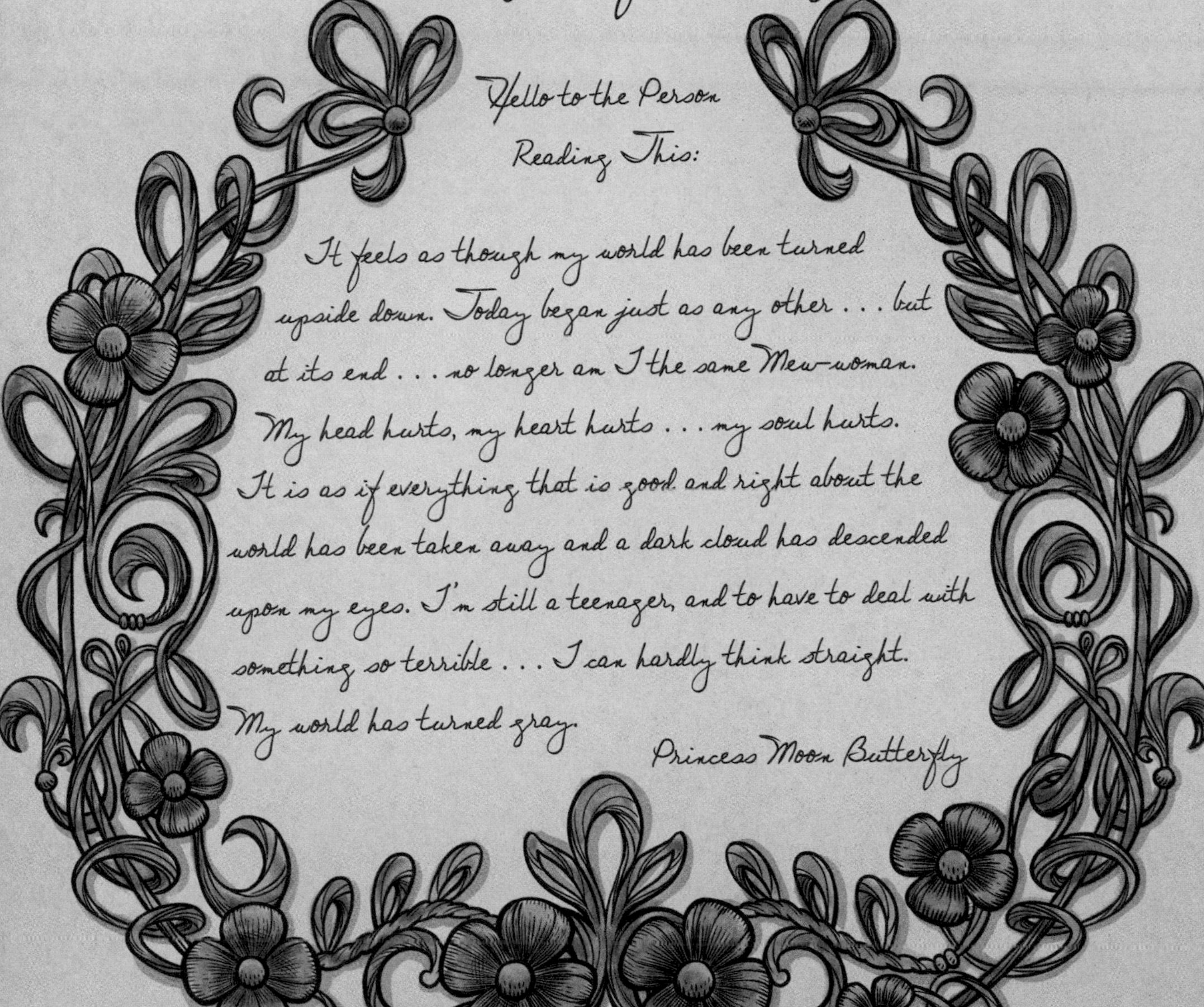

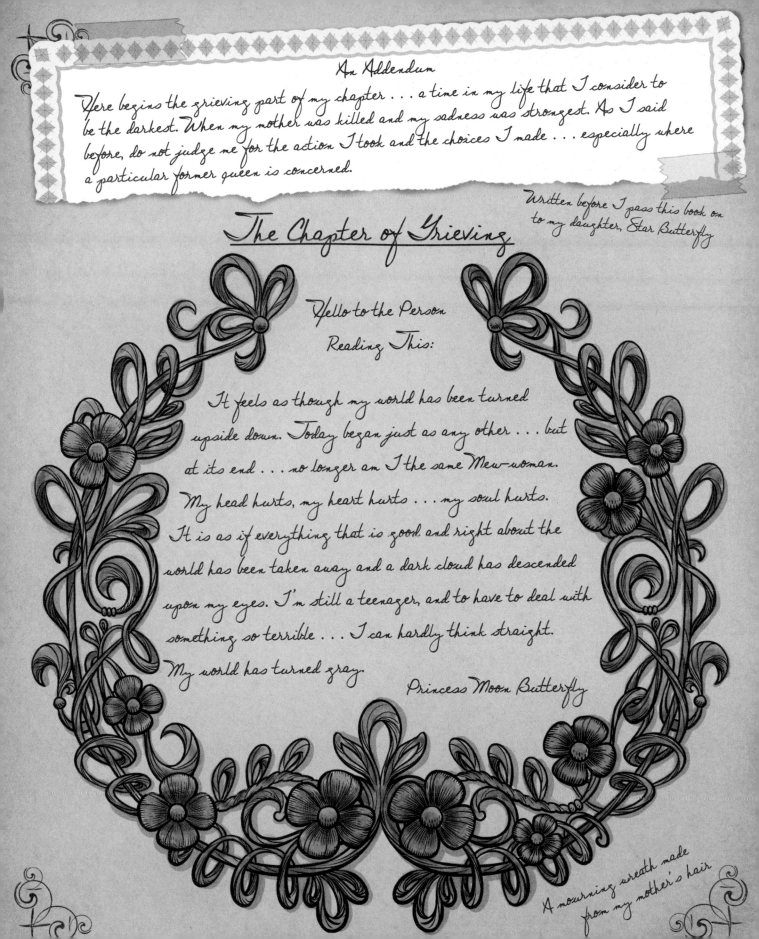

Hello to the Person
Reading This:

It feels as though my world has been turned upside down. Today began just as any other . . . but at its end . . . no longer am I the same Mew-woman. My head hurts, my heart hurts . . . my soul hurts. It is as if everything that is good and right about the world has been taken away and a dark cloud has descended upon my eyes. I'm still a teenager, and to have to deal with something so terrible . . . I can hardly think straight. My world has turned gray.

Princess Moon Butterfly

A mourning wreath made from my mother's hair

Hello to the Person Reading This:

I am now queen of Mewni . . . and I hate it.

Queen Moon

Hello to the Person Reading This:

I could not sleep. Each time I closed my eyes, I saw my mother's face. I cannot bear it. There is no rest for the queen. The Magic High Commission and my other councillors want to go to war with the monsters who killed my mother. I am not sure war is the answer. But I am not sure that it is not. I am so terribly confused.

Queen Moon

Hello to the Person Reading This:

Loss and grief are terrible to deal with—even before you are compelled by propriety to throw out every stitch of clothing that is not black. I am not allowed to wear anything that does not reflect my grief—though it is terribly sad to get rid of so many lovely dresses and cloaks and the like . . . all of which I will very much miss.

Queen Moon

Hello to the Person Reading This:

I went to see a particular someone today. . . . A deal was struck and my mother's killer will be punished. This I swear.

Queen Moon

Hello to the Person Reading This:

I did not use the spell to its full potential, or that unnamed former queen would have been freed. But I have done enough to stave off further war with the monsters . . . and for that I am ever grateful.

Queen Moon

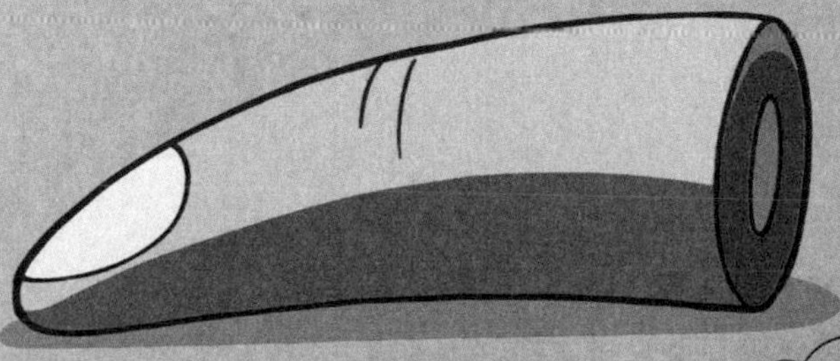

Reign of Moon the Undaunted: Moonglow Diamond Days

Hello to the Person Reading This:

Running a kingdom is difficult work—but not as difficult as laying siege to a monster horde. Which was exactly what was called for directly after the reception. Glossaryck is right; I must learn to "dip down" (as he calls it) or I will suffer the same fate as my mother. My magic must get stronger if we are going to continue to keep the monsters at bay.

Queen Moon the Undaunted

Hello to the Person Reading This:

I am so confused. I cannot decide which boy I like. I know it seems rather shallow to worry about dating so soon after my mother's death. I think I might wait until I no longer have to wear the dark cloak and dresses of the mourning period, which ends two years from now. At that time, I think I will have a better idea of who is a better match.

Though I must say—as much as River Johansen does not make the ideal companion for a queen, he very much makes me laugh. Which, in these sad days, is a talent worth its weight in gold. I do wish his family was not so . . .

enthusiastic. An hour spent with the Johansens is like a week spent with any other family. And Count Mildrew . . . well, there is something about him, and when I am in his presence, I just cannot relax. Oh, sigh. The heart is a fickle thing.

Queen Moon the Undaunted

Hello to the Person Reading This:

Glossy misses my mother almost as much as I do. He spends his days crying inside of my mother's chapter and—in a move that is patently unlike him—he has not eaten anything with the word "corn" in it for three weeks. I am truly beginning to worry. He is also remiss in helping me with my magical studies, and there is only so much I can do on my own without his help. Sigh . . . if only Mummy were still alive, I would not be so sad and my magic would not suffer so.

Queen Moon the Undaunted

Hello to the Person Reading This:

Big news. I almost cannot believe it myself. Stay tuned!

Queen Moon the Undaunted

Queen Moon the Undaunted and River Johansen were married today at Butterfly Castle in the Mewni Grasslands. In attendance were the most prominent Mewni families, which included the Lucitors of the Underworld, the Pony Heads of Cloud Kingdom, members of the Spider Bite family, and members of the Johansen family. Even the kingdom of the Waterfolk sent emissaries to celebrate this momentous occasion.

Queen Moon the Undaunted recently became queen in the wake of a family tragedy—the death of her mother, Queen Comet, who was assassinated during peace talks with the monsters. The bride was given away by Mina Loveberry and Lekmet (from the Magic High Commission)—her estranged father, the famous multiverse chef Lazlo Marmalade, was not in attendance—and wore a beautiful heirloom lace gown that has been in the Butterfly family for centuries. The groom ate his weight in roasted meat and fell asleep before the reception ended.

Wings of Style and Magical Battle Armor

I feel, as queen, that part of what is asked of us royals is to maintain propriety at all costs . . . so it is rare that I take on this form. Though, if truth be told, I am rather fond of the butterfly wings. They are such lovely shades of blue—and the fact that the diamonds on the upper wings match the diamonds on my face (though they are different in color), well, makes them rather fancy in my mind.

Arms That Taste—An interesting fact that I will share with you: whatever I touch with my four additional hands, I can taste. Which is why it is always best to wear gloves. You never know what strange tastes are lurking about.

Battle Tiara—a moonglow stone with magical healing properties
Arm Gauntlets—woven by the Waterfolk from virgin kelp
Butterfly Wings

Breastplate and Battle Skirt—cast from zidanium (only to be found in the Crystal Dimension), they are almost indestructible.

Turning Your Wand into a Magical Neon Whip

A spell in three parts

Part One
(Must be done at sunrise)

1. Clasp hands together, wand held between palms
2. Lift clasped hands and wand in the air above your head
3. Think these words: "I am a lion tamer"

Part Two
(Must be done at bedtime)

1. Place wand under your pillow
2. Go to sleep for the night

Neon Whip Spell

Part Three
(Must be done immediately upon awakening)

1. Retrieve wand from under pillow
2. Clasp hands together, wand held between palms
3. Lower clasped hands and wand so they point to the ground
4. Think these words: "I am a lion tamer"
5. Your wand will instantly become a magical neon whip

From now on, any time you think the words "I am a lion tamer," the wand will instantly become a magical neon whip. Please don't do this spell often, because wand radiation under your head isn't safe.

Reversing the Spell:

To turn your magical neon whip back into a wand, think these words: "Lion tamed."

Turning Your Wand into a Light Sword

Light Sword Spell

1. Point wand straight ahead
2. Swish it back and forth four times
3. Think these words:

"Light of power, draw to me
Fill my wand with majesty
Flames that burn with molten cold
A light sword form of blue-white gold"

Use light sword accordingly.

Important note:

Of course, it is very important to know how to reverse each and every spell you use. Without the ability to change what you have done, you are only half a magic wielder. Returning things to their natural state is a magic trick of its own.

Reversing the Spell:

To turn your light sword back into a wand, think these words: "Now's the time to cease your glow; let your magic wand be sword no more."

The Making the Royal Bed Spell

It is a rare day (as rare as being born under the Bozslug aureole sign) that my husband, King River, makes the bed. I think the last time I saw his hands fluffing a pillow was when our daughter, Star, was born—and that was only because she and I were both crying hysterically because the bottle he gave me was too hot. So I might use this spell occasionally to "encourage" his participation in household chores. The beauty of the spell is that after the task is complete, River forgets entirely that he even did the chore in the first place.

1. Wave your wand in the air—wave it like you really do care.
2. Twirl in place three times.
3. Think these words:

The bed must be made
The task falls to you today
But once you are done
You can go and have fun
Forgetting you ever
Touched a bedcover

Bed making spell

Reversing the Spell:

This is the only spell I will never need to know how to reverse.

My Dearest Star:

I hope this book will treat you as kindly as it treated me. Enjoy the fruits of your forebearers' labor—there are some amazing spells inside these pages for you to make your own. Please be respectful of Glossaryck and do as he says. Without him to guide you, your magic will become a curse and not a gift.

Your loving mother,
Queen Moon Butterfly

PS: Beware of Eclipsa's chapter—there is powerful dark magic inside.

STAR
THE UNDERESTIMATED

Star the Underestimated
was queen for just four days.
Her one decision on the throne:
to give it all away.

My wand crystal—
It's yellow!
The handle—
It's lavender!
It's actually Amberized Starglass.
Very rare.

Star the Underestimated
Aureole Sign: Pig-Goat
Height: 5' 2"
Attributes
Strength: 13
Intelligence: 16
Wisdom: 11
Dexterity: 16
Constitution: 15
Charisma: 18

F?? ?ORD
S??M

ugh. I'll get back to this later.

My Millhorse—
It smells!

His name is Pumpkin and he was your mother's. He was actually sired by a brother of Stephandipity.

HEY!

I did it. I broke through. I've had this book since my 14th birthday a couple weeks ago—well, it wasn't my REAL birthday; we don't celebrate my real birthday because it falls on Stump Day, ALL HAIL THE STUMP :)—and I couldn't bring myself to write in it. After reading all my grandmothers' chapters, it's a little intimidating. There's so much cool stuff that my grandmas—and apparently an uncle, too—wrote in here. . . . It's a lot to live up to.

You stopped reading after Skywynne's chapter!

Hey! I skimmed!

Anyway, my mom told me I have to write in here. "Just start somewhere, Star," she said. And each day that I wasn't writing in it I was aware I wasn't writing in it and then I started to worry about worrying about not writing in the book.

And then I had this dream that no one loved me and my teeth fell out and it was suddenly okay to wear food pants (pants with food printed on them), and I sprang up in bed, ran to the book, opened it to Glossaryck's room, and yelled "GLOSSARYCK, WHAT IN THE WHAT DO I WRITE IN THIS COCKAMAMIE BOOK?!"

I guess I scared him because he yelled "HEY!" at me.

Then I realized that was the perfect thing to write in the book. :)

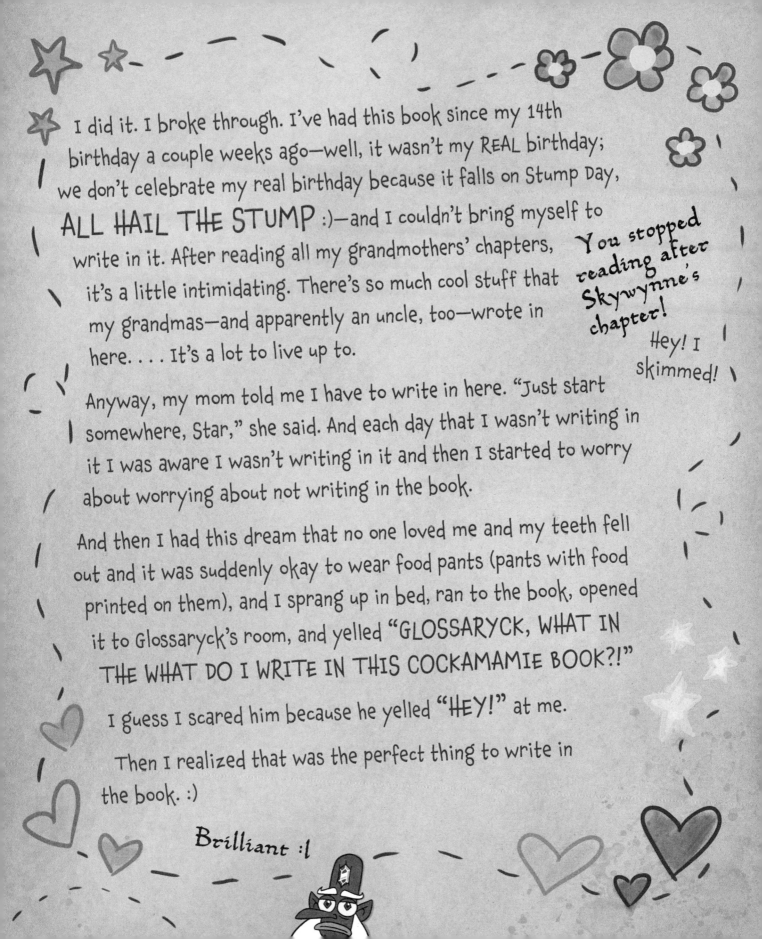

Brilliant :|

The Silver Bell Ball

At the request of Queen Moon Butterfly,
Your family is cordially invited to attend

The Silver Bell Ball

Welcoming the Pigeon Family to
The Kingdom of Mewni on
The 28th Moon of Norvath, Year of the Heart

I wasn't looking forward to the Silver Bell Ball this year. First of all, Pony Head wasn't going to be there because they were on a family trip, and second, there's this new family in the kingdom—the Pigeons—and they're . . . uh . . . pigeons. My mom wanted to make sure that we welcomed them into the kingdom properly because they're new, so she decided to center the ball around them.

I'm not exactly sure what happened—my parents have been vague on the deets—but basically I think the Pigeons completely took over old Mukwald Manor. Problem is, the Mukwalds were still living there, so there was a lot of war and destruction and bird poo and now the Mukwalds are gone and the Pigeons are the new ruling family of Mukwald Manor.

Anyway, I'm not really into birds, BUT, I am SO glad I went to the Silver Bell Ball like a good princess, because I got to meet Sir Tomas Lucitor, prince of the Underworld. He's the first prince to attend the Silver Bell Ball to be both close to my age and NOT:

A. A bird

B. A Fish-person

C. A Mukwald

D. A relative

As if those things alone weren't enough, he's also a hot demon with a swimmer's body. Before you criticize me for being shallow, we also had a ton to talk about. I don't know what yet, but I know it's there, ya know?

Anyway, at the end of the night, he sorta asked me to go to the Lava Lake Beach Boardwalk for cornshakes!

Tom Lucitor

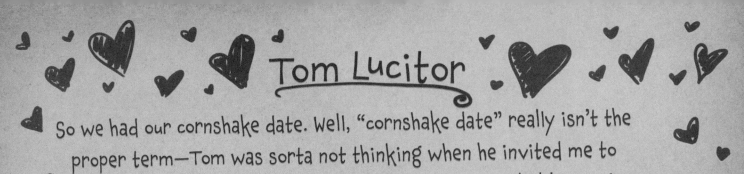

So we had our cornshake date. Well, "cornshake date" really isn't the proper term—Tom was sorta not thinking when he invited me to have cornshakes in the Underworld, cuz as you can probably imagine, cornshakes don't really last long down there, ya know, because of all of the molten burning stuff. So we ended up with cups of melted cornshakes. Kinda gross. BUT! The date was great. OH!

I bought these on the boardwalk!

SPECIAL
ONLY $14.99
OR THE SOUL OF YOUR SECOND BORN

What do you think?

Who are you talking to?

I like them, but I don't want to come across as one of those people who goes on vacation to the Underworld and comes back and is all like "Yeah, so I'm basically a demon now"—know what I mean?

Anyway, we had a really good time and I think we're gonna go out again, this time maybe somewhere aboveground where the cornshakes won't melt.

Tobitt and Me

By Star Butterfly

As long as I can remember, my dad has always hated Tobitt.

No matter what defenses we put up in the kingdom, this dirty cyclops always seems to get through them and into our corn bins. I'm talking force fields, magical traffic cones, enchanted moats, etc.—Tobitt always gets through. No other monster can penetrate our defenses, but for whatever reason, dirty old Tobitt can. His name has even become somewhat of an insult within the kingdom. The meanest thing you can call someone is a "son of a Tobitt."

My dad wakes up screaming his name sometimes.

My dad has sort of made a sport of going out in the kingdom and battling Tobitt, sending him scurrying back into the Forest of Certain Death. My mom decided that this vendetta my dad has against Tobitt is unbecoming of a king, so it's been up to the knights to chase him off.

UNTIL . . . I got the Royal Magic Wand! My mom doesn't know, but I've made it my personal mission to carry on the tradition of the Butterflys being Tobitt butt-kickers. After all, it's only natural to inherit your parents' hatred!

I don't really know any of the spells in this book yet, but I've made a few of my own. Nothing fancy, but some good strong blasts that really give Tobitt a run for his corn!

Me, Tom, and my new headgear!

Me and Tom right after the Silver Bell Ball!

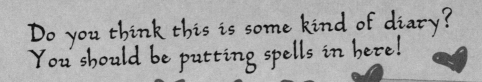

Do you think this is some kind of diary?
You should be putting spells in here!

Tom Lucitor 2.0

Photobooth Noob!!
Say Cheese!

Been hanging out with Tom regularly for the last few weeks, and tonight we made it official that we're a thing! He surprised me and picked me up in this wicked carriage and took me to the field to climb trees. We spent the day looking in birds' nests and picking tree slime out of our hair.

It was SO romantic! We can have fun kinda doing whatever. Pony Head thinks I should be careful because she said she dated a demon once and they have "issues." She gave me this old demon dating guide that she got from a school counselor. I showed it to Tom—he thought it was hilarious.

So He's a Demon . . .

A Dating Guide

by Gladdy the Vexed,
love doctor and founder of
Gladdy's Life-Coaching and Anger
Intervention Centers for
the Underworld

So you've decided to ignore the advice of your parents, friends, and anyone else with any sense at all, and you're going to date a demon. Here are some things you will want to know about your new demon beau:

Understand His Anger

It's true that demons are notoriously angry. My research in this field has led me to conclude this anger is a result of living in a state of constant burning. Imagine your world. Now imagine it on fire. Doesn't that make you angry?

Embrace His Mascara

Those aren't tears of soot. Demons put a lot of time into face makeup. Chances are, that's why you like your demon in the first place. However, sometimes we forget to notice his efforts to beautify himself, so remember it does his ego good and softens his anger if you remind him how nice his eyes look.

Respect His Mama

Demon boys tell their moms EVERYTHING, so make sure that you respect that relationship. Demon moms are known to be protective, and they have a lot of sway over their demon sons' decisions.

Remember that his anger is his problem, not yours. Remind him when he's raging out that he's being a jerk, but do it in a supportive way. Ask questions. Instead of more accusatory statements like "You're being a raging jerky-jerk!" ask about his needs. Consider this adjustment: "Is there anything I can do to help, you raging jerky-jerk?"

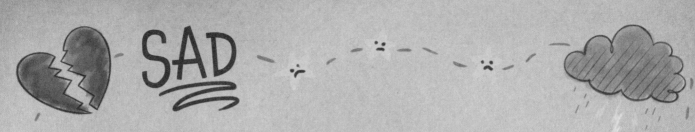

SAD

I guess I blew it. Tom and I got into this huge fight. It's a long story, but we broke up and so I went to the Forest of Certain Death to blow off some steam and kick some Tobitt butt.

Apparently some ding-dong villagers actually live like super close to the Forest of Certain Death, and they're telling me now that one of my flamebows maybe sorta burnt down their "village."

As if.

Anyway, I got in trouble. My mom asked to see my spell book, realized I wasn't writing anything in it but "scribble-scrabble," as she called it, then yada-yada-yada they are sending me away. Don't know where yet; prolly Saint O's.

Dad came to me privately and told me that while he hated Tobitt, too, he thought maybe it was best to have me train somewhere without so many distractions. He said they were still scouring the multiverse for the right place.

Also: I heard my mom tell my dad she's worried I'll end up like Soupina the Strange.
Who?? What?!?

SAD

Earth

I know I'm supposed to be putting spells in here, but I guess I just need a listening ear at the moment.

Mom and Dad sent me to Earth. From what I can tell there are no monsters here, and people seem sorta friendly. It doesn't seem to be a big deal that I'm a magical princess from another dimension.

I'm going to this school called Echo Creek Academy, and they put me up with these nice people, Angie and Rafael Diaz. Their son, Marco, is one of my classmates. He's nice—sorta neurotic, dresses cute, and he's into martial arts.

I certainly miss Mewni already, but this place is much better than St. O's. It's probably good to get away from Tom and get my head clear.

My going-away party!

HAVE AN EARTHASTIC TIME

Angie and Rafael told me to help myself to whatever I need in their house . . . and I NEEDED THIS!

GLITTER GLUE!
Magic from the walls! (do not eat)
More horns!
OMIGOSH LOOKIT WHAT THEY HAVE ON EARTH!
BOBA TEA!
QUEENS!
WARRIORS!

Food that isn't corn!
Put them together!
BURRITOS!
SUGAR!
SUGAR
Boys with these
and these
And their babies!
Tiny edible animals!
Magic Looky Box!
People you love even though they don't know you!
Ball sports

Well, now that Marco knows where I keep my journal, I'm gonna have to stash these pages in here. Not that I wrote anything embarrassing I'm embarrassed about or anything. He'll never look in here . . . he can't stand Glossaryck. HEY!

CHAPTER 11

MY THOUGHTS ON MARCO:

I met Marco on the first day of school. Somehow the principal knew we'd be the best of friends, and it's true, we are!

But not at first.

Marco is very particular. He likes things a certain way.

I sorta picked up on that right away, so I just pretended like I didn't know what I was doing. Earth's a new, crazy place, so I can sorta get by just by acting like I don't get it.

Look, I'm not gonna lie to you, Diary, there's a lot I don't get about Earth. They have buttons you push to cross the street, and everyone pushes them many times. Why? Either the

button works or it doesn't.

Imagine the little man who is connected to the other end of that button. . . . He must be terribly annoyed.

Look, this isn't my first other dimension, 'kay? I get that I'm not gonna understand things right away, so I just roll with it. It's kinda cute when I don't necessarily understand things, so with Marco, I let it all hang out.

I think it helps him to

help me. When we're together, he sees the chaos in the world and sort of embraces it.

I've never connected with another person in that way. I know what you're thinking, you naughty diary, and NO, I don't have a crush on Marco! I can have a boy friend. Not a boyfriend, but a boy who is JUST a friend. He can even be cute and it's no big deal. I mean, take Marco—case in point. Totally cute, totally just friends. Totally.

Thank Baby Dolphin Giggles for Marco Diaz. I almost destroyed the school today, but Marco helped me, or I guess he just sorta got outta my way, and I got my Mewberty wings!

yay
good time
happy Besties
Go out of town!
POOF
I ♡ friend
DUCKFACE
STYLEZ 4 MILEZ
Super KAWAII
HAY
PARTY LIFE
GURL!
WE ARE COOL!!
#1
OH NO
SHE DINT!

This is from the night my two besties became besties! I think it went well!

I'm trying to be mad/not mad at Marco. I'm mad because he ambushed my date with Tom to the Blood Moon Ball. I know, I know . . . I probably shouldn't have gone in the first place, but it's one of those things where I had to go to know, ya know?

Anyway, Marco sabotaged what would have been a perfect failure of a date and it made me mad. Marco and I danced together, and I didn't know it was him at first . . . at least I don't think I knew. I'm not mad that I got to see how good of a dancer Marco is.

Wand 2.0

So! I guess this is a big deal—this creep, Toffee, was trying to steal my wand, but it turns out he wasn't trying to steal it and he really wanted me to destroy it! So I did! But, SURPRISE! My wand blew up AND blew up Toffee and then my wand came back to life!

Yeah, this has never happened before. . . . You're sorta on your own now, but I guess you always were. Born alone, die alone, I always say!

My wand crystal—It's sorta split in two, but it's still yellow!

Cleaved Amberized Starglass. Still rare, but now there are two.

The handle—It's still lavender, but now it has a purple stripe!

Apparently.

My Millhorse—Still smelly and I can't understand anything he says.

His name is Vincenzo and he is quite possibly the weirdest Millhorse ever.

Aargh! I'm getting that feeling again, the same one that I had before I ever wrote a single word in this book; I feel like I need to be writing in here more. I haven't even tried to jot my spells down. There'll be time for that after this weekend. Janna and I are going to have a séance in the cemetery to try to communicate with the spooky old clown named Bon-Bon the Birthday Clown.

Apparently, he died tragically, in a trick-candle accident.

Can't wait!

Will he come back . . . JUST LIKE HIS CANDLES?

I promise to write more soon!

Janna cut this out of a book from the Echo Creek library!

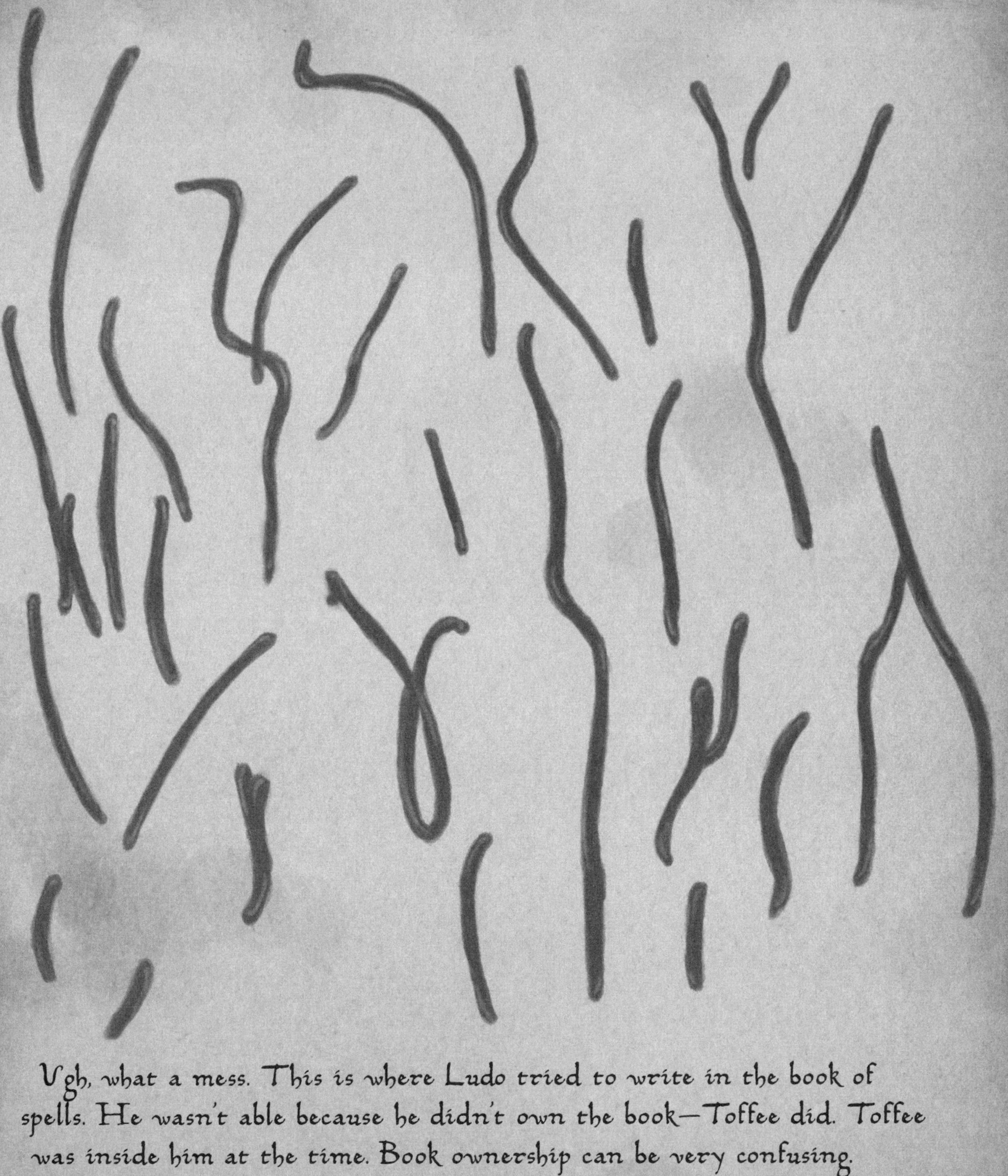

Ugh, what a mess. This is where Ludo tried to write in the book of spells. He wasn't able because he didn't own the book—Toffee did. Toffee was inside him at the time. Book ownership can be very confusing. Anyway, please don't write in the book unless you own it.

Once again, hello, new owner of this book—and new custodian of yours truly, Glossaryck. For your courage under fire (did you abscond with this book when no one was looking?) or pure dumb luck (maybe you just happened to find this book lying on a park bench somewhere in the environs of Echo Creek, Earth?), you have earned yourself a round of applause. And also a chance to curate your own chapter.

I feel the time is ripe to create a portrait. Please add your visage to the pantheon of book owners before you. C'mon, you know you want to.

Tell us your tale. On the next page is the perfect spot to draw your portait and craft an epic poem to show the world—or, at least, me and you—how special you are. Because you know you're special. Yes, you do. You know it. Don't act like you don't.

There's also room to draw your wand and Millhorse. Please add colors. I love color. And flavor.

You've got spells. I know spells. Let the synergy flow. Dip way down and document all the amazing stuff swirling around at the bottom of the soup. These pages are for sticking your spells on and letting them breathe.

I know there are more spells inside of you. I feel it. Put them right here so I can see!

Now don't be stingy with your spells.
Let yours truly, Sir Glossaryck of
Terms, have a peek.

Glossaryck's Thoughts on the Future

In closing . . . now that you've made this book your own, it's time to think about the future . . . of this book. Because as we all know, it has a funny way of catching on fire. And whenever it burns again, as we all know it's going to, its owner—that's you—will be tasked with its reconstitution.

So just keep any old piece of the book and then place one of my lovely little silkworms on top of that piece to bring the book back into existence. It doesn't matter how charred it is; my silkworms aren't too picky.

Might I recommend Silky? She's got a real eye for detail and is just as sweet as a piece of Comet's *sob* pudding pie. Now that's a lot of sweet.

Now, of course, I want all my kids to have equal opportunities. Stinky could definitely help a new book owner out, but you'll have to proofread like a hawk. He could accidentally/on purpose give you a false entry or ten.

Don't bother with Sassa-Sassy-Pants Sassafras. She's not one to be told what to do. You might end up with a ceiling fan instead of a spell book.

Cover Art by Drake Brodahl
Additional art by Daron Nefcy, Drake Brodahl, Cindy Plourde, David Brueggeman, Amanda Thomas, and Alison Donato

Design by Lindsay Broderick
Editorial by Erin Zimring

A very special thank-you to Andrea Atencio, Tatiana Bull, Britta Reitman, and Jenna Hicks for all their help in making this book happen

For information address Disney Press,
1200 Grand Central Avenue, Glendale, California 91201.

Printed in the United States of America
First Hardcover Edition, September 2018
1 3 5 7 9 10 8 6 4 2

FAC-038091-18208
ISBN 978-1-368-02050-3

Library of Congress Control Number: 2018936736

For more Disney Press fun,
visit www.disneybooks.com
Visit DisneyXD.com

SUSTAINABLE FORESTRY INITIATIVE Certified Sourcing
www.sfiprogram.org
SFI-00993
Logo Applies to Text Stock Only